It had been a long time since he'd gotten so wrapped up in a woman...

He'd paid for his misdirected attention with a cut that might leave a scar, too. Will found a mirror, getting a better look at his injury. Hadn't today's sacrifices deserved more than Sara's chaste kiss of thanks? He shut his eyes, imagining...

"I didn't thank you for saving my life." Same words as before but this time Sara's gaze would hold his longer. He'd make no effort to touch her. It was up to Sara. "Will..." Her voice was a low, throaty purr. "Thank you." She leaned forward and kissed him....

It might be a fantasy, but such a kiss would shake him to his core. Under its influence, their roles in life would be reduced to the simplest common denominator: the hunter and the hunted.

Dear Reader,

They're rugged, they're strong and they're *wanted!* Whether sheriff, undercover cop or officer of the court, these men are trained to keep the peace, to uphold the law. But what happens when they meet the one woman who gets to know the man *behind* the badge?

Twelve of these men are on the loose...and only Harlequin Intrigue brings them to you—one per month in the LAWMAN series. This month meet Will Riggs, P.I., in *Hero for Hire* by Laura Kenner.

Born and raised in Alabama, Laura now calls northern Virginia/Washington D.C. home—that is, until Uncle Sam tells her otherwise. A military dependent, she sees each new assignment as not only an opportunity to guess how many cardboard boxes it takes to pack up her family (at last count—214), but as a potential location for new books. She extends an invitation to all to visit her newest "home," the one on the World Wide Web: http://www.erols.com/lhayden

Be sure you don't miss Will's exciting story—or any of the LAWMAN books coming to you in the months ahead...because there's nothing sexier than the strong arms of the law!

Regards,

Debra Matteucci
Senior Editor and Editorial Coordinator
Harlequin Books
300 East 42nd Street
New York, New York 10017

Hero for Hire
Laura Kenner

Harlequin Books

TORONTO • NEW YORK • LONDON
AMSTERDAM • PARIS • SYDNEY • HAMBURG
STOCKHOLM • ATHENS • TOKYO • MILAN
MADRID • WARSAW • BUDAPEST • AUCKLAND

To Alison Ramsey for being ready, willing and able to fan the idea when it first sparked and to the Wyrd Sisters for keeping it burning, even when I smoldered.

ISBN 0-373-22405-2

HERO FOR HIRE

Copyright © 1997 by Laura Beard Hayden

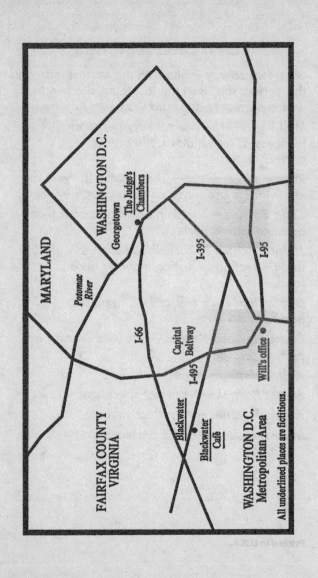

MARYLAND

WASHINGTON D.C.

Georgetown

The Judge's
Chambers

Potomac
River

I-66

I-395

I-95

Capital
Beltway

I-495

Will's office

FAIRFAX COUNTY
VIRGINIA

Blackwater

Blackwater
Café

WASHINGTON D.C.
Metropolitan Area

All underlined places are fictitious.

CAST OF CHARACTERS

Sara Hardaway—She had the perfect man and the perfect job, and the last thing she needed was a perfect stranger to walk into her life.

Will Riggs—The perfect stranger made it his business to turn himself into any woman's perfect match.

Raymond Bergeron—The divorce lawyer who knew things are never as perfect as they seem.

Celia Strauss—The woman who proved that practice makes perfect.

Judge Michael F. Russell, Retired—He used to find perfection in justice; now he finds it in food.

Martin and Lucy Hilliard—The perfect partners.

Diane Howard-Barnes—She was seeking the perfect divorce.

Anita Rooney—A perfect tool.

Blazer Barnes—A perfect specimen.

Archie Koeffler—A perfect square.

Mimi and Joanie—The perfect secretaries.

Chapter One

Friday, late morning

The elevator door opened and conversation spilled into the quiet foyer. "—one to screw in the light bulb and five to sue for deprivation of darkness."

Sara Hardaway spared the two women standing in the elevator car only a cursory glance as she juggled her boxes and stepped in. To her relief, the eleventh-floor button was lit, eliminating the need to free a hand or ask for assistance. Somehow, she didn't think either of the women would think to offer some help. They were already deeply mired in soft conversation, ignoring her.

The woman in the navy suit lowered her voice. "You're supposed to laugh when someone tells you a joke."

"I don't feel like laughing." The other woman crossed her arms and her bottom lip trembled for a moment. "And I wish you'd have given me time to change." She looked decidedly self-conscious as she adjusted the skirt of her teal silk dress. "I don't think this is the right outfit for such a serious situation."

Was it Sara's imagination, or did the women glance at her as if assuring themselves that no matter what, at least they looked better than she did? She winced inwardly, not willing to give them the satisfaction of knowing they'd made her feel uncomfortable.

Sure, she was wearing jeans, a sweatshirt and a Redskins baseball cap to cover her dirty hair, but there was a good reason to look so…so bad. A really good reason, she wanted to tell them. After all, it wasn't fair; even when she dressed nicely, she usually took the freight elevator and slipped in the back of the office. But just her luck—the *one* day when she didn't want to be seen by anyone, the freight elevator was broken. The Otis Elevator Corollary to Murphy's Law?

She'd had no other choice but to walk around to the elegant marble foyer and use the regular elevator, doing her best impression of a messenger making deliveries. She shifted uncomfortably, wishing the hole in the knee of her pants wasn't so big or so frayed.

The women in the elevator spoke around her as if she didn't exist. The one in the navy suit performed an elegant, careless shrug. Her shoulder pads didn't even shift out of place. "It's only a preliminary meeting. Consider it the weigh-in before the big match. Both camps check each other out, sizing up their candidates, wanting to know if both competitors can go the distance."

The woman in the silk dress shuddered. "You make it sound like a boxing match."

"That's exactly what this is."

Sara couldn't help but glance at the woman in the navy suit. With her slightly wide stance and one hand curled into a fist, Sara had no doubt this female could have stood toe-to-toe for several rounds with Muhammad Ali in his prime. Maybe even go the distance.

"Divorces are all like that," she continued. "You spar a little, size up the competition, figure out their weakness and then go in for the kill."

Bingo! A divorce lawyer and her client. Sara knew she should have recognized the look of steely determination on one face and the caught-in-the-headlights look on the other.

"And remember—" the woman in the navy suit lowered her voice a notch "—if his lawyer asks about the '91 property purchase, we show both the original deed of trust, the California tax records and the affidavit from the insurance company." She patted her expensive leather briefcase. "But we don't volunteer any information about the property in Arizona. Understand?"

The female in the silk dress nodded, tugging at the collar of her outfit. "Okay. But I still think—"

The elevator dinged, signaling their arrival. As the doors slid open, all three started for the exit at the same time. Sara paused, taking a deferential step back, but she received no acknowledgment from the two women. Typical. They pushed ahead, having assigned her to the ball-cap-and-jeans level of the hierarchy of life. Ball cappers evidently ranked right below waitresses with beehive hairdos and above flower children still living in tie-dyed VW buses.

The woman in the silk dress turned to the other female. "Have you ever met this attorney before? This…R. S. Bergeron?"

A chill zipped up Sara's spine.

The one in the navy suit shook her head. "I've heard of him. Do you know him?"

Sara strained to hear the answer. It would be much too obvious if she followed them right to the office door. Wouldn't it put a nice snag in their panty hose to know they were headed for the same place? Instead, Sara went to the service corridor and rang the back-door bell with her shoulder as she balanced the boxes of food.

"Yes?"

"It's me, Joanie," she called into the intercom. "I have lunch for the huddled masses." She paused for emphasis. "And baklava for you."

The door buzzed in response. Sara headed straight for the conference room, hearing Joanie thunder in from the vestibule. They arrived at the same time.

"Thank heavens, you're here. Raymond called earlier to say he might be running late, and his clients just arrived." She helped to pull the food containers from the box.

Since the conference room was used as much for entertaining clients at lunch meetings as anything else, Sara pulled out the china she and Raymond had selected expressly for such occasions. She began to set the table for four. "I know they're here. I rode up the elevator with them." Pausing to check one of the knives for spots, Sara tried to ignore the distorted reflection of the woman in a baggy sweatshirt and faded cap.

"Is it dirty?" Joanie nodded toward the knife.

Sara dragged her attention from the utensil back to the task at hand. "No. I was just marveling at how bad I look. It also makes me wonder if the lawyer I saw in the elevator was one of those people who can't see their reflection in the mirror."

Joanie giggled. "A real Vampira? Funny…she didn't strike me that way."

Sara shrugged. "Maybe I saw her true personality because to her, I was just some old bag lady in the elevator. But she certainly makes a person wonder if part of the attorney-client privilege means surrendering information about your blood type." Sara stuck a finger in her sweatshirt collar and pulled it out to demonstrate where a vampire might strike. "It gives a new meaning to the concept of a working lunch."

A stentorian voice echoed throughout the room. "Don't give me any ideas.…"

Sara spun around and spotted her fiancé, Raymond Bergeron, standing in the entrance to the conference room.

Well over six feet tall, he filled the doorway as easily as he filled the room with his smiling charm.

"Ah, Sara...my sweet. And speaking of a tasty morsel—" he swooped toward her, his arm raised as if he held a cape at his face "—what's on the menu today? Besides you, that is?" He leaned down, pretending to nibble her neck.

She batted him away. "You didn't give me much prep time so I had to go with what was available. It's your basic soup, salad, sandwich and dessert combo. White chili with chicken, house salads with walnuts and honey-mustard dressing, turkey club sandwiches and a chocolate cheesecake. And baklava for Joanie." Sara smiled at Raymond's secretary. "I know you don't like cheesecake."

Joanie pulled the small container of Greek pastries toward herself with a possessive gleam in her eye. "Boss, I hope you realize it's a rare and wonderful woman who'll go into work on her day off just to make a meal for her forgetful fiancé."

He crossed his arms and narrowed his gaze. "Like I told you—I didn't forget this meeting. It just came up suddenly." When he saw Joanie's silent censure, his expression melted into a hesitant grin toward Sara. "And I really appreciate this, sweetheart. It's more of a help than you could ever really know." Although he wasn't usually a demonstrative person in front of others, Raymond surprised Sara with a hasty kiss. Before her shock could subside, he broke away. A slight red tinge colored his cheeks as he turned to Joanie. "Is everybody here, now?"

She raised an eyebrow and nodded. "Mrs. Howard-Barnes and Ms. Rooney are already in your office and Mr. Barnes is on his way up."

"Good. We've forced her into making the first concession." Raymond rubbed his hands together in obvious satisfaction. He elaborated, as was his usual custom. "Ms. Rooney has a reputation for trying to play hardball on first contacts. I'm sure she expects lunch with the infamous Blackwater Barracuda to be a matter of either raw fish or, at the very least, rare meat, not a froufrou girlie meal like this. It ought to really throw her off-balance.''

"Froufrou? Girlie?" Sara picked up a towel and snapped it toward him. "I'll have you know, Mr. Barracuda, that the Honorable Judge Michael Russell came by the restaurant just last night and tried to charm the recipe out of me for my white chili. Again."

"I'm surprised he didn't try to serve you a subpoena to get it. He still thinks he's on the bench." Raymond's face tightened a little, a warning of something unpleasant yet to come. "And speaking of Judge Russell, I have a small problem."

"Problem?" It was her turn to give him a narrowing gaze. "What kind of problem?" She could see the answer in his body language, which read *I don't want to tell you this but—*

"I don't want to tell you this, but it's about dinner at his place, tonight."

There goes our dinner date. Disappointment flooded through her. It had taken almost a court order for her to get a Friday night off. Schedules had to be juggled, shifts covered, bribes made, promises exacted, everything short of donating a heart, lung and kidney so that she, the boss, could have a rare but leisurely Friday night out with her fiancé at their favorite restaurant. And now?

"Oh, Raymond…"

"Don't 'Oh, Raymond' me!" He leaned forward and pecked her cheek. "I'm not canceling it. I simply have a short meeting scheduled at six and may be running a little late. Why don't you go ahead to the judge's restaurant and I'll meet you there around seven-thirty. Okay?"

She looked down at the polished conference table. In its reflection, she saw two business professionals with busy lives, trying to balance work with love and love with work. And to complicate things, they both loved their work. So far, they'd been successful, juggling it all. And in the Great Book of Potential Disappointments, being a little late for a special night out didn't rank up there with earthquakes, volcanic explosions and forgetting an anniversary.

After all, she reminded herself, he'd anticipated her disappointment; based on her experience with men, most of them didn't usually think *that* far ahead.

She adopted her best "I'll survive the disappointment" smile and faced him. "Promise you won't be too late?"

He drew a cross over the red handkerchief peeking from the pocket of his charcoal suit. "Promise."

Friday evening

"PROMISE..."

Sara wadded her cocktail napkin into a sodden ball and sneered. "Some promise." Taking careful aim, she tossed the ball, beaning the man behind the bar who had bent over to retrieve something from the bottom shelf.

"Hey!" The Honorable Judge Michael F. Russell, retired, straightened and plucked the damp wad of paper from his collar. "Didn't your mother ever tell you it wasn't nice to shoot spitballs in school?"

Sara held out her empty hands, demonstrating her lack of ammunition. "One. It's not a spitball. Two. This is a bar, not a school. And three. I wasn't aiming at you." She smirked at him. "I was aiming at the trash can."

Mike flipped the paper into the trash can several feet away. "I find it difficult to believe you missed such an easy target." He picked up her empty glass, wiped away the damp ring beneath it with a clean cloth and placed a new drink in front of her. "If I didn't know better, I'd say you were taking out your frustrations on the nearest man."

"Hardly." She took a tentative sip and allowed herself a reluctant smile. The drink, nicknamed a "Public Defender" was the judge's trademark, a secret concoction that reputedly relied less on alcohol than on special mixer ingredients. She suspected that he was playing his usual fatherly role and that this third drink was most likely a virgin Public Defender. Of course, some of the less reputable characters who hung out at the bar always proclaimed that you couldn't use the word *virgin* with anything remotely connected to the law profession. Sara refused to use the unsavory nickname they'd coined for the virginal version of the drink—something about defending a woman's anatomy....

She contemplated the orange-pink concoction, then lifted her glass in salute. "Here's to conscientious divorce lawyers who seem unable to divorce themselves from their work."

The judge lifted his bottle of Evian water. "To divorce lawyers."

"To *conscientious* divorce lawyers," a voice corrected.

Sara spun around on her stool and stared at the source of the intrusive voice. It belonged to a man who stood a few feet down the bar.

He didn't look like a typical bar patron.

Although all the other male customers had loosened their requisite power ties, they still wore the stamp of regimentation that branded District patrons who used Friday nights at their local watering holes to wind down a long week. Mike had once quipped that Friday night was Stupid Tie Night and he gave a weekly award for the bravest attempt to induce a little originality in the otherwise-staid politicians' dress code.

But this man standing by her at the bar wore no tie. Unlike the other male patrons, he was dressed in a white sweater over jeans as if he'd spent a casual afternoon playing Frisbee on the Mall rather than playing political hardball on a federal court.

She supposed most women considered him handsome…not that she noticed or anything. But it was evident at first glance that it was his infectious smile that animated his basic features. He was definitely not a politician. Their smiles never reached their eyes. His did.

She eyed his haircut. *He's not military, either. A tourist? On the make?*

He regarded her with a nod as he lifted his glass in salute. "Of course, that assumes you believe in such a thing as a conscientious divorce lawyer. Which, in turn, means you accept the absurd notion that a lawyer could have a conscience in the first place. So far, I've never met one, myself." The man turned toward the judge and gave him a broad smile. "Evenin', Mike."

The judge grinned back. "H'lo, Will. So *you* were the other person who ordered a Public Defender. I wondered if I was going to have a run on them tonight."

Sara glanced at the familiar-looking orange-pink liquid in the man's glass as he took a healthy swig of his drink. He looked more like a guy who would order a beer rather than a cocktail heavier in juice than rum.

"Vitamins," he declared after lowering his glass. "It's the only sure source of vitamins I get these days." He fiddled with his cocktail napkin, folding under one edge. "I wish you would tell me what's in this thing, Mike, so I can figure out how many of them it takes to meet my minimum recommended daily allowance."

Sara shook her head, knowing the utter futility of his request. "He won't do it, you know. I've been trying for years to get the recipe out of him, but the good judge won't budge."

Mike drained his bottle of water. "Not even for you, Will."

Will moved closer to her, placing his drink next to hers

and giving both their glasses a fierce appraisal. "It doesn't look like it would be so hard, does it? Divining the ingredients used to make this thing?"

She contemplated her own glass. "It's not as much figuring out what's in it as how *much* of each ingredient."

"Starting with orange juice?"

She nodded. "And grapefruit juice."

"Fresh lemon?" he challenged.

"Just a twist. Maybe even some orange rind."

He nodded sagely. "I thought so. And what about the pink?"

She shrugged. "Probably grenadine."

Mike continued to putter behind the bar, listening to their list of proposed ingredients without comment. Sara wondered how his poker face would react if they hit on the winning combination.

Will shifted his attention, staring intently at the judge rather than his drink. "And what about that all-important secret ingredient, Mike?"

The judge merely shrugged.

Will lifted his glass, turned his scrutiny to the liquid, then took a tentative sip. Sara followed suit.

Their gazes met above the rim of their glasses. For a moment, a thousand thoughts and images careened through Sara's mind. An unexpected-yet-familiar shivery sensation started at the base of her neck and shot down toward her legs. After one frozen-but-mesmerizing moment, she blinked, using the distraction to tear her attention from him and hopefully guide it back to where it belonged. She stared at the drink, her focus blurring.

What was I doing? A second tremor rocked her. *What am I doing? I have a man, thank you very much. A wonderful man who loves, cherishes and, best of all, trusts me.* She closed her eyes, conjuring up an image of Raymond, resplendent in his charcoal suit and red power tie.

With a wicked grin, he began to take off the tie. He tossed the deep cranberry silk onto the bed. Cranberry?

"Cranberry..." she whispered to herself.

Will leaned slightly toward her. "Pardon?"

She took another speculative sip of her drink. "Cranberry juice," she said to him in a low voice.

He quirked an eyebrow. "Cranberry?" He tasted the word in the same manner he tasted his drink. Sudden enlightenment flooded his face, and he winked. Shielding his hand from the judge's view, he started a countdown.

Three.

Two.

One.

"Cranberry juice!" they said, their two voices blending as one.

To her utter surprise, Mike blinked.

It was a simple, almost-involuntary gesture that would have meant absolutely nothing had it been performed by practically anybody else. But this was Judge Michael F. Russell, a man with a long, illustrious career on the bench where he had been nicknamed "The Rock" for his almost-blatant lack of emotion.

In him, such a minor reaction as a blink spoke volumes.

Sara wondered if the same could be said about her. She felt a reminiscent frisson cross her shoulders.

Her cohort in culinary crime stared at her for a moment. "You okay? You look...cold."

"It's the ice," she lied.

Will turned to the judge, his concern fading to a mixture of awe and triumph. "Do you have a pen? We need to immortalize this moment in time."

Having overcome his momentary lapse in composure, Mike produced a small yellow pencil stub. "Will this do?" he asked in a noncommittal voice.

Will accepted the pencil, grabbed a cocktail napkin and

started writing with paper-tearing enthusiasm. Sara shamelessly read over his shoulder.

"On this day, the eighteenth of October in the year 1996, I, William Brian Riggs, and—" He nudged the napkin toward Sara and after a moment's hesitation, she obliged by writing in, "Sara Hardaway."

"Do both solemnly swear that they witnessed the former-but-still-Honorable Judge Michael F. Russell perform in such a manner that could be described as an overt physical reaction displaying the emotion called 'surprise.' Said judge was neither under the undue influence of alcohol, exhaustion or any known drug or intoxicant."

Will signed his name with an indecipherable flourish and handed the pencil to Sara, who signed as well.

The judge glanced at the napkin, shook his head and began to polish a glass that was already clean. "I neither confirmed nor denied that cranberry juice is a key component in my drink. However I *am* willing to admit that a Public Defender is made up of twenty-seven ingredients. So, looks like it's seven down—" he paused to give them the full benefit of his benign, unruffled smile "—and twenty more to go."

Will turned to Sara, his grin fading a little. "I think Mike guards his formula closer than they do Coca-Cola's."

"Coca-Cola?" She took another sip. "I don't think it's one of the ingredients."

The smile broke free as he lifted his drink in salute. "I don't think so, either. So here's to secret formulas, close-mouthed judges and—" he paused as a fresh glint entered his eyes "—lovely ladies with foam mustaches."

Sara snatched her napkin and dabbed at the residue of drink that dotted her upper lip. "Did I get it?"

His critical glance seemed to encompass more than just her lips. He shifted closer to her and reached over, pulling the napkin out of her hand to gently blot her cheek. "There…"

Had his hand lingered one millisecond longer, Sara might have looked for an excuse to leave. She didn't want to be guilty of implying that she was available, nor did she want to place herself under any undue strain in having to correct his assumption. She found her watch a suitable diversion until she realized it indicated Raymond was over an hour and a half late.

"Don't tell me you're getting stood up, too." Will consulted his own watch, tapping it with a sudden grimace. His eyes widened suddenly and he took another glance at the napkin they'd signed. "'Sara Hardaway,'" he read. "You wouldn't also go by the pseudonym of Harmony Kent, would you?"

She shook her head. "If you ever heard me sing, you'd know the answer was no."

He shrugged and finished his drink. "If you're not Harmony Kent in disguise, then it's official. I've been stood up." He added a sigh. "On a blind date, no less."

"Sorry."

Watching the way he started fiddling with his napkin, Sara wondered if he was going to hit her with the old "Since neither of us have anything better to do tonight, why don't we…" routine. To her surprise, he shot her an almost-embarrassed smile, then turned and asked the judge for the phone.

Mike handed him the cordless unit and Will consulted a piece of paper from his wallet before dialing.

Mike leaned closer to her. "Did Raymond tell you he was going to be late?"

She nodded. "Yeah…but not this late."

"I'm sure he realizes how hard it is for you to get a night off. Especially a Friday night."

She shrugged. "But will he be as understanding when he realizes I can't get another Friday off until the next blue moon?'' As she spoke to Mike, she watched Will out of the corner of her eye. Whatever the nature of his conversation, he didn't like what he was hearing.

"Sure, he will. An infamous attorney like the Blackwater Barracuda understands the pressures of running a business."

"He says he hates that nickname, you know."

Mike shook his head. "No, he doesn't. You and I both know he secretly loves it." His sympathetic smile widened. "Anyway, you need to eat. If you can hold off for another forty-five minutes, I can break loose from here and join you for an intimate, however platonic, dinner for two. Raymond trusts me."

She reached over and patted his arm. "He's not the only one. Thanks...but no, thanks. I think it would be better if I just went on home and used this time to get some extra sleep."

"If Raymond shows up later or calls, you want me to—" Mike made the appropriate twisting gesture "—dig the knife in a little?"

"It's not necessary." She winked at him. "Of course, it might not hurt, either. If you really feel a pressing need to make Raymond understand my overwhelming sense of disappointment...then who am I to stop you?"

Mike shot her an "Okay" sign. "You got it."

Will stepped closer, handing Mike the phone. "Thanks."

Sara turned around, took one look at Will's crestfallen face and felt a pang of sympathy for him. Not a shred of amusement remained in his expression. She leaned toward him slightly. "Everything okay?"

He stared at his empty glass, waving away Mike's offer to refill it. Turning back to her, Will adopted a pale imitation of his earlier grin. "Halfway through the conversation, Harmony couldn't remember the excuse she'd just offered for standing me up. Either she had to wash her hair or her favorite aunt just died. By the time we finished, it sounded as if she had to wash her dead aunt's hair.'' He didn't wait for their reaction. "Mike...will this cover my tab?'' He reached into his wallet and pulled out a ten.

Mike nodded, taking the money as well as the empty glass. As he reached for the discarded napkin, Will stopped him, the grin gaining some strength. "Nope, this is an important legal document. I think we need to put it someplace safe. Who knows when it might come in handy.'' He stood, folded the paper, placed it in his pocket, then held his hand out to Sara. "Miss Hardaway, it was a pleasure meeting you.''

She accepted his handshake, "And it was nice to meet you, Mr.—er—''

A pleasant tinge of color brightened his features. "We were never formerly introduced, were we? I'm Will Riggs.''

"Pleased to meet you, Will. Maybe between the two of us, we'll eventually figure out Mike's secret formula.''

When Sara reached to the back of the chair and retrieved her coat, Will immediately offered to help her put it on. "Are you leaving, too?'' She felt his hand brush across the back of her neck as he deftly lifted her hair from beneath her collar. Goose bumps rippled down her arms.

"Yes. I've run out of patience.''

He hesitated for a moment. "Well...if you have nothing to do tonight...and I have nothing to do, why don't we stay here and eat? Or go to a movie?''

From a lesser man, those words would have sounded like a cheap line, but Will made it seem like a natural response when two people found their plans had changed. However, Sara didn't actually consider his offer for more than a second or two.

Happily engaged women didn't do things like that.

However, happily engaged women did have a responsibility to turn down nice guys in a kind and considerate manner.

"Uh, as much as I appreciate the offer..." She stumbled over the words, trying to find the right balance between pacifying his ego and making sure he realized she was a staunchly loyal woman.

"Thanks, but no thanks?" he supplied.

She nodded. "Something like that."

"The divorce is still too fresh?"

"Divorce?" She thought back to their earlier conversation and suddenly understood Will's confusion. "Oh...the divorce-lawyer reference. No, I'm not in the beginning, middle or end of a divorce. My fiancé is a divorce lawyer who is almost unforgivably late for our night out."

"'Almost unforgivably,' meaning he will be forgiven?"

She shrugged. "Eventually. However, I do reserve the right to put him on the hot seat for a while. Just on general principle, you know."

Will adopted a conciliatory smile. "Please...let me walk you to your car. It's the least I can do." He tossed a glance toward the judge who was listening openly to their conversation. "Mike can vouch for my good character, right?"

The judge nodded. "He's a good 'un, Sara, and he knows if he got out of line, I'd wipe the floor with him." Mike caught her gaze and held it for a moment. "It's okay. Really."

She smiled. "Thanks. I'd appreciate an escort."

Will blazed a crooked path through the knots of conversing people and led her toward the door. Halfway there, he leaned back and said something to Sara, which was swallowed up by the crowd's noise.

"What?" she prompted, moving closer to him.

"The cranberry juice. Now that I think about it, I don't know how I could miss something so obvious."

She nodded. "Weird, eh?"

Even once they got outside, they were still surrounded by a throng of noisy people.

"Where's your car?" Will shouted above the roar.

She pointed into the darkness. "A block to the left and down the side street. I parked in the alley beside a dry cleaners."

"I know exactly where that is." Will threaded them through the last group of people who congregated under the canopied entrance to The Judge's Chambers. He placed a steadying hand on her elbow as they walked down the short flight of steps. "I'm glad you're not out here by yourself. The lighting isn't good in that area." Although he didn't remove his hand after they reached the street level, she decided his gesture fell under the auspices of a gentleman's code of manners.

Once they strolled down the sidewalk a half block, the noise level went down significantly, but a passing ambulance quickly filled the void. Sara flinched at the sound.

Will leaned closer. "You okay?" His breath made a frosty cloud in the air.

She nodded. "Sure." The cold October wind whistled around the corner and down the collar of her coat. But Will was the one to shiver.

"If I had known it was going to be this cold tonight, I would have brought a jacket," he complained.

It seemed only natural for Sara to shift closer to him, in order to prevent some of the wind from passing through his thin sweater. His hand tightened on her elbow as she took a jostled step.

"Watch out. These brick sidewalks are killers."

She nodded. "Potholes and high heels. They automatically attract each other, yet they're natural enemies."

His grip tightened again as they left the brightly lit main

avenue and stepped into the shadows lining the darker side street. Although they shared innocuous small-talk as they walked, she felt as if he spent more attention on their surroundings than he did on her. He carefully scanned every shadow without being overt, and she found his protective instincts reassuring.

As they approached her car, she fumbled in her pocket and pulled out her keys, then thumbed the remote unlocking button.

Nothing happened.

Will stared at her keys. "Something wrong?"

"It didn't work." She held the unit out at arm's length and pushed the button again. "I don't understand."

"Push it again," he instructed. To his credit, he didn't wrench the remote out of her hand and try it himself. Instead, he released her elbow and scanned the darkness with sudden intensity. A moment later, he took her by surprise with a sudden burst of laughter.

She pivoted and glared at him. "What?"

"This isn't your car." Will turned and pointed at another vehicle in the distance. The car's interior lights were on but no one was inside. "I bet that one's yours."

She squinted in the darkness, belatedly realizing that the car they stood beside was black, not dark green like hers. She allowed herself one self-exasperated sigh. "Oh, brother..." Maneuvering around the parked car, Sara stepped out into the empty street. Pushing the remote button merely confirmed her error; the other vehicle's interior lights flickered off, then on again.

"Ain't technology great? Wait—" Will stopped in the middle of the road and stooped down. "I think you dropped something when you got out your keys."

Sara reached into her pocket. "I don't think so." She stepped closer to him, squinting to see what had captured his interest in a pothole in the middle of the road.

An engine roared to life. Headlights suddenly flared in

her eyes. In one blinding moment, sound and light united, swelling to deadly proportions. A shriek of rubber on asphalt blended with Will's shouted warning.

"Sara...look out!"

Chapter Two

There was no time to weigh possible options.

Will hurled himself at Sara, knocking her out of the way. As they tumbled between the parked cars, he tried to absorb the worst of their momentum and impact-force by twisting in midair and landing on the bottom. A split second later, he learned exactly how much pain such altruism could generate.

When his head hit the curb, a swirling rainbow of stars blotted his vision. To make matters worse, Sara hit him squarely in the solar plexus, forcing the air out of his lungs. He heard the thrumming echo of a badly tuned engine over his own gasping attempts to regain his breath. Even after the loud vehicle disappeared down the street, it was still hard to hear the anxious voice calling his name over the hammering of his heart.

"Will? Will? Are you all right?"

He refused to move until he could recall the fundamental difference between up and down. Once he remembered, his next reaction was to make sure Sara hadn't been injured. But he quickly learned her initial instinct was to administer the same treatment to him. After a confusing moment of dueling first-aid attempts, they both realized they'd survived their ordeal relatively unscathed. Will helped Sara up from the gutter and propped her against a nearby car.

He rubbed the lump forming on the back of his head and tried not to wince. "You okay?"

Her teeth began to chatter. "That c-car came out of n-nowhere. He c-could have hit us."

"But he didn't." Although earlier, she'd made it perfectly clear she wasn't interested in him, Will surrendered to an instinct to put his arm around her shaking shoulders. For one incredible moment, everything felt...right. It was as if having this woman in his arms was the most natural thing in the world for both of them. She shuddered and his doubts crept back. Was her reaction a matter of delayed stress or the sudden realization that she was in *his* arms and not her fiancé's?

He orchestrated her release by gingerly probing his second most demanding injury: a bruised chin. "Did you see the driver?"

She shook her head. "The headlights blinded me. I couldn't tell you whether it was a Volkswagen or a Mack truck."

He closed his eyes and leaned against the hood of the parked car, trying to recall the details the flash of headlights had etched into his brain. "It was a Mercedes—dark, maybe black. But I couldn't make out which model or the license." He opened his eyes. "I couldn't see the driver, either."

"You're pretty observant." Her look of dawning admiration turned rapidly to concern. "Will...you're bleeding."

He glanced at the faint smear of color on his fingers, and the bowling ball in his stomach took a counterclockwise spin. *I hate blood.*

"Will?"

"I hate blood," he repeated, this time aloud for her benefit. He swabbed the cut on his chin and tried not to look at the residue left on his fingers. Knowing that the better part of valor was maintaining the facade of bravery, he managed what he hoped wasn't too pasty a smile. "It's nothing. I've done worse to myself shaving."

Sara pawed through the purse still slung around her shoulder and pulled out a small packet of tissues. "Here."

After swabbing away the worst of the blood with a tissue, Will lifted himself from the car bumper, then offered her a hand. To his surprise, she accepted, slipping her cold fingers into his. To his further amazement, she stood without removing her hand from his grasp.

"Should we call the police?"

Will dragged his attention back to their predicament, almost embarrassed that he could even consider invasive personal feelings when the meting out of justice should be the foremost thing on his mind. He squinted into the shadows. There wasn't much to go on. They had only a vague description, too much elapsed time and a major interstate escape route only a few blocks away. He glanced at his watch, then looked up at her only to be momentarily mesmerized by her dirtied features, her mussed hair and her magnificently disheveled dress.

"Will?" she prompted.

He glossed over his temporary misdirection. "I—I was just thinking…it's almost ten o'clock on a busy Friday night. We don't have much of a description of the vehicle and we can't identify the driver. Other than my chin and your stockings—" she followed his glance to her grimy knees "—and our collective dignity, no real damage has been done."

Despite the pink halo of the streetlight, he could tell she was truly blushing. Pulling her hand from his, she suddenly busied herself, flicking away the sodden leaves stuck to her dress. "My collective dignity is going to be very sore in the morning."

He stuffed his hands into his pockets and winced. "Mine, too."

She took one last look down the street. "I guess the best thing to do now is simply head home." Suddenly she straightened, then blinked. "I didn't thank you," she whispered. He started to protest, but she cut him off with a quick gesture. "You saved my life and I want to thank you for that."

He stared down at his shoes, wondering how long it would be before he uttered the immortal words, "Aw, shucks, ma'am. T'weren't nothin'."

"Will?"

He looked up.

"Thank you." She caught him by surprise by stepping closer, standing on her tiptoes and placing a warm but very chaste kiss on his cheek.

The whisper-soft sensation played havoc with his already shaky equilibrium. He stared into her eyes, wondering if he would find some evidence of restraint hidden in their depths. Could an unpretentious gesture of gratitude mask a more complicated emotion? In the split second that their gazes locked, he created an entire life for them.

Together.

He blinked.

And his fantasy world faded into the oblivion from which it rose. *Pipe dreams,* he reprimanded himself. *Nothing but stupid pipe dreams.*

She groaned as she flexed her shoulders. "I'd better go now. If I don't get into a hot tub soon, I won't be able to move tomorrow."

A hot tub?

His pipe dreams surfaced for one last go at it.

"But…" His voice trailed off as the truth smacked him in the face. No matter how charming, how attentive, no matter how attracted he might be to her, her heart belonged to another man.

It was as simple as that.

He dragged himself back to the business at hand. This was definitely conduct unbecoming a gentleman...but he wasn't there to be a gentleman; he was there as a businessman, hoping to ply his unsavory trade.

He took a deep breath. If charm couldn't win, perhaps logic had a chance. He bent down and retrieved her keys from the leaf-strewn gutter, gallantly wiping them off on the leg of his jeans. At least he could appear to be a gentleman whether he truly was one or not. "Can I at least follow you in my car? Just to make sure you make it home all right?"

The look she gave him contained more concern and confusion than fear. "It's not necessary. This really was...an isolated incident. I think I'm over the worst of it." She held out a remarkably steady hand and he reluctantly gave her the ring of keys.

"You're absolutely sure?" He held her fingers just a tad longer than necessary.

She ignored his gesture, gracing him with a small but genuine smile. "I appreciate the offer, but I'll be fine."

He walked with her in silence to her car, holding the door for her as she settled into the driver's seat. A more persistent man might push a little harder, but Will decided she wasn't the sort of woman who respected being unduly pressed. He knew a compromise was in order if he wanted one last chance. Closing the door, he motioned for her to roll down the window.

"Does Mike know where you live? Does he have your phone number, at least?"

Her eyes widened.

That got her attention!

Her smile faded a bit. "Look...you're a nice guy and I appreciate what you did but—"

"Don't worry, I'm not trying to pick you up." Will stooped and rested his arms on the window opening. "It's just that it would make me feel a whole lot better if you called Mike when you got home. Just so he and I...so we both know you got home safe. If he knows where you live, then he'd be able to call the cops if there were any problems or you felt uncomfortable."

She took a moment to mull over his logic, then nodded and sighed. "Yes, Mike knows where I live."

Will thumbed over his shoulder toward the restaurant. "Then after you roll up your windows and lock your doors, I'm going to go back and tell him what happened so he'll know to expect your call." Will consulted his watch. "How long will it take you to get home?"

Sara shrugged. "Twenty, maybe twenty-five minutes. There's not much traffic this time of night."

"Then I'll tell him to expect your call within the half hour. Anything later than that and we call out the guys from 'Dragnet,' okay?"

She nodded. "Sounds fair." She glanced up, nailing him with a look that under any other circumstances, he would describe as beguiling. But Will realized there was no guile involved.

No hidden messages.

No engaging offers from the engaged lady.

He stood, accepting defeat as graciously as he could manage. "Drive carefully."

For a moment, their gazes locked. Even though the window slowly rolled up between them, the glass failed to slice through their riveted attention.

"Thank you," she mouthed.

It wasn't until her car disappeared around a corner that Will allowed himself to release the breath he held. He'd made a mistake. A big mistake.

And he was going to have to think fast to place the blame elsewhere. But William B. Riggs could tap-dance around guilt with the best of them. He stuffed his hands into his pockets and whistled a tuneless melody as he headed back to the restaurant.

SARA TOLD HERSELF she wouldn't look at the answering machine when she got home, but curiosity demanded to be served. While she called Mike from her phone in her office, she tried valiantly to ignore the steady red light, which indicated no one had left a message.

No one including Raymond.

Mike burst onto the phone line. "Sara! Will told me what happened. Are you okay?"

"Yes, Mike, I'm fine. I didn't notice any cars following me or men in trench coats waiting outside my door."

"You're sure?" he shouted over the background noise. "I could find that no-good fiancé of yours, read the riot act to him and he'd be over there in two seconds flat."

"No, Mike. Like I said, I'm fine. And don't you dare bother Raymond. He must be tied up in business or he would have shown up tonight." She paused, girding her courage. "Uh...what about Will? Is he okay?"

"I sent him home with an ice pack for his head."

Her heart took an extra beat. "His head?"

"Yeah, he took a pretty good crack on the noggin when you landed on him. But don't worry about him—the guy's got a hard head. He bounces back fast. Now, you...you go check your doors, then head to bed. Okay, doll?"

"Thanks for caring, Mike. Bye."

After she hung up, Sara realized she had two options: fear or anger. Both would keep her up all night, either worrying that something terrible had happened to her fiancé or furious over his apparent inconsideration. However, she knew Raymond was neither careless nor thoughtless. She surrendered to the logic of fatigue, which whispered that he would call the next day with some reasonable excuse why he'd been unable to make their date.

Whether she chose rage or panic, either would be better dealt with after a good night's sleep.

But sleep didn't come easily, nor did it come without a price. She tossed and turned all night, and when she awoke in the morning, she suffered from vague memories of several erotic dreams that tiptoed around the edges of her mind.

As she propped herself on a stool in the kitchen, Sara tried to dredge up those dreams from their forgotten corners. It was no fair having her subconscious provide what must have amounted to distracting entertainment all night and not be able to remember much of it. It had something to do with—a sudden shiver made her slosh coffee on the newspaper—a knight in shining armor using a Frisbee to disarm a white-eyed mechanical dragon holding a scale in his claws.

Sara didn't need a Freudian theorist to explain the obvious symbolism; her knight in shining armor was Will and the white-eyed mechanical dragon was the oncoming vehicle that had nearly run them over. The scale? The symbol for the legal system, which could represent either a retired judge or the Blackwater Barracuda. Which one? Did it really matter? She didn't believe that every dream bore the responsibility of carrying a message from the subconscious mind.

But...what about the Frisbee?

Blowing into her coffee, she watched ripples destroy the reflection of a sleepy woman who held no deeply rooted attraction for Sir William of Riggs.

Sometimes a Frisbee was just a Frisbee.

She left her mug on the counter and searched the refrigerator for something bland for breakfast. She spotted a jar of a marmalade—his favorite marmalade. Well, if he wanted to eat it and not wear it the next time she saw him, Raymond S. Bergeron, attorney-at-law, had quite a heartfelt apology ahead of him. When he eventually surfaced, she would make sure to put him through his paces.

Make him toe the line.

Or walk the plank.

She would...scan the headlines, looking for some sensational story, which would explain that Raymond had single-handedly saved twelve people from a burning bus and had been whisked to the White House for an awards ceremony.

She actually trotted down the driveway and retrieved the paper. But there was no story...so far.

Twice she reached for the telephone, but each time, she forced herself to stop. Raymond was the one who needed to make that all-important apologetic call, not her.

But what if he's hurt...?

Sara ignored the little worrywart voice in her head. However, she did continue to find excuses to linger at home: lounging for an unusually long time in the hot tub and changing her mind twice about her outfit. Finally running out of delaying tactics, she dressed and headed to the restaurant where she figured some hard, tedious work might distract her.

Entering through the back door, she dodged a deliveryman hauling in trays of fresh bread.

"You're late, again," she complained as she held open the door for him. She couldn't help but enjoy the whiff of freshly baked bread as it passed by.

"Yes, ma'am. But this time I called."

But you're still late. Sara stepped into the kitchen and spotted her partner, Lucy Hilliard, who was busy overseeing the morning crew. Lucy raised her hand to cut off Sara's further protests. "I know he's late. But he called."

"So he said. But it's the third time this week. One of these days he's going to cut it too close and we'll be serving burgers with no buns." She tried to maintain a stern front but the aroma of fresh bread overtook her. She snagged one bun, sampled it and sighed. "But we'll never find anybody who makes them like this guy." She took another bite. "Just as long as he called…"

Lucy's husband, Martin, squinted at Sara through the steam of the large pot he was stirring. "You look too rested. What happened?"

Sara released another sigh. "Nothing."

Lucy stopped slicing lemons long enough to give Sara a critical once-over. "Nothing as in 'nothing much' or as in 'nothing at all'?"

Sara felt the tips of her ears redden. "Nothing as in Raymond never showed up."

"Never?" Lucy and Martin blurted together.

Sara shrugged. "He told me yesterday he had a six o'clock meeting that might make him a little late. But it must have lasted longer than he expected. I left Mike's place around ten—" she didn't dare look at Martin "—after waiting almost two hours." But in avoiding Martin's glower, she made the mistake of glancing at Lucy. The woman's look of shock was almost more than Sara could bear.

"And he simply never came?" Lucy uttered in disbelief. "Or called? Or at least left a message?"

Sara sighed yet again. Was it entirely necessary to relive that humiliation simply for the enlightenment of her friends? And she still had Martin's reaction yet to survive.

As expected, he slammed a lid on the pot he was tending; Martin always reacted physically when he got upset. But it was his second motion that took Sara by surprise. When he reached for the phone hanging on a nearby wall, she didn't quite understand what he was doing until he punched the fourth digit—of Raymond's number.

"Oh, Martin…don't."

He shook his head, listened to the receiver, then spoke in his usual low, controlled tones. "Raymond, it's Martin.

I think you'd better explain to Sara why you missed your date last night.'' He shoved the phone in her direction.

That was Martin for you. No frills, tell-them-what's-on-your-mind Martin. Usually she found his directness refreshing; this morning she found it damn near unappealing and she made sure he had an opportunity to read her opinion plainly in her face as she took the receiver from him.

Raymond sounded sleepy. ''Honey, I'm sorry but you have to understand that the meeting ran long.''

She tightened her grip on the receiver. ''I figured that's what happened. I explained that to Martin, but you know how he is.''

Martin crossed his arms and glared at her.

She knew what his expression meant: *Tell him how you really feel.* And she also knew Martin Hilliard wouldn't let her rest until she confronted Raymond, which she didn't want to do, even if she knew it was the right thing to do. She drew a fortifying breath. ''I just wished you'd called so I wouldn't have worried—''

Martin cleared his throat loudly.

She glared at him. *You aren't going to let me get away with anything, are you?*

She picked up the thread of her conversation. ''Then I wouldn't have felt as if you'd forgotten all about me.''

''Forget you?'' Raymond made a noise that reminded her of a stifled yawn. ''Not bloody likely. Listen, sweetie, I know Martin's standing there, tsk-tsking and muttering under his breath. He's pretty hard to ignore when he gets a head of steam. Just tell my esteemed cousin that I agree with him. I'm a louse. I'm a two-bit four-flusher who doesn't deserve an angel like you. Tell him I'm the lowest of the low and he can be sure I'll do any and everything I can to make it up to you.''

She glanced at Martin who crossed his arms and glared back. Although the two men were cousins, they shared an animosity that was almost as strong as the family bond between them. Martin gave her another steely-eyed glare, which was eerily reminiscent of his cousin's. "Has Ray apologized, yet?"

A voice buzzed in the receiver. "Is Marty glaring at you?"

Sara nodded, trying to sort out the three-way conversation. "Yes, Marty's glaring," she said into the phone. "Yes, Ray apologized," she informed Martin. She glanced at Lucy who leaned against the wall, evidently enjoying the spectacle. "Mary Margaret Lucille, do *you* have anything to add?" Mary Margaret Lucille twisted the imaginary key which locked her lips shut, then raised both hands in mock surrender. She turned her attention back to her lemons.

Raymond's voice settled into a silken hum in her ear. "Listen honey, I really want to make this up to you. How about we take a long drive in the country? You know…somewhere quiet, where we can admire the fall colors. I bet I could pull a few strings, call in a few markers and get reservations at that little bed-and-breakfast you like out toward Manassas."

Her heart quickened. "The Lakeside Inn?"

Lucy nodded her furious agreement while Martin shook his head. Husband and wife caught sight of each other's opposing reactions and began a hissing conversation in low tones. Sara imagined a scale balancing each side's arguments against the other's. The pans teetered one way and then the other.

Blind justice strikes again….

The receiver purred, "Well, how does it sound, angel?"

She shivered in spite of herself. "It sounds…lovely—"

Lucy punched her fist into the air in silent triumph. "Yes!" she mouthed in celebration.

"But I'm afraid I have to work."

As Lucy's spirits sagged, Martin straightened, crossed his arms and gave Sara a satisfied nod.

Closing her eyes to block out their silent expressions, Sara continued. "Raymond, you have to understand…I had to move heaven and earth to get last night off. And part of the agreement was for me to take both the lunch and dinner crowds today." She forged ahead, hoping to forestall his next argument. "And you know how busy we are on Saturdays."

The Blackwater Barracuda, a recognized master of debate, launched his rebuttal. "Ah…but if Lucy and Martin are already there, then I bet you could talk them into—"

"Lucy and Martin have a special anniversary to celebrate tonight and there's no way I'm going to mess up their plans." Raymond tried to interrupt her again, but Sara continued. "Look, I'm really sorry, but I'm going to be busy all today and tonight. We'll talk tomorrow, okay? Bye." The receiver hit the hook a bit harder than Sara had intended and the echo filled the kitchen.

Martin's smug expression faded as he split his attention between Sara and his glowering wife. "An-anniversary? Did I forget…?"

"It's just like a man to forget something important like an anniversary." Lucy snapped a towel in Martin's direction. Her expression faded to a half smile. "Jeez, don't have a heart attack, Martin. You didn't forget anything. It's not our anniversary. It's just Sara's way of making excuses. Right?"

Sara reached over and retrieved a slice of lemon from Lucy's cutting board. Tearing off the rind, she used it to form a yellow ring on the steel countertop. "I didn't know what else to do. If I tell him I'm upset that his meetings always seem to get in the way of our plans, then I get accused of not understanding the demands of his career."

"But you do understand," Martin supplied. "But…" His voice trailed off, inviting her to finish the unspoken sentiment.

"But...he needs to remember I have responsibilities, too."

Lucy rushed to Raymond's defense, something she'd been having to do more often than usual. "I'm sure he understands how demanding it is to run a restaurant. But you know how single-minded he is. Most good lawyers are."

Martin cocked his head toward his wife. "To hear Lucy talk, you'd think he was *her* cousin rather than mine. But listen, I'm the one who knows all about Raymond. *I* grew up with him. We didn't call him single-minded when he was a grubby five-year-old who hogged all the crayons. We called him selfish."

Lucy stood her ground. "But Raymond did apologize, right?"

Martin harrumphed with gusto. "Bet it wasn't much of an apology, was it?"

After suffering a bellyful of their bickering, Sara threw her arms up. "Stop it, you two! It's my life. Okay?"

Her tactics didn't dissuade Martin one bit, proving that the cousins had at least one "stubborn" gene in common. He crossed his arms and shot her a look that was hauntingly familiar. "You didn't answer the question. Was it a real apology or did he give you some half-assed 'I'm sorry, *but...*' answer?"

Sara thought back on Raymond's quick dismissal of her complaints. A romantic weekend might make a nice bandage to cover the wound, but things could fester under a bandage if left untreated. She allowed herself a resigned shrug. "You're right. It wasn't much of an apology."

A boiling pot demanded Martin's attention for a brief moment. When he turned back around, he wore a new expression; he was almost smiling. "Exactly how mad are you?"

Mad? Being mad didn't hurt quite like this. "I'm more disappointed than mad."

A new twinkle entered Martin's eyes, a visible sign of a mind and wit that both worked at lightning-fast speed. "So...are you disappointed enough to want to avoid him tomorrow, too?"

She shrugged. "Maybe."

"Well, then..." Martin reached over and grabbed his wife's hand, lifting it to his lips for a quick kiss.

Lucy shot him a dubious look and took a step backward. "You have one weird sense of timing, Martin Hilliard."

"Nonsense." He reached forward and pulled her into his arms. "It's our duty to keep our dear friend, Sara, from making a liar out of herself." His smile dripped with condescension. "Right?"

Sara knew Lucy was no match for Martin's hundred-watt grin.

Lucy blushed. "Well..."

"We mentioned something about seeing a movie tonight, but why don't we do something else, instead." He gave Lucy such a look of undisguised adoration that Sara felt like a spectator—an unwelcome spectator at that.

Martin lifted Lucy's hair from her ear and whispered loudly enough for his audience to hear, "Why don't I call and see if there are any vacancies at the Lakeside Inn?" He turned and winked at Sara. "I understand they might have had a sudden cancellation."

Sunday, late afternoon

THIRTY HOURS AND four hundred and twenty-three meals later, Sara discovered her cohabiting hostess and bartender weren't speaking and one of the new busboys was stealing tips. Her biggest worry was how to keep the thief from becoming a victim once the aggravated waitress realized why she'd had a miserable day, monetarily, and how to keep the bar from becoming a battle zone.

After three stern lectures, one threat and a dozen roses, things were back to normal at closing time. Sara watched the hostess, Melissa, pitch in and help her boyfriend, Charlie, tally his bar register. Once the misunderstanding between them had been assuaged by flowers—from the only florist in the area who was open at three on a Sunday afternoon—and a sincere apology, they fluttered around each other like lovebirds, cooing and eyeing the bar as a possible roost.

Kids, Sara told herself with a sigh. Then she stopped short. Since when did romance become a matter of age? And when did age become a factor here, anyway? Charlie and Melissa were graduate students, not sixteen-year-olds enthralled with the idea of being in love.

Sara caught sight of herself in the mirror behind the bar. Thirty-two wasn't old. Thirty-two didn't mean that romance had to take a back seat to the other aspects of love—like compatibility, strength of devotion....

Her analogies of love fizzled as she watched the two lovers join in a steamy kiss.

Passion...

Maybe I made a big mistake not accepting Raymond's offer. Sure, it was a bribe, but it might have been just what we needed, to— she allowed herself a quick glance at Charlie and Melissa and wondered why the mirror behind them hadn't fogged up —*to get back on track.*

Sara turned and watched the waitress and busboy shake hands. Their dispute turned out to be a misunderstanding rather than a case of out-and-out thievery. The busboy had cheerfully presented her tips to her, having labored under the misbelief that he was supposed to collect them for her when he cleared the tables. Although his apology was hard to understand since English was his fourth or fifth language, the sincerity was unmistakable.

With all of the restaurant's problems having been easily

reconciled, it was time for Sara to go home and see if she couldn't work the same kind of magic in her own life.

But Raymond's only response was, "Hello, you've reached 555-9476. I can't take your call right now, but leave your name and number...."

And she continued to get that same message all seven times she called him the rest of that day, evening, and night.

After she undressed for bed, she picked up her latest book from the bedside table. It seemed almost unconscionable that she could get lost in someone else's love story when hers was stuck somewhere in the middle chapters.

She put the book aside and tried to lose herself in a cooking magazine, but to no avail. Switching off the light, she sighed and stared into the darkness cloaking her ceiling.

Wherever you are, Raymond, I hope you feel as miserable as I do.

Sunday night

"YOU WHAT?" He rubbed his right temple with the palm of his hand.

"What can I say? I panicked."

"Panicked? You didn't panic. You went absolutely friggin' crazy." His head started to throb. "Only a lunatic would try to run someone down in broad daylight."

"It wasn't daylight. It was nighttime. Friday night."

"I don't care if it was during a total eclipse of the sun. Someone could have seen you, identified the car. Then where would you be?" The pain pulsated through his head, down his fingers and headed toward his heart. Or was it the other way around? Up from the heart and into his fingers, then his head?

He dropped onto the barstool, squeezed his eyes shut

and dragged his attention back to the problem at hand. "Promise me you won't try something stupid like this again. Okay?"

A faint answer pierced the darkness. "I promise, honey."

Chapter Three

Will looked up at the ceiling above his bed. Another well-placed crack and he'd have a perfect Big Dipper staring down at him in all his misery.

He flipped over and punched his pillow for the fourth time. Small pinfeathers spewed from a minuscule rip in the seam, fluttered in the air for a few seconds, then floated down to land on his nose.

He sneezed, destroying his last fleeting hope of sleep.

"Damn it!" Will sat up, grabbed the pillow and hurled it across the room. It landed against the door with an unsatisfactorily dull thud, leaving a trail of feathers to mark its trajectory. "Why can't I go to sleep!"

The sudden rush of adrenaline coursed through his veins, flooding his sluggish body and making it respond with the same sense of alertness as his mind. He groaned. *I'll never get any sleep now!*

No sleep. No sleep. The words matched the heavy thrum of his heart. No sleep...

Until I call him tomorrow and make my report.

And? his conscience prompted.

"And make him happy and me, miserable."

And what about her?

The words echoed in his mind.

What about her…?

Sara Marie Hardaway, brown hair, brown eyes, five foot six, no police record, excellent credit rating, restaurant owner, all-around nice person…would wear white when she married Raymond S. Bergeron, Esquire, in the requisite large church wedding.

And William Brian Riggs would continue to wear black as he skulked around the shadows, trying to get the goods on the guilty.

He sighed.

Why did life have to be so monochromatic?

Monday, almost sunrise

"ALREADY?" SARA SQUINTED, then fumbled with the clock at her bedside. Then she realized the insistent sound came from her telephone. She jammed the receiver somewhere in the vicinity of her ear. "H'lo?"

"Good morning, glory!" Raymond's voice boomed with unearthly enthusiasm.

She groaned. "What time is it?"

"Five forty-five. I wanted to talk to you before I went out for my racquetball game."

She pulled the pillow over her head and released a string of oaths she'd learned from the garbageman one slippery day in January.

"What? What?" he shouted. "I can't understand you."

"You could have called me *after* your game. I don't go into work until after lunch on Monday."

"Oh, jeez…"

Illumination dawns, she grumbled to herself, *one ringing phone call too late.*

"I didn't remember your schedule," he continued. "I'm sorry, hon. I really am. Why don't I call back later and—"

"I'm awake now, Raymond." She ground her fist into the flowered pillowcase. "Why don't you simply tell me what you want, then let me go back to sleep, okay?"

"Sure, sweetheart. All I wanted to do was apologize again for Friday night. It really was inexcusable, but this Howard-Barnes divorce is becoming a real bitch of a case. It's gotten to the point where I think she's trying to get the towels monogrammed "His" just for the sheer pleasure of screwing him over. But...I didn't mean to spend all Friday night arguing with them. You know I'd rather have been with you."

She opened her eyes. *He apologized.* Astonishment evaporated her ability to speak.

Raymond misinterpreted her lack of response, evidently thinking it was his cue to grovel some more. "You had every right to be mad at me. I should have called you. Hell, I should have simply walked out and let Blazer face both of them by himself. Then maybe he'd appreciate how much I shield him from the harsher realities of life."

"Blazer? Your client's name is Blazer?"

Raymond emitted a snort of laughter. "Sounds like a character from some soap opera, doesn't it? But it's his real name."

Sara allowed herself a first morning giggle. "What? Did his father own a Chevrolet dealership or is he some sort of no-neck football jock?"

Raymond's laughter increased. "Both."

It was good to hear him laugh, to share a joke with him. Laughter seemed an endangered commodity in their relationship, so when it occurred spontaneously, she remembered all the reasons why she was attracted to him.

And in the time it took to wipe a tear of laughter from her eyes, all was forgiven.

"I feel better now," he confessed. "I hated feeling guilty all weekend and not being able to clear the air like this."

"Me, too."

"What now?"

Sara thought for a moment. "Got plans for lunch?"

"Do I?" His voice dropped to a throaty growl. "You tell me. By lunchtime, I ought to have a hell of an appetite."

"Raymond," she warned. "I'm talking about bringing you lunch, sharing a meal. I'll bring something... interesting."

"You're interesting."

She ignored his obvious meaning. If they played their cards right, there would be time enough for fun and games as well as food. "Noon?"

"I'll clear my calendar and my desk. Or the conference room if we need a little more maneuvering space."

"Raymond Bergeron, you're incorrigible."

"More like insatiable."

A little over six hours later, Sara stood in the lobby of his building, balancing a basket of food on her hip. She wore a very prim-and-proper flowered dress that buttoned up the front. It was a calculated choice, selected because it was one of Raymond's favorites. She figured it had something to do with the less-than-prim-and-proper undergarments she always wore beneath.

As she punched the elevator call button, she thought about her last trip here. It was just her luck. Now that she was presentable enough to use the lobby elevator like a paying customer, Friday's lawyer and her milquetoast client were nowhere to be seen. When the elevator car arrived, Sara had it to herself for a speedy trip to the eleventh floor.

Joanie saw her coming and held open the glass door. "I don't know what happened this weekend, but if you're the reason why he's in a good mood for a Monday morning, you'll be my best friend forever."

Sara followed her into his office, surprised not to see

him working studiously at his immense desk. "How good a mood?"

Joanie nodded toward his empty chair. "Instead of ordering flowers to be delivered or sending me to get some, he went down to get them, himself. He said something about picking up a suitable bouquet of orchids."

"Orchids?" Sara placed the basket on his spotless credenza. "Orchids sound…serious."

Joanie alternately rubbed her hands and wrung them. The secretary knew something and it was eating away at her. She swallowed hard and glanced toward the door. "Sara, we've been friends ever since you guys started dating, right?"

"Sure."

"And I don't want to spoil any surprises, but I also don't want you to get caught off guard, either."

"Now, Joanie—" Sara began.

"Please…hear me out. Something's up. I can't tell what. But Raymond's gone to get orchids and he's been running around here, humming and acting strange. Sara—" The woman leaned forward in conspiracy. "I think he's going to ask—"

The telephone rang, making both of them jump.

Joanie made a face and reached over to grab the instrument on Raymond's desk. "Raymond S. Bergeron, attorney-at-law, may I help you? Oh…hi. Yeah? Right now? But Sara's here and… Well, yeah, I'm sure she would, but… Emergency? It better be an emergency. Be there in a minute." Joanie hung up and turned to Sara. "I'm sorry. There's a new secretary on nine and she's the most mechanically-challenged person I've ever met. The Xerox machine has eaten her report and it's the only copy. She's got ten minutes to deliver thirty collated sets of notes to a board meeting and she's starting to panic. I've got to give her a hand."

"No problem. You want me to man the phones?"

Joanie shot her a look of gratitude. "Would you... please?" Sara followed Joanie to her desk in the outer office where the woman reached into the drawer and retrieved a small screwdriver. She held it aloft. "Sometimes the machine spits stuff out if you threaten it with dismantling." She trotted toward the glass door leading to the hallway.

"But what about Raymond's big secret?" Sara called out to her.

Joanie paused in the doorway. "I think he's going to propose."

The door swung shut and Sara stared at the retreating figure.

"But we're already engaged."

Joanie didn't hear her and continued toward the exit stairs.

Orchids?

Sara returned to Raymond's office, contemplating this unexpected side of his personality. Orchids were nice, but not necessarily her favorite flower. When she thought of orchids, she thought of junior proms, Mother's Day and bridal bouquets.

Bridal bouquets?

Bridal?

It hit her. Raymond had been the one who espoused the concept of the long engagement and she couldn't help but understand his sense of caution. Surely a divorce lawyer realized the wisdom of two people getting to know each other well before getting married. It was his chief complaint about the cases he handled; it was far simpler for two people to make a legal commitment than a moral one.

In support of his justified sense of hesitation, she'd never pressured him for a wedding date, preferring the more open-ended engagement for the same reasons he cited. But if Joanie's instincts were right—and they usually were—changes were in store.

Maybe he wants to set a date....

Sara wandered blindly back into Raymond's office, her thoughts lost in a maze of conjecture and flights of imagination. Thoughts of orchids became bridal bouquets. And bridal bouquets led her to thoughts of white gowns, a church full of people, a tableau of friends dressed to the nines watching her step down the aisle. An organ would blare out "The Wedding March," church bells would chime.

Bells?

Sara glanced at the ringing telephone. After a moment's hesitation, she punched the flashing button and stuttered past her usual "Blackwater Café" greeting to a more appropriate, "Raymond Bergeron, attorney-at-law. May I help you?"

"May I speak to him, please?"

"I'm sorry, Mr. Bergeron's not in the office at the moment." She scrambled in Raymond's lap drawer, looking for a sticky pad and a pencil. Knowing his sense of organization, she realized all she probably had to do was look in the file drawer under 'P.' However, the lap drawer yielded what she needed. "May I take a message?" she said in her best secretarial voice.

"Would you have him call...uh—just a moment." A second later, she heard a muffled sneeze on the other end of the phone. He came back on the line. "I'm terribly sorry. I didn't mean to sneeze in your ear."

"You didn't, sir. The name again?"

"That's double U-B-R-I-G-G-S. He has the number."

"I'll ask him to return your call, Mr. Uubriggs." She stood and stuck the note to the headrest of his chair, where it showed quite plainly. As she stepped back into the outer office, she spotted Joanie heading in her direction.

"That was quick. Did you avert disaster?"

"Yes, only because she's a hopeless case."

"What do you mean?"

"She forgot where the output tray was. When I arrived, there were thirty perfect collated sets sitting there and her original still sitting on the glass."

Sara winced. "She's that inexperienced?"

Joanie lifted one eyebrow. "She assured me she had other assets to offset her lack of secretarial skills. I was afraid to ask what they were." Joanie made a grand gesture of looking around the office. "Anything exciting happen the three whole minutes while I was gone? Any wedding-gown deliveries? Have the champagne and cake arrived yet?"

"Hardly." Sara led the way into the conference room where she raided its cabinets for two place settings. Joanie helped carry the pieces into Raymond's office. "However, you'll be glad to know that I can take a phone message with some accuracy. I left it on Raymond's chair."

Joanie raised her eyebrow again. "On his chair?"

Sara reached into her basket and drew out a tablecloth. With one practiced snap of her wrist, she spread it over his desk. "I didn't want to lose the little piece of paper under all this. He has a funny name—sounds Swedish or something like that." As she started pulling food containers out of the basket, Joanie examined the sticky note. Her sudden burst of laughter caught Sara by surprise.

Joanie pointed to the note, then to the container of cashew-chicken salad. "You'd better stick to cooking and leave the message taking to me."

Sara craned over the secretary's shoulder. "What did I do wrong? He said you had his number."

"It's nothing—just an easy mistake to make." Joanie pointed to the name, "Mr. Uubriggs." "It's not double *U-B-R-I-G-G-S*." She picked up the pencil and corrected the spelling. "It's *W. B....R-I-G-G-S*. W. B. Riggs."

Riggs? "Riggs?" she repeated for Joanie's benefit. "W. B. Riggs as in Will Riggs?"

Joanie shot her a grin that could almost be described as lascivious. "You know him?"

Sara shrugged. "We've met." She eyed the note again, then broke away for a moment to slap Joanie's hand away from a foil-wrapped package. "Those rolls will get cold if you unwrap them. Does Raymond know Will Riggs?"

Joanie consoled herself with a stolen slice of carrot. "Sure. Raymond uses him all the time."

"As what?"

"A private investigator. He's our 'When in doubt, check them out' investigator."

Suddenly, Sara became aware of her surroundings: the sounds of the clock ticking on the opposite wall, the hum of Raymond's computer, the hiss of air through the ventilating system. "'When in doubt…'" she repeated. "You mean like looking into people's backgrounds and making sure they don't have a string of broken hearts or maybe a police record?"

Joanie nodded. "That and more. He tests what Raymond calls someone's 'loyalty rating.' You know, he talks to the female client about her fiancé, then hires a sexy woman to give the guy the come-on. If he falls for it and tries to make the moves on the bait, then the client knows what type of jerk he is *before* they get married."

"And I suppose—" Sara swallowed hard "—it can work the other way, right? This Mr. Riggs provides this service for…male clients, too?"

Joanie's grin broadened. "Will hires a real studmuffin to give the woman the business. If she accepts the offer, then she's busted. The cat's out of the bag before the bag becomes community property."

"He hires someone? He never…handles the case himself?"

Joanie perched on the edge of the desk. "Not that I'm

aware of. Of course, it's not for the lack of good looks. He's a good-looking son of a gun, but not in a flashy way. But as far as I know, every time Raymond's used his services, Will has hired someone to be the bait.''

A chill danced across the back of Sara's shoulders. ''And Raymond uses Mr. Riggs's services frequently?''

Joanie laughed. ''Sure. It's part of what Raymond calls his continuing-education program for his recently divorced clients. So they don't make the same mistake twice. If you ask me, it's a mistake because he's killing his repeat business. But Raymond says he still gets enough business from those clients who won't listen to the truth and continue to make bad marriage decisions.''

The phone rang again and instead of disturbing the lunch preparations to get to the phone, Joanie skidded out the door to her desk and took the call there.

Sara stared at the little yellow square of paper sticking to the leather headrest.

Surely Raymond wouldn't have...

He couldn't have suspected she would...

Did he trust her so little?

Her stomach began churning, her heart pounding. The blood rushed in her ears, almost obliterating the sounds of Raymond's arrival in the outer office. She sensed his presence behind her one moment before he nibbled her ear.

''Hello, gorgeous.''

''Hi.'' She didn't turn around, for fear of exploding with questions.

He wrapped one arm around her waist, leaning forward to place his chin on her shoulder. ''Hmmm...you smell nice. Almost as nice as these.'' He reached around and held a bouquet of flowers in front of her.

She looked down at the collection of white orchids; they were arranged in a perfect bridal bouquet. Perfectly presumptuous, at the moment.

"Orchids don't smell." She made no move to take the flowers from him.

His hot breath scorched her neck. "They don't dare try to outshine you, sweetheart." He started kissing the spot below her ear, which usually made her forget her name, lose track of where she was, disregard everything but what desire demanded.

But this time, no wave of passion swelled up to blot out her control. She held up the yellow message slip where Raymond could see it. "Tell me about this."

Raymond stopped long enough to look at the paper, slip it from her fingers and crumple it into a ball. "It's nothing." He started kissing her again.

Disappointment solidified into anger; she stiffened at his unwanted touch. "You sent him to test me Friday night, didn't you?"

The bouquet of flowers lowered for a moment, then the kissing stopped.

"You set up the whole bogus Friday-night date," she continued. "Stood me up on purpose, then sent in your slimy detective to see if he could entice me into a little extracurricular activity."

"But you didn't fall for him."

She turned around, appalled at what sounded like a sense of pride in his voice. "And now you're going to reward me for my faithfulness?" She batted away the bouquet. "This is supposed to make me forget that although I've never given you a single reason to distrust me, although I've never even looked at another man, you felt the need to test me? To try to trick me into infidelity?"

His look of shock melted quickly into a haughty anger. "I didn't think you would sleep with the man."

"Was I supposed to give him my phone number? Let him buy me a couple of drinks? Was I supposed to notice he was attentive, interesting, handsome, intelligent?"

Raymond drew a deep breath. "Evidently you did pay him some attention."

"That's beside the point." She reached down and retrieved the crumpled note, holding it in the palm of her hand. "For three years, I've given you no reason to distrust me, but evidently you do."

"But I don't distrust—"

"It doesn't matter, Raymond." Searching for her purse, she snatched it from the credenza. "It doesn't matter if you don't trust me because I no longer trust you."

"But..." He reached out, grabbing her arm in a too-tight grip.

She pinned him with her steeliest glare. "Don't touch me."

He slowly released her arm. "You're making a mistake, Sara. I love you." He glanced down at the flowers in his hand. "I want to marry you."

She stared at the white orchids, reminded once again of white wedding gowns, towering cakes with white frosting and tiny net bags of white rice. The mind's eye discolored them to match her black mood. "You wanted to marry me only after you were sure I passed some sort of stupid loyalty test."

The lingering warmth in his eyes faded. "But I haven't spoken to Riggs, yet."

Sara pulled the tablecloth back to expose the phone. "Then you'd better call him." She knew it was a cheap shot, but right now, only a low blow would suffice. She drew herself to her full height and gave him the most sinfully satisfied smile she could muster under the circumstances. "Call him, Raymond. You might be surprised at what he reports."

Monday afternoon

HE CONTEMPLATED the smooth brown cylinder of glass that he rolled between his hands. Beads of condensation clung to his skin. Or were his palms sweating? He couldn't tell. "What next?"

"We wait."

"Wait? Are you nuts?" He gripped the beer bottle in one hand. "We need to do...something."

"We don't do anything. That's rash. Until we understand how badly our position has been compromised, we simply hold back."

The glass warmed beneath his white-knuckled grasp. "Hold back? You've got to be kidding." Suddenly, the glass bottle cracked. He released an expletive and dropped the bottle, revealing a thin crimson slash that creased the palm of his hand.

"See what sort of damage wanton force can cause?" a silken voice purred in his ear. "You won't do anything until I tell you to. *If* I tell you to. Understand?"

He watched the single drop of blood swell and spread.

He understood now.

Chapter Four

Will scanned the report given him by his operative team. It never ceased to amaze him how greedy people could become when they thought no one was watching. Under the guise of collecting boxes for an upcoming move, a stock clerk had systematically looted every division of an electronics warehouse, building what Will's operative described as a ten-thousand-dollar computer system, one stolen component at a time.

Will leaned back and laced his fingers behind his head. This type of case was the backbone of most private investigating agencies. As long as people were paid minimum wage but had maximum tastes, greed thrived and crime lingered in its wake. Lucky for the investigators, their only job was to discover the criminal, not to apprehend him, which made their job that much safer.

Safe.

That was Will's byword, his mandate for himself as well as the people who worked for him. The best way to get yourself out of a dangerous situation was to never get into one in the first place.

He rubbed at the sudden telltale twinge above his temple.

Do as I say, not as I do.

Part of staying out of danger was remaining alert—another Riggs mandate, which he himself had painfully failed to remember. It had been a long time since he'd gotten so wrapped up in a woman—a subject—that he failed to see oncoming danger, like the speeding car. And he was paying for his misdirected attention with a beaut of a headache, not to mention a cut that looked as though it might leave a small scar on his chin as a souvenir. He dug into his lap drawer and found a small flat mirror, which he angled to get a better look at his injury. His imagination took off on its own, providing a far more satisfying ending to the case. Didn't such a sacrifice deserve more than a chaste kiss of thanks?

He closed his eyes and imagined Sara tangled in his arms, her look of fear fading to something more powerful, more personal.

"I didn't thank you for saving my life." Same words as before, but this time with a totally different meaning. This time, her gaze would hold his longer, with gratitude mixed with something infinitely stronger. He would see challenge in her eyes—a challenge born...out of desire, perhaps?

He would allow himself to meet her gaze directly but make no effort to touch her. There were rules to this; rules that prevented him from responding to implied challenges. It was up to Sara; she had to make the first move.

"Will..." This time, there was no question in her tone. There were no unanswered questions between them. Her voice was a low, throaty purr. *"Thank you."* She leaned forward and kissed him.

Ah...*the* kiss. Not the chaste little thing he'd called a kiss where she pressed her lips against his cheek for a split second, then disappeared from his life, leaving not as much as a glass slipper in her wake. Their kiss would be tender at first, even tentative. But inhibitions would fade under the heat of undeniable attraction.

He would respond. He couldn't help but respond.

Simultaneous desire would turn a simple gesture into a complex tangle of emotions. Gratitude would become seduction somewhere along the...

You're dreaming, Will, he reminded himself. *This is nothing more than fatigue leading your imagination astray.*

He smiled. *So what if it is?*

It would be the type of kiss that would shake him to his core and make him forget everything. Under its influence, their roles in life would be reduced to the simplest common denominators: the hunter and the hunted.

But what of the hunt?

Will opened his eyes and dragged himself away from his unforgivable dream. *Grow up, Riggs.* She was his prey, all right, but the rules of the hunt were different in this case. *And,* he reminded himself, *this is nothing more than a case.*

Bergeron should be thrilled. After all, Will's failure meant the lawyer's success. Now the man could run off and marry the woman of his dreams.

Will drew in a sharp breath, remembering how he had regained his senses and found himself stretched out in the gutter with his arms wrapped around Sara Hardaway. Soft curves, fragrant hair, her heartbeat throbbing wildly against his chest.

But what if she's the woman of my *dreams, too?*

Will shook his head, destroying the image that was starting to capture his imagination again.

Business. Not pleasure. All business.

He glanced at the file spread across his desk. The warehouse theft. He tried to concentrate on his operative's final assessment of the case. Several things had tripped up the guilty computer thief: good investigative technique, un-flagging attention and a stroke of luck.

Dumb luck.

Just like the dumb luck he'd had, saving Sara from a potential hit-and-run driver. He would never have chanced something potentially dangerous like a runaway car to in-gratiate himself with her, to make her feel appreciative of his selfless act and to force a wedge into the temporary crack that gratitude could create. He never worked that way with inherently dangerous gimmicks. However, he wasn't beyond taking advantage of an unforeseen oppor-tunity to make one last effort to get under her skin.

But...Sara had done everything she was supposed to; she'd turned him down flat. Thanks but no thanks. She'd even refused him with a classy sense of style and grace.

But why did he still feel uneasy?

He shouldn't, Will told himself. Bergeron was ecstatic and probably had spent the weekend with the lovely Miss Hardaway, shopping for wedding rings. And, Will sup-posed, what she didn't know, really wouldn't hurt—

The intercom buzzed. "Call on line one. It's about the Bergeron case."

"Got it, Mimi." Will picked up the phone. "Thanks for returning my call, Mr. Bergeron. We're working on the final bill and I wanted to ask you—"

"I'm not Mr. Bergeron."

Uh-oh... It was a familiar voice. A familiar *female* voice.

"This is Sara Hardaway—"

Here's the windup. The pitch. It's aiming for the fan....

"Mr. Bergeron's *former* fiancée," she continued.

Direct hit! The Good Ship Matrimony *has sustained major damage.* Will cleared his throat, deciding to side-step the personal ramifications of the words "*former* fi-ancée." Business. Always business. "What can I do for you, Miss Hardaway?"

"It was 'Sara' at the bar the other night."

He swallowed hard. No more Ms. Nice Guy; this was the voice of the Ice Maiden incarnate. It froze out every warm thought he'd had during the past hour or so. "You're right. It was Sara. What can I do for you?"

"I want you to explain the system to me."

"The system? What system?" he repeated, stalling for time.

"The investigating procedure. Explain to me your role in this little…charade." She paused for a moment, then spoke with an air of forced detachment. "Were you supposed to try to get me in bed?"

Will closed his eyes, momentarily distracted by the very scene she so coldly described. Under the influence of his overactive imagination, he could picture bed activities with her being damned near volcanic. Something clogged his voice. "Er…not at all, Miss Hardaway."

"Wasn't that the whole purpose of the act? To entice me into some compromising position so you could rush back and report on my disloyalty? Were you eventually going to try to pressure me to go with you to some sleazy hotel or perhaps your apartment? Some suitable place where someone would take photographs of us to prove to Raymond I'm unfaithful?"

"Nothing like that at all."

"Then what?" Her voice sank to almost a whisper. "What were you supposed to do? What was *I* supposed to do? Decide to sleep with you out of spite just because Raymond had stood me up—again?"

Will drew a deep breath. He could try to lie his way out of the mess, but there was something unacceptable about lying to Sara Hardaway. Maybe it was because he truly liked her. Maybe it was because he felt like a complete louse for trying to catch a woman at a crime she seemed incapable of committing. The moment after her lips had chastely brushed his cheek he'd known just how wrong Bergeron had been about his fiancée.

Will cleared his throat. "All I was supposed to do was set up a situation where you would meet someone you'd likely be attracted to and simply see what happened. I never offered to drag you to a hotel. I never mentioned sex at all. Hell, I didn't even get your phone number!" He blurted the last fact a bit louder than he intended.

A sudden revelation slammed him between the eyes. Was he more disappointed by his own failure than he was hers? He'd done his best and she hadn't even given him a second look. Was his life so shallow? Was he so wrapped up in the fictional macho-stud-P.I. mentality that he based his personal self-worth as a man on whether he'd wormed Sara's phone number out of her or not?

"I wonder," she continued, oblivious to his confusion, "if you had gotten my number, would you have gone to the next level?"

Will swallowed hard, hearing his own thoughts reflected in her words.

"Maybe make a date with me?" she continued. "Hope for a little innocent necking at first base, all for the sake of appeasing Raymond's irrational fears? Or would you have tried to go directly to home plate just to prove to him he'd chosen a...a gold digger as a fiancée?"

Her voice broke and with it went Will's control.

"Please...Sara...I never intended to go to bed with you. And I can guarantee your fiancé certainly never said anything of the sort when we discussed the case. Our standard operating procedure is not meant to force or lure someone into committing an indiscretion. I only provided a basic opportunity. The decision was up to you. And we substantiated the fact that you couldn't be seduced into an...indiscreet act with someone to whom you couldn't help but be attracted."

She sniffed, regaining some of the composure in her

voice. *"To whom I couldn't help but be attracted?"* she mimicked. "You think very highly of yourself, Mr. Riggs. What did you and Raymond do? Sit down and discuss my tastes?" She picked up momentum with each question. "Figure out who I might likely be attracted to? What qualities? What looks?"

The conversation echoed in Will's head. Bergeron had stiffly pointed out that Will had the basic qualifications when it came to looks, manner, personality type.

"And quite frankly—" the lawyer had leaned forward across the table and lowered his voice "—I don't trust this case to just anybody. I don't want you to turn this over to one of your sleazy operators. They're sufficient for my clients' needs but not for mine. I don't trust them with her. I want you to do it."

"Me?" Will had stared at the man. "But I never handle these types of cases myself. I have operatives with acting experience who—"

"Actors?" Raymond had dismissed them with a wave of his hand. "They're the worst. They're oversexed men with no morals at all. Like I said, I want you to do it. I trust you. And considering how much business I throw your way…"

Will dragged his thoughts back to the present conversation. As much as he hated justifying the actions of a man like Bergeron, the lawyer deserved some defense in this case. He cut into her tirade.

"Miss Hardaway—"

"—you might believe you're God's gift to women but I really am upset about the stunt with the car. It could have been dangerous—"

"Miss Hardaway!"

"I can't believe anyone would stoop that low as to—"

"Sara!"

Silence.

His hand tightened on the receiver. "First, I had noth-

ing to do with that car. I don't believe in adding an unnecessary ingredient like danger, real or perceived, into a
case like this. Secondly, your fiancé is a divorce lawyer;
he can't help but see the seamier side of marriage and
divorce. Is it any surprise that he might be more cautious
than the average person? Maybe even overly cautious?
But you have to understand his perspective even if it
might be a bit skewed.''

"You don't have to tell me about the skewed perspec-
tives of a man surrounded every day by disintegrating
marriages and couples locked in mortal combat." She
sounded tired, almost resigned; and if Will wasn't mistaken, he could hear the first note of begrudging accep-
tance in her voice.

He closed his eyes against the harsh sun pouring
through his window. "Have you spoken to Mr. Bergeron
about this?"

"Yes." She released a long sigh. "I spoke. Well—"
she paused for a moment "—maybe I yelled. And he
never listens when I yell. He probably thinks our engagement is still on."

"Then why don't you take advantage of the situation
and let yourself cool down before you talk to him again?
In the end, all I did was confirm his suspicions—that
you're a beautiful, trustworthy woman who's proved she's
faithful to her fiancé. Okay?"

There was a long moment of silence on the phone.
"Maybe." There was another period of silence before she
spoke again. "May I ask you a question, Mr. Riggs?"

"Please…it's Will."

"How long have you been a private investigator?"

"Eight years."

"In light of your eight years of experience in your business, do you really think the ends justify the means?"

"Sometimes." He opened his eyes, wincing at the
strength of the afternoon sun. "Most of the time."

At least, I thought so up till now.

"But what if the ends don't justify the means, Mr. Riggs?"

Blood rushed in his ears, making them buzz.

Her quiet voice repeated the words above the roar. "What if they don't?"

Monday evening, rush hour

FOUR HOURS AND A HALF-bottle of antacid later, the phone rang again. Having already dismissed his secretary, Mimi, Will had opted to hang around his office. He pretended to examine case files and read notes on ongoing cases, but in all honesty, he was trying to regain some of his business composure. Sara Hardaway had asked an all-important question, which he was still trying to answer to himself.

Do the ends justify the means?

Had he needed to go through the whole—what did she call it—charade? Had it been necessary to orchestrate a situation in hopes of catching her in mid-discretion? He'd investigated her past and found nothing that would indicate she had left cuckolded lovers, broken hearts or empty wallets. Why had he let Raymond Bergeron bully him into a full-blown loyalty test? Will only used that as a last resort to get the goods on someone who already had a history of using and abusing their lovers' trusts.

Sara Hardaway simply wasn't that type of woman.

He dropped into his chair, tired of finding busywork to assuage his ego, his libido and his pride. He glanced out his window at the setting sun. No use leaving now. He would just get tangled in the traffic. He stepped out of his office and into the reception area where the window faced south. He glanced out at the traffic and sighed.

I-95 was a vast parking lot of vehicles. Red brake lights flashed in uneven rhythm as trucks and cars played musical lanes. It was the same tune every day, "Going Nowhere Fast in the Key of D.C.-Sharp."

It made no sense to join the unhappy throng of rush-hour drivers when he could sit in his nice quiet office, grab a beer and try to forget all about divorce lawyers, warehouse thieves and other unsavory people.

The phone rang as he pawed through Mimi's yogurt containers and retrieved a beer. He reached for the phone, then withdrew his hand.

That's why God made answering machines.

The machine clicked and he listened to Mimi's dulcet tones:

"You've reached the offices of Riggs Investigations. Our hours are 9:00 a.m. to 6:00 p.m. Monday through Saturday. We are closed on Sundays. If you have an emergency, please call 555-4212. If not, you may leave a message at the beep."

The machine hiccuped and beeped.

"Uh...this message is for Mr. Riggs."

Will recognized the voice.

"This is Sara Hardaway and I'd like to apologize, er, speak with him...at his convenience. My...my number is—"

Will snatched up the phone. "Sara? It's me. Just a minute." He fumbled with the answerer, turning it off. "There. Sorry, it was after hours and I was letting the machine catch the calls."

She spoke in a quiet, unemotional voice. "I want to apologize."

"You don't need to do that."

"Yes, I do. You were doing your job. Raymond made great efforts to explain that to me."

"You spoke with him?"

"Yes. We...discussed the situation."

"And?"

"He told **his side** of it. I can understand...to a

point...why he felt as if he needed further reassurances. I disagree with his method but I understand why he acted the way he did. I just wanted to apologize to you. All in all, you were very professional about the whole thing and I appreciate that."

He swung his feet up to the coffee table, adopting a more comfortable position. "I *am* a professional, Sara. That's why Mr. Bergeron uses my services." Will contemplated the beer bottle for a moment. *At least, I hope to God he still wants to, after this debacle.* He twisted off the beer's cap.

"That's another reason why I called. I wanted to assure you that this case won't affect your working relationship with Raymond. Despite the rather emotional outcome of this case, he still intends to use your company's services in future proceedings."

"Thanks for letting me know." Will lifted his beer in salute. Bergeron might be a pain in the ass, but he was a well-paying pain in the ass. "He brings me a good deal of business. I'd hate to lose his steady paycheck."

She made a noise that didn't sound much like an agreement. He drummed his fingers against his knee. Why had she called him? Sure, she'd apologized, but that was no reason to call back so soon. Somehow, he didn't think she'd meekly accepted Bergeron's philosophy of using the same means to validate his own relationship as he did his clients'. Will lifted his beer bottle and almost took a healthy swig before stopping himself. He didn't want to have a convenient excuse like alcohol, on which to blame his next actions.

He drew a deep breath. "He's not my only client, you know."

"What do you mean?"

"I have individual clients as well who want to verify their partners' loyalty before getting married."

There was an uncomfortably long silence on the other

end of the phone. Finally, she spoke. "Am I that transparent?"

"No." He allowed himself one small sip of beer. "I just thought I'd make the offer. After all, you're entitled to know if your fiancé can live up to the same standards he sets for you."

"What's good for the goose..." Her voice trailed off.

"Could really piss off the gander," he supplied.

"Then let's do it, Mr. Riggs." A new tone edged her voice. "Let's take our chances on pissing off the gander. Maybe if I could make him understand why I'm upset, why I feel so...so betrayed, then maybe we can start over again." She released a sigh. "Let's do it. The sooner the better."

"Not so fast." He swung his legs back off the coffee table. "These things can't be rushed."

"Which means?"

"Which means you have to be ready to accept whatever I find out about him. Good, bad or otherwise."

"You won't find out anything about him I don't already know."

"But can you be sure?"

She hesitated for one telltale moment. "I've known Raymond for six years. We've been together for three. I know his family. His cousin is even my business partner. But...I suppose you know all that."

Will contemplated his beer bottle. "Uh...yeah. But that's not what I'm talking about. What do you do if I find something? What then? What if he takes the bait? Can you handle the truth?"

"What I can't handle is a lie, Mr. Riggs. You do what you need to do, hire whomever you need in order to give him a dose of the same medicine. I'll cover all the expenses."

Will pushed away his worst doubts, which hinted that he would soon be losing Raymond Bergeron's account.

He left the beer bottle on the table and crossed to the front of the desk where he found Sara Hardaway's case file in the To Be Filed basket. "What about the cost?"

"I expect you to charge me the same rates you charge Raymond. If you need a retainer, I'm willing to write you a check right now."

He flipped open the file, immediately riveted by a picture of her clipped inside the folder. "No. Uh...no retainer is necessary. We'll just let this be covered by Mr. Bergeron's retainer. I'll send you the paperwork and a questionnaire to fill out concerning your fiancé." He glanced at a similar paper Bergeron had filled out on her. How would the two compare? A perfect match?

"Do I need to come by your office to pick it up?"

"No...I can have it delivered to you. I have—" he glanced at the information sheet "—your address."

"Yes..." There was an awkward moment of silence. "I suppose you do know everything about me, don't you?"

The dial tone's mocking sound buzzed into Will's brain for several moments before he remembered to hang up. As he stared across the room, a small smile started inside him and slowly battled its way out.

The tables had turned.

He snatched his beer from the table and carried it to his desk. He sat down at his computer and pulled up a blank initial case-description form and began to type.

Client: Sara Hardaway
Target: Raymond Bergeron.
Concerning: Loyalty test.
Possible operatives:

Will tapped his fingers against his keyboard for a moment. Then he allowed himself a full-fledged smile.

Celia Strauss aka The Black Widow

Will laughed and pushed away from the desk.

Wednesday morning

"NOT BAD. NOT BAD at all." Celia's scarlet fingernail left a neat half-moon indentation in the corner of the picture. She allowed the paper to slip from her fingers and flutter toward the desk.

Will caught the photograph before it landed. "This isn't just *any* case, Celia."

She shot him a stunning smile. "They never are."

In any other circumstance, with any other woman, Will's heart would have made an involuntary leap. To the casual observer, Celia was a classically beautiful woman: dark-haired, peaches-and-cream complexion, violet eyes.

However, Will knew better than to be fooled by the packaging. She was an expert in her particular field, a master of seduction, a virtuoso of implied virginity. She knew instinctively when to make eye contact and when to look away, when to speak and when to listen and, most important of all, how to find that one spark of libidinous desire within a man and how to fan it until it burned away his self-control.

She was, with all intents and purposes, Will's secret weapon. But he always paid a price for her expertise; when Celia walked into a room, you never knew what you were going to get: a siren on the make, a shy coed, a frustrated housewife looking for fun, a young urban professional trying to forget the pressures of the job. She didn't simply play the roles; she became these people with an almost-psychotic immersion into character. Sometimes, he wasn't sure whether she was a consummate actress or a borderline schizophrenic.

Today, evidently, she'd decided to play the role of

femme fatale. Will swallowed hard and played along because with Celia, there *was* no other option.

She leaned back in her chair with the grace of a lioness on the prowl. When she drew a deep breath, her dress slipped to artistically reveal a tantalizing bit of cleavage. It was no accident. Nothing Celia ever did was accidental. She looked up at him from beneath a fringe of dark lashes and widened her intoxicating smile.

Will's sense of caution went on full alert. "Forget it, Celia." He shook his head. "I've had my shots."

She released a husky laugh. "That's what they all say." She moved from the chair, draping herself across his desk as if it was a grand piano and she was a torch singer with a mission. "But no one is totally safe." She pursed her lips, kissed her finger and ran it down his cheek. "You, of all people, should know that by now."

Will stiffened. Given another time, another place, another woman, the sensation would be provocative, enticing, undeniably sexy. But not with Celia. Not anymore.

The cure to Celia had indeed been Celia, herself. After a very brief but torrid liaison, Will had discovered that beneath her Snow White exterior lay the manipulative heart of the Wicked Queen, herself. Always aloof, she seemed to derive her greatest pleasure from attaching the strings to a man's heart as well as other parts of his anatomy and sitting back, watching her puppets dance to her own psychotic choreography.

Luckily Will escaped; or was released—he was never quite sure which. He'd recovered well enough to identify her innate abilities to adapt and had helped her channel those talents in a more acceptable vein. To his relief, she'd seemed thrilled to have a chance to work *for* him instead of *on* him. Her mission had become to "protect the women of America from the scumbags out to use and abuse them."

And Will felt as if he owed it to the men of America to limit her firing range.

Celia traced the outline of Raymond's photographed face with her delicate finger, licking her lips slightly. "He looks as if he could be quite a...challenge." Her too-perfect smile deepened as she turned toward Will. "I do so love challenges." She shifted toward him, displaying even more cleavage. "What does our quarry do for a living?"

He cleared his throat and studied the picture. "Remember the Curry case I told you about? The lady who owned the car dealership?"

She nodded. "I was so disappointed that he confessed to his little indiscretion before I had a chance to meet him." She glanced at the photo again. "Is *this* Mrs. Curry's prospective husband?"

Will pushed the rest of the file across the desk toward her. "No. Our 'quarry' is Mrs. Curry's divorce lawyer, Raymond Bergeron."

"The divorce lawyer?" A glint of animation flashed in her eyes as she straightened. "How deliciously appropriate! The divorce lawyer gets a taste of his own medicine." She rose gracefully from the desk and scooped up the file. "This will require a very special touch, you know."

"That's why I'm putting you on the case, Celia. He hired me to run a check on his fiancée and she found out. Now she wants to return the favor and test him, as well. Since he knows all about the process, he may be as suspicious as hell. You have to be twice as careful."

"I'm always careful, sweetheart." She tucked a manicured hand into her purse and pulled out a small nickel-plated gun. "Always."

The hackles rose on the back of Will's neck. "Jesus Christ, Celia! What are you doing with that?"

She trailed her finger down the length of its shiny barrel. "Birth control?"

Will shuddered, then held out his hand. "May I?"

She handed him the weapon, grip first. "Nice, eh?" The first look of genuine expression crept into her face: pride. "It's small but it does the job."

He hefted the gun, feeling its weight, the sensation of the knurled handle in his palm. He slid open the chamber to find it empty. But when he pulled out the clip, it held a full load. Drawing in an uneasy breath, he debated the idea of confiscating the ammunition, but after a second thought, he pushed the clip back in place and nudged the gun gently back across the desk to her. "New corporate policy—if you're on the clock for me, leave this at home."

She reached for the weapon. "But—"

His hand closed over hers for a moment. "I don't care, Ceil." He pulled back, allowing her to retrieve the weapon. "You know the rules. You never put yourself in a position to need a gun. If it's dangerous, get the hell out. With this thing—" he pointed to the gun "—you're putting *your* license in jeopardy as well as mine. I'm your employer, remember?"

Celia shrugged and returned the gun to its place in her purse. "You, William Riggs, have turned into an old sourpuss. Whatever happened to the guy who wanted to stay with me in the hot tub all night? Did your sense of adventure prune up with the rest of you?"

Will shrugged. The Celia he'd first met had been quiet, studious, strong, funny and caring. It turned out to have all been an act, a personality she had created to attract him because she intrinsically knew that was what he wanted in a woman. Her ability to perceive and then to morph into the ideal woman constantly amazed and repelled him simultaneously. From what he could determine, every time she triumphantly proved a man's beastly infidelities, she was actually reliving the sense of revela-

tion and control she'd never achieved with some erstwhile
lover.

Cuckolding by effigy. Some people required such release.

He cleared his throat. "What was between us...all that
is past history, Ceil."

She leaned across the desk, coming so close to him that
he could smell the delicate aroma of heated perfume rising
from the neckline of her low-cut silk blouse.

"History?" she whispered. He caught the slightest
whiff of alcohol on her breath. "I never made good grades
in history," she continued in a husky voice, her lips skim-
ming his cheek as she spoke. "But biology? That's my
subject. Birds, bees..." She leaned closer. "Flowers,
trees..." She nipped him on the earlobe. "Cross-
pollination..."

He closed his eyes, not because his control was weak-
ening, but because it was getting stronger. Three years
ago, her proximity would have driven him wild, and her
touch would have resulted in spontaneous combustion.
Right then. Right there.

On the desk.

But after viewing The Black Widow's methods and
having literally survived her bite, he was forever immune
to her charms, however provocative, however enticing. He
sat perfectly still, determined to prove that his body
wouldn't betray what his mind had already learned to re-
sist.

"Will?" Her hot breath left a thin layer of moisture on
his cheek.

"Yes?"

"I hate men." She waited a moment before continuing.
"And sometimes I think I hate you most of all."

He swallowed, momentarily remembering the loaded
gun in her purse. "I know you do, Celia." He pushed
back in his chair so that they could face each other rather

than remain nose-to-nose. "You hate me because I know exactly who and what you are."

Her expression betrayed her, revealing how close he'd hit to the truth. He pressed his luck and continued. "And despite it all, I like you. And as much as you hate to admit it, you like me."

Her bottom lip trembled for a second before her posture changed, eradicating all weakness from her face and body. "Of course, you like me. You're a man. I'm a woman. It's the nature of the beast."

His imagination supplied the missing connector of logic: *And all men are beasts.*

Celia glanced down at the file and photo, gathering up both in one smooth motion. When she looked up again, their gazes locked and a thousand questions poured through Will's mind. A majority of them concerned what kind of bastard could so thoroughly scar the psyche of an intelligent, beautiful woman like Celia Strauss.

As if in response, Celia placed a finger against her pursed lips and then pressed the same finger to his lips. "This guy, Bergeron? Consider him snagged, bagged and tagged." She shot him a perfect smile and turned, leaving a hint of expensive perfume in her wake.

As soon as the door closed behind her, a shudder coursed up Will's back. Celia was wildfire. Capriciously consuming, controllable only with a lot of planning and hard work.

God help Raymond Bergeron if he had the merest proclivity to stray.

Will smiled, in spite of his professional need not to.

Chapter Five

"We need to talk." Quiet desperation filled the voice on the phone.

"Why?"

"Because there are things I have to explain to you, Sara. Reasons why I feel the way I do. We really do need to talk."

Sara swallowed hard. *Be cool. Don't jump at the opportunity....* "When, Raymond?"

"How about tonight?"

"Where?"

"I don't know. Someplace quiet." After a moment of silence, he spoke, his voice sounding a little bit hopeful. "How about the Frisco? I can get reservations there. The owner owes me a couple of favors."

It didn't surprise her that he would select one of the finer restaurants in Georgetown. Even in the worst of times, he insisted on eating well. At least, she could be thankful he hadn't suggested they return to The Judge's Chambers; the last thing she wanted to do was associate her friend's place with the phrase, "the scene of the crime."

"Well..." She sighed.

"Please, Sara? It's important to me. *We're* important to me."

Her grip on the phone tightened and she convinced herself that her sense of hesitation was nothing more than a theatrical pause. After all, she was supposed to make this sound convincing. "Seven o'clock. I'll meet you at the bar."

"But I can come pick you up—"

No! Take control! "I'll meet you there, Raymond. At the bar."

The phone clicked, then she heard a dial tone that sounded suspiciously similar to the blood thrumming in her ears. It had taken a long time to gear herself up to call Raymond, to prepare her story, to gird herself to purposely set up a meeting for which she would fail to show. And now, to have *him* call *her* first and create the perfect opportunity was more than her nerves could take. Just as she thought she might give in to indecision, fate had marched in and carried through with her end of the plans.

Her hand shook as she replaced the receiver in its cradle. Leaning back against the headboard, she tried to adjust the pillow behind her. After a few halfhearted attempts, she snatched the pillow from behind her and buried her face in its flowered cotton case.

Once upon a time there was love, trust and loyalty, all hopelessly entangled just as they should be. But somewhere along the line, the three concepts had started to unravel.

When had trust become doubt?

When had loyalty become suspected perfidy?

And how could love survive without the others?

She ground her fist into the pillow. How long would she have to wait to find out how Raymond reacted? Sara glanced at the bedside clock: 4:00 p.m.

IT WAS 7:36 p.m.

Will turned his glance from his watch back toward his

quarry, noticing how Bergeron squirmed on the barstool. Sara was right. She'd predicted exactly what her fiancé would do—show up twenty minutes late for their date, expecting to find her waiting like a dutiful fiancée.

Once he'd discovered she wasn't at the bar or in the restaurant, the attorney had experienced a variety of visible emotions over the next fifteen minutes or so: irritation, concern, frustration. In Will's learned opinion, Raymond had slid past "concern" all too quickly.

Bergeron pivoted on his stool, turning away from the door. He ordered a second whiskey sour, again just as Sara had predicted. A few moments after being served, he looked up in surprise as the bartender returned with a cordless telephone, indicating that the attorney had a call.

Whatever Sara was telling him, it elicited the right mix of emotions to increase the lawyer's general sense of irritation, presumably at her. After he shoved the phone back in the bartender's direction, he picked up his drink and downed it in one easy gulp.

In Will's expert opinion, Raymond Bergeron was primed and ready to be taken on a little joyride called "Celia in Wonderland."

And Celia, being the consummate professional vamp that she was, had also observed his emotional spiral.

She made her move.

For Will, it was like sitting back and watching a play—without being able to hear the dialogue. But the imagination supplied what couldn't be heard.

"Excuse me, but is anyone sitting here?"

Bergeron almost said something curt without looking up, then he caught sight of Celia. His expression as well as his body language altered drastically, and he uttered something evidently witty. She replied with an enchanting peal of laughter, one of her specialties. After the proper amount of reflection, she perched daintily on the edge of the stool and ordered a drink from the attentive bartender.

Within twenty minutes, she and Bergeron had shifted from barstools to a table in a dark corner of the bar. Celia had already made the transition from reluctantly accepting a seat to gazing with undeniable attraction and rapt attention at her quarry. In the midst of one serious recitation, she reached out and touched Bergeron's arm with a look of searing compassion.

Will caught Raymond's lascivious reaction—a look of undisguised lust coupled with a slobbery knuckle-nibble—by immortalizing it on film, courtesy of his best camera, a telephoto lens and some professional low-light film.

Click: Bergeron whispering something in her ear.

Click: Celia throwing her head back in laughter.

Click: Bergeron making a play for her exposed neck.

Click: Bergeron pulling Celia into what might be construed as an intimate embrace. Were secrets passed? Acceptances made? Will couldn't quite read it in their faces.

Click: Bergeron grasping her by the hand and helping her to her feet.

Click: the rear views of Bergeron and Celia as they headed out the door, arm in arm.

Crack: the sound of Sara Hardaway's heart breaking.

Will tried to ignore the sinking feeling in his stomach as he grabbed his jacket and headed out the back door, in hot pursuit and in cold dread. He chided himself; he knew nothing would go wrong. Celia knew the drill; she normally utilized the old "There's something wrong with my heel" routine to allow him enough time to get around to the front of the bar and tail them on foot to the next bar or restaurant.

But by the time he stepped out of the alley, ready to follow them to any of the quieter Georgetown bars, Will spotted them standing beside a red Porsche.

His car? Damn it! Will ducked back into the shadows. "Don't get in...don't get in..." he chanted under his breath as he watched Celia rub up against Bergeron. He'd been very careful to explain to her that this wasn't a case where they needed pictures of her leading her prey into the hotel room for a night of "Who's on first?" She knew that at most, they needed only a couple more incriminating intimate photos to wrap the case.

Will's imagination provided a conversation along the lines of what Sara needed to hear.

Celia would purr, "Maybe you and I can get together sometime."

Bergeron would hesitate for one moment, then make his admission. "Although I'm quite flattered by your attention, I'm afraid...I'm in a relationship."

"Oh, well..."

But the scene Will imagined bore no resemblance to the one being played out before him.

Actually, it would be hard to carry on any type of conversation when two people were playing a spirited game of "Your Tonsils or Mine." Will figured Bergeron might have pulled his new lady love right into the back seat of his sports car for further medical inspection if a passing vehicle hadn't illuminated their passion in a rather revealing beam of light.

Will pushed back into the shadows, wondering if *this* would be the moment when the man's sense of loyalty would kick in. As Bergeron pivoted to deliver a rather inventive curse in the direction of the retreating car, Celia turned toward Will's position and shot him her best seductive smile.

Then shot him the bird.

He lowered the camera. *Aw, Celia...not now. Don't go crazy on me, now!*

He shook his head. Maybe he should have been expecting something like this. For all her strength, all her ability, Celia had a fragile side and unfortunately, it seemed evident she'd chosen tonight of all nights to let her control shatter. And without her self-control, Celia became one big rampant id, running amok.

Will felt the cold of the brick wall seep through his jacket. He could see it all so clearly now. For some inexplicable reason, her steady pilot light of hatred for men had suddenly been transformed into a Molotov cocktail and she was going to gleefully lead Raymond Bergeron down a primrose path. And it wasn't just any old road—this one had been booby-trapped with mines by a professional demolitionist of love.

Before Will could make a decision on whether to put a stop to the whole case, Celia wrapped herself around Bergeron's thigh and her hand disappeared inside the attorney's jacket.

Bergeron responded with a smile and another expression, which said, "When you can't be with the one you love..." His lascivious grin widened as he pulled her toward his Porsche.

From the look on Celia's face, Will knew she was a woman with a mission: to demonstrate exactly how far a supposedly loyal man will fall.

And no doubt, Bergeron would fall—hard and fast.

Will scrambled into his car, not really caring if his quarry spotted him or not. Bergeron might be a royal, pompous pain in the neck and maybe he didn't deserve to snare Sara Hardaway—seemingly the last honest woman in America—but no one deserved to be the sole personification of Celia's hatred of all things testosterone.

Bergeron pulled his Porsche into the flow of traffic with more speed than was called for. Will managed to tail him without undue notice until Bergeron hit the on-ramp to the interstate. The attorney demonstrated the Porsche's celebrated acceleration ability by hitting the top of the ramp doing 110 miles per hour.

Will didn't stand a chance.

He smacked the steering wheel with the heel of his hand as he watched the Porsche weave between cars and fade from sight.

You poor bastard.

Saturday, the wee hours of the morning

SARA TRIED HARD NOT TO look at the phone. A watched phone responded to the same logic as a watched pot; the harder you stared at it, the longer it would take to boil.

Or ring.

Especially after midnight.

She decided a cup of tea would best soothe her jangled nerves, and prophetically, the teakettle and the phone sounded at the same moment. In the process of silencing one to hear over the other, she burned her hand.

"Ow... Damn it.... Hello?"

"Sara?"

"Raymond?"

"No..." There was a long pause. "It's Will Riggs."

"Oh..." Her heart wedged itself in her throat. "So? What happened?"

There was a second protracted silence, during which Will spoke volumes.

Her heart unwedged itself and, turning to lead, landed at her feet with a thud. "Oh, no..."

"Don't jump to any conclusions, Sara."

Her eyes began to flood with tears but she exerted all her self-control to keep her voice steady. "I won't. Just tell me what happened."

Will cleared his throat and spoke in a dry, professional-sounding tone. "The subject arrived at 7:23 p.m. and took a seat at the bar. He ordered a drink, finished it and at 7:37, he ordered a second drink. He received a phone call at 7:41. Prior to the call, he appeared impatient and mildly upset. But after the call, he appeared much more upset. He ordered a third drink, this time a double. My... operative made her move as he was being served. They talked at the bar for approximately twenty minutes, then shifted to a table toward the rear of the restaurant. They stayed there, ordered two more rounds of drinks, then departed at 9:46.''

"Together?"

There was a moment of hesitation—long enough for her heart to jar her chest with several rapid beats.

"Yes. They climbed into a red Porsche 911 Targa, Virginia license plate—"

"ECROVID," she supplied. "It's Raymond's car. It's 'Divorce' backward." She shivered, despite her desire not to. "Did you follow them?"

Will's professional demeanor deflated with a prolonged sigh. "I tried to, Sara, I really did, but he outran me." Emotion crept into his voice. "It wasn't because he saw me—I know how to tail a car without being spotted. But I'd only planned to follow him, not expecting it to turn into a chase. But he pulled out fast and hit the intersection doing fifty and the interstate ramp at over a hundred. I didn't have a chance in hell of catching up with him without completely tipping my hand."

"It's not your fault. Raymond has a tendency to drive fast when he's had a couple of drinks. That why I usually commandeer his keys when we go out—" She swallowed hard, knowing she had to ask the next question whether she wanted to hear the answer or not. "Did he...respond to your operative?"

"Sara—it's a matter of interpretation—"

"Look," she snapped. "Either he did or he didn't." Righteous indignation arose in her, allowing her analytical side to take temporary control of her building emotions. "Did they touch each other at all?"

Will hesitated for a moment, then spoke. "Yes."

"Did he hold her in what one might construe as a provocative manner?"

"Yes."

"Did he initiate any of these actions?"

"Yes."

"Did they kiss?"

There was another pause. "Yes."

"Are we talking a quick peck on the cheek or—" she faltered "—or something more...intimate." Her logical control began to waver.

"Sara I don't think we need to—"

"Yes, we do!" Emotion returned with blunt force. "I need to know every dirty little detail. Every touch, every caress, every promise he made, every—" She forced herself to stop, to regain what little self-control and self-esteem she could manage and to take a gulp of air. "Was their kiss of an intimate nature?"

"You sound like a lawyer."

"I've hung around long enough with one to pick up some of the tricks of the trade. Was their kiss of an intimate nature?" she repeated.

"Define 'intimate.'"

"Damn it, Will! You know what I mean! Intimacy—increased intensity, prolonged contact, obvious emotion, heightened awareness, a sense of—"

"Yes. It was an intimate kiss."

She gripped the receiver so hard her hand began to shake. "Damn! Damn him and damn her and especially damn me for setting up this whole stupid thing in the first place!"

"Sara...don't do this to yourself."

"Don't what? Delude myself? Keep the candle burning in the window while the rest of my life goes up in smoke? Forgive, forget and accept the fact that the standard of loyalty differs between the genders? Well, I'm afraid it's not all right for him to play tongue-hockey with a total stranger while I'm feeling an incredible sense of guilt for a simple kiss of gratitude because you saved my—'' She stopped, unwilling to contemplate how close she came to hitting the truth in her emotional tirade.

During the resulting silence, she wondered whether Will was demonstrating a sense of grace by not commenting on her outburst or was simply stunned speechless.

A muted siren's wail filled the air and Sara realized the sound came through the phone from Will's location. It provided a suitable diversionary tactic for her. ''Is that a siren? Is everything all right?''

''Yes.'' He waited until the noise started to fade away. ''It was just a police car.''

''Police? Aren't you at your office?''

''No. I'm at Bergeron's place, staking it out. I figured there might be a shot of catching up with him here, but no one's home right now. No lights are on and the Porsche isn't in the garage. So, I figured I'd hang around here because they—he might come back.''

''Don't.''

''Don't what?''

''Don't stay there. I don't want to know how late he stays out with her, where they are, what they're doing. The damage is done. This relationship is over. At least, it will be tomorrow when I confront him with the truth.''

''Sara...we need to talk about this before you make any rash decisions. Why don't I come over and—''

''No!'' The word blurted out, stronger than she'd expected. ''No, don't come here. I need to...to think. I promise I won't make any earth-shattering decisions that involve getting drunk, getting revenge or anything like that. I won't call his machine and leave threatening messages. I just need to be by myself, to think over the chain of events. Alone. Okay?''

''Well...'' He hesitated, then released a sigh. ''I guess

I can understand. But if you need anything, call me. Please? You know, just to talk or whatever.''

"I'll be okay—"

"You have my pager number and you can call absolutely any time. Day or night. Okay? It...it would make me feel better."

She closed her eyes. "Okay—thanks, Will. I appreciate your offer. Maybe tomorrow I'll be ready to talk. Just make sure you go home, now. Raymond's a big boy—he can make his own decisions, live with his own consequences.''

She placed the receiver in the vicinity of the hook before her knees gave out. Squatting on the kitchen floor, she huddled against the nearest cabinet, wondering when and how her world had shattered into a handful of small sharp pieces. All her plans, hopes and dreams had been shared ones. At least, she'd thought Raymond had shared them with her. But if she was wrong about him, then what other concepts, ideas, dreams did she have that were also wrong?

Damn you, Raymond.

Damn all men.

She corrected herself. It was an easy trap to fall into, condemning all men for the sins of one. Look at Will....

Sara had a flash of memory, of him holding her in his arms, concerned over her possible injuries. Even though they'd landed in a rather compromising position, she hadn't been guilty of any impropriety with him. After all, she'd turned him down. Even if he was funny and handsome and intelligent and well-mannered and...

And the kiss—it was simply one of gratitude, of appreciation; the sort of kiss you would give your cousin, or your grandmother or...

Sara suddenly realized why she'd vehemently told him not to come over.

It wasn't about the kiss she'd given him. It was all

about the kiss she'd *wanted* to give him; the type of kiss you gave a very handsome, witty, intelligent, attractive man who had saved your life....

"Damn it...I'm no better than Raymond."

She began to cry.

WILL HUNG UP THE phone and stared at the darkened windows of Raymond's McLean home. Sara might not want to know all the details, but Will did. After all, it was his operative who'd blown the whole case to hell and when he fired her, he wanted to be able to cite all the facts and figures to back him up.

He stared down the street, almost wishing he would suddenly see the Porsche crest the small hill and head in his direction. But no headlights split the night. No prodigal son headed home. And unlike the Prodigal's father, Sara didn't seem the type of person who would find it terribly easy to forgive and forget.

As a mental image of Sara danced around the edges of his imagination, Will made himself a solemn vow: Never, under any circumstances, would he ever put himself in the same position again. No matter how enticing or intriguing the woman sounded, he would never play the role of attentive suitor, again.

Hell, that was why he hired actors—people who made it their business to play a role with feeling, then walk away from it, no strings attached. Professionals like Celia could pour all their energies into the apparent seduction of a person, then leave, never bothering to take a second glance backward to what they left behind.

In his eyes, he was no better than Celia; he simply wasn't as brazen.

Or as successful.

Will sighed and started his car.

He couldn't help but have noticed the note of panic in Sara's voice when she said she didn't want him coming over to comfort her. Which role did she think he was playing? The intrigued suitor like he had at the bar? Or did she think he was one of those guys who enjoyed preying on women when they were caught in the throes of emotional upheaval?

He pulled away from the curb.

She must think I'm a real bastard.

THAT BASTARD!

Sara bolted upright in bed, responding to the strident noise that rescued her from a particularly hideous nightmare. Remnants of her anger-filled dream clung to her mind as she fumbled for the alarm clock sitting on her bedside table. In the dim light, she saw it was only a little after two. Had she been so upset when she went to bed that she couldn't even set her clock right?

The noise exploded again, and Sara realized it came from the telephone. *Three guesses as to who's on the other end.* He didn't even bother to identify himself.

"You stood me up." Raymond's words lacked his usual careful precision of speech.

Drunk. I'm not surprised. "How could you, Raymond?"

"How could I what? Get mad because you stood me up? Well, baby, I've got the right to get mad and drunk, too, if I want to."

"No, that's not it. I want to know why you decided it was fair for me to be required to meet a standard that you yourself were unable to reach."

"What in the world are you talking about?

"I'm no fool, Raymond. If you thought it was okay to use Will Riggs to test my loyalty, then I had the same right to test you. I hired him to return the favor. But there is a difference. I passed the loyalty test, Raymond, and you didn't."

"You mean—"

"She was a plant, Raymond, an operative he uses to see just how far a man will fall if given the opportunity. Not a push, just merely the opportunity. Well, *baby*—" she mimicked his words without mercy "—you fell, all right. So where are you? Your place, hers, or some cheap motel on the Beltway?"

Sara heard something that sounded exactly like a woman's tinkling laughter, but she jerked the phone from her ear as a louder noise suddenly replaced the giggles. Although it sounded as if he'd dropped the phone, his words were still distinct: "You conniving little bitch."

Raymond spoke with more force, more violence than she expected. As a rule, he seldom lost his self-control; it was one of his great attributes as a divorce lawyer—staying calm under fire, even when caught between warring factions. But now he used words she'd never heard him utter before, even when drunk. To her further confusion, she wasn't sure whether his comments were directed toward her or his female companion.

Sara heard the woman say, "Don't be so rough on—"

"How dare you?" Raymond's shouts vibrated through the phone. "How dare you test me! After all I've done—"

"How dare you test me!" Sara shouted back. "I did nothing to—"

"You heartless bitch. And *you!* I can't believe that you'd—"

This is useless. Sara's sense of self-preservation kicked in and forced her to hang up. She didn't want to be a part of an escalating three-way argument. It was becoming impossible to understand which comment was directed where—whether Raymond was arguing with the woman with whom he slept or with Sara.

And the absolutely last thing she needed to listen to was his feeble excuse about his momentary lapse in judgment. No apology, no explanation, no alibi he could offer would begin to offset the fact that he'd called to make his

accusations of her while he still was in the company—
perhaps even the bed—of another woman.

I hope she was worth it, Raymond.

Sara hurled the phone across the room.

Chapter Six

Saturday, very early morning

"I took care of the problem."

Her heart hammered as the reality of the situation sank in. She looked into her companion's face, seeing exactly what kind of heady mixture was formed when triumph, fear, bloodlust and apprehension combined. "But I thought you said—"

"I said I didn't want *you* barreling in there and doing something stupid like the stunt with the car. Let's just say that an opportunity presented itself and I took advantage of it."

"An opportunity?"

"I had a chance to eliminate the only witness as well as plant a couple pieces of evidence that'll take the police on a merry chase in the opposite direction. God knows, I've sat in enough courtrooms to understand the rudiments of how to redirect their attention."

"What kind of evidence?"

"Does it really matter to you? All you need to know is that they'll never find a connection between that woman and us." Her companion paused to scan the room. "Fix me a drink."

She stumbled to the counter, her fingers shaking as she

poured the whiskey. Moments later, she refilled the empty glass. "You're...hitting the sauce a bit hard, aren't you?"

Her companion shot her with a steely-eyed glare. "I just killed a woman. I'll damn well drink however much I want." The second whiskey disappeared as quickly as the first. With a flick of a finger, the empty glass toppled over.

She scrambled to intercept the glass, but failed to reach it in time. The remaining liquid spilled across the polished counter in a thin golden stream.

It reminded her of a trail of blood.

"As much as I damn well want..."

Saturday morning, later

"Oh, Loo-cee... You got some 'splaining to do...."

Sara closed her eyes and shook her head. Whenever Martin and Lucy went off on a weekend, they were insufferable for days, afterward. But it had been a week since their impromptu vacation and they were still buzzing around each other like bees around the hive.

The last thing she needed on a day like today was to be surrounded by lovebirds and bees.

But they were everywhere.

Martin and Lucy. Charlie and Melissa. Even the new busboy brought his girl by to see where he worked. They were all over each other, whispering, giggling.... Sara could barely tolerate all the cooing. The only fowl she could consider at the moment were dead ducks, stool pigeons and maybe, some Wild Turkey.

"Oh, Loo-cee!" Martin called from the storage room.

"Lucy ran down to the wholesale house to pick up that special shipment of napkins." Sara picked up a cleaver and ruthlessly slammed the blade into the chicken, which was spread-eagled across the cutting board in front of her. Another type of fowl with which she was willing to deal.

"Ouch!"

Sara spun around.

Martin stood in the storage-room doorway. He winced, nodding toward the chicken. "Someone I know?"

She pulled the blade out and whacked the bird one more time, turning a half chicken into two quarters. "You could say that." Whack. Two eighths.

"Someone I'm kin to?"

Whack. Two sixteenths.

Martin sighed. "Tell me what my idiot cousin did before our specialty of the day becomes chicken hash."

Whack. Two thirty-seconds.

"Oh, nothing much."

Whack. Stir-fry.

Tears blinded her and she stepped back from the cutting board, cleaver in hand. "All he did was hire a private investigator to run a check on me."

Martin took a step toward her. "He what?"

"That's not the half of it." She buried the cleaver in the untouched half of the chicken and shifted to the sink to wash her hands. "The private investigator he hired specializes in testing people to see if they're faithful to their spouses. They set me up to see if I'd react favorably to a proposition from a handsome stranger." She stared at her soapy hands. "I didn't accept."

"Of course not," Martin supplied in indignation.

She shrugged and finished rinsing her hands. "So, in retaliation, I decided that Raymond should have to prove to me he could pass the same sort of loyalty test."

Martin handed her a paper towel. "That serves him right. You needed to show him how it feels to be doubted."

She nodded. "But there was only one problem I didn't anticipate. Raymond failed the test."

Martin stared at her. "F-failed? You mean..."

She drew a shuddering breath. "I arranged to meet

Raymond last night, then didn't show up. The private investigator sent a very beautiful woman to make a pass at him, to see if he could be persuaded to join her in a one-night stand. They took off together.''

Martin closed his eyes and sighed. "Why am I not surprised? Raymond's my cousin, but I never really liked him. He's been a manipulative son of a bitch all of his life. I always thought you were the best thing ever to happen to him."

"Martin, I'm sure—"

"No. I really mean it. You brought out so many of his good qualities—attributes I never thought he possessed. I figured that with you at his side, he might actually make himself a suitable member of the human race. For a divorce lawyer, that is."

Tears choked off Sara's ability to respond.

Martin pulled her into an embrace. "Look, honey, if he's not smart enough to realize how important you are to him, then don't waste your time on him. He doesn't deserve someone as wonderful as you."

She pulled back, dabbing at the wet spots she'd left on the shoulder of his shirt. "Thanks. I came to the same conclusion around four o'clock this morning. It's nice to hear it from somebody else."

"It's the truth." Martin glanced at the clock hanging over the steel-doored refrigerator. "Four o'clock. God, you must be wiped. Why don't you take off today? I can call someone in to help."

She shook her head. "Nothing doing. The last thing I need to do is go home and mope. Hard work is the answer." She turned to the cutting board, picked up the knife and eyed the chicken. She tried to smile, but failed. "So, do you have a good recipe for chicken hash?"

"I do."

Sara turned at the sound of the familiar voice. Will

Riggs stood in the kitchen doorway. "The bartender said I could come on back. How are you?"

Martin took a step forward, literally moving between her and their guest. Sara conjured up a brief smile, thankful for Martin's inclination to protect first, ask questions later, even if Will was a couple of inches taller than him.

Martin stood his ground, making up for stature with demeanor. "I don't know who you are but I think Sara's not in any mood to—"

She reached up and touched his arm. "It's okay, Martin. This is Will Riggs, the private investigator who…helped me." She ignored Martin's overt, near hostile glare. "Will, this is my partner, Martin Hilliard."

Will returned a glare, which matched Martin's in intensity. "Bergeron's cousin." He pronounced the name like he would the word *cockroach.*

They remained in a typical testosterone standoff until Martin made the first concession by sticking out his hand. "Don't hold being Ray's cousin against me." He offered a half smile. "You pick your friends—" he nodded toward Sara "—and your business partners and if you're really lucky, you find someone who is both a partner as well as a friend. But you can't pick your family. Raymond's ours whether we want him or not."

Will accepted Martin's hand, the gesture breaking the tension in the room. "I understand. I have a second cousin I'd just soon forget existed, too." He turned to Sara. "The reason I came by was to see how you were doing."

She crossed her arms. "Okay. Considering."

"Get any sleep last night?"

The lingering echo of her wee-hours-of-the-morning phone call made her close her eyes for a moment. "Some, until Raymond called."

"What did he say?" Both men spoke simultaneously.

"Oh…nothing much." She shrugged. "He tried to blame everything on me, but he lacked the conviction to make it stick. Evidently, the Blackwater Barracuda decided he couldn't face an in-depth cross-examination alone.''

"What do you mean?" Will asked.

"Just that—he wasn't alone. *She* was with him when he called. I could hear her giggling in the background." Sara wiped away an errant tear that dared to form in the corner of her eye. She squared her shoulders. "Do you think she was there for moral support or did he simply roll over in bed and suddenly remember he had a fiancée to pacify with a quick call?"

"Aw, Sara..." Martin stepped forward as if he wanted to put his arm around her, but he didn't. "I'm so sorry," he whispered.

"Me, too," Will added. "I don't know what got into Celia. She's always followed her instructions like a professional." He reddened visibly as he ran his hand through his hair. "But she didn't act like a pro last night. She should never have gotten into the car with Bergeron." Will ducked his head and paid inordinate attention to his shoes. "I know it's small consolation, in light of everything that's happened, but I'm firing—"

An electronic ping interrupted him. He plucked a beeper from his belt, glanced at it and looked up sheepishly. "Sorry. Uh...could I use your phone?"

Sara nodded toward a black telephone hanging on the wall.

As Will dialed, Sara thanked God for the momentary reprieve. She didn't want to be forced to utter some useless platitude about Celia's status as newly unemployed. She couldn't forget the throaty giggles providing the background music to Raymond's call.

May she choke on her laughter.

Martin picked up the cleaver and started his own angry dissection of the chicken. He muttered something unintelligible under his breath as he diced the raw meat into neat cubes.

Will had his back to her but she couldn't help but hear his part of the conversation.

"Riggs... Yeah... No... Last night. Why?" There was an uncomfortable pause. "Are you sure?"

Sara looked up, instantly aware of an alarming note of concern in Will's voice.

He turned around and glanced at her. "Well...er...yes, of course. I'll be right there." He reached into his jacket pocket and pulled out a small notebook and pen. "Give me the address again." He scribbled something in his notebook, then stuffed it back in his pocket, pausing to consult his watch. "Ten minutes. Fifteen, tops."

He hung up the phone, then turned to Sara. His sheepish look had transformed into something much more serious. "I...uh...have to go." He fumbled with his pager, dropping it as he tried to clip it on his belt.

They both knelt in an attempt to retrieve it, their fingers grazing as they reached simultaneously for the errant beeper. Sara watched him swallow hard and her instincts went on full alert.

"I'm sorry. I mean...I—"

"What is it, Will?"

He placed a hand under her arm and helped her stand. After a moment's hesitation, he released a sigh. "That call...it was from a friend of mine who works in the homicide division of the Blackwater Police. He asked me to come view a crime scene."

"A crime scene? A murder?"

Will nodded, his expression set in granite. "They need me to identify a victim's body."

Sara glanced down at his hands, which were tightened into fists, betraying his building emotion. The very worst fantasies danced on the edges of her imagination. "A body," she repeated. She crossed her arms, pleating her sleeves nervously between her fingers.

He nodded, then reached out to cover her hand with his in a move that she couldn't help but take as conciliatory. "I'm sorry, Sara."

Her stomach twisted and her knees grew watery. "Raymond?" she whispered.

"No." He sighed. "Celia."

Sara pressed her hand against her mouth. "Oh, my God…"

"I have to go now." He turned toward the doorway but Sara shifted so she blocked his path.

"I'm coming with you."

"No, you're not." He turned to Martin. "Tell her she's not coming."

Martin paused with the cleaver in his hand. "Don't look at me." He used the blade to scrape the pieces of cubed chicken into a bowl. "I can't stop her. Never could."

Sara reached for her purse. "I said I'm going. If it is your associate, then she died while she was working on a case that involves me. And Raymond." A horrible thought passed through her mind. She sagged against the counter to support herself. "Oh, no…"

"Sara?" Will grabbed her by the arms. "Are you okay? You aren't going to faint or anything, are you?"

"Last night…the threats. I thought it was just heat-of-anger type of stuff…that he'd calm down, eventually. But it was confusing, with her in the room with him. I honestly thought he was yelling mostly at me." Sara looked up, wishing, hoping, praying that Will would dismiss her worst thoughts with a careless wave of his hand.

He didn't.

She drew a deep breath. "Will…what if he was screaming at her, instead?"

THEY DROVE IN SILENCE. Will forced himself to concentrate on the rigors of traffic rather than the look of pale concentration on Sara's face.

Trainor, his contact in the homicide division, said the body had been discovered a couple of hours earlier in an upscale Fair Oaks hotel room, only a few miles west of Sara's Main Street restaurant. Will appreciated the call, but prayed his friend was wrong, that the female victim only bore a passing resemblance to Celia Strauss. After all, Trainor had only met her once, so there was ample room for mistaken identity—Will hoped.

Traffic complicated what should have been an easy drive, snarling his nerves with the same efficiency that tangled the commuters into a crawl.

As they sat still in the gridlock, Sara finally spoke. "If it... If the body is the woman you hired to be with Raymond last night, then will he be a suspect?"

Will shrugged. "You're the one who heard them argue. Did he sound as if he might have become violent?"

She stared out the side window. "He yelled. Everybody sounds violent when they yell."

"No, they don't. You yelled at me over the phone when you found out who and what I am."

"That was different. I'm not a violent person."

"Then you think Bergeron *is* a violent person?"

She released an exasperated huff of breath. "You're twisting my words. I never said that."

"Either he is a violent sort of man who might kill with enough provocation, or he isn't. Make up your mind." Will hit his horn, causing the car in front of him to inch up. He pulled around the stopped vehicle and turned into a side street that led to the hotel parking lot.

Sara gripped the door handle for support as he wheeled sharply into a parking place. "Why are you doing this?"

He drew a deep breath before turning to face what he expected would be her expression of tearful confusion and dismay. But to his surprise, the look in her eyes said she already knew the answer. "Because these are the sorts of questions the police are going to ask you...if that body is Celia's."

If the body is Celia's...

Those words haunted their wordless trip into the hotel lobby. Will spotted a plainclothes detective who gave him directions to the room where Trainor was working. In deference to the high-class hotel, there were no overt signs of an investigation, but he knew one was being conducted, nonetheless. Trainor usually worked the upscale cases where a dirty business like murder was whispered rather than shouted about. He specialized in quiet questions designed to solicit the same clues and information as a regular investigation but without ruffling corporate feathers in the process.

They didn't speak until the elevator reached the fifth floor. An officer stood guard by the elevator and stopped them before they could step off. Will pulled his P.I.'s license from his wallet and showed it to the man. They were allowed onto the floor and given directions to the room.

After following a right-angled turn in the hallway, they could see a quiet bustle of people hovering around the last room on the left. Will stopped, knowing what his next duty was. He placed a hand on Sara's shoulder, stopping her before she could take another step forward. "You wait here."

"But—"

"Sara, it's a crime scene. It could be rough."

She gulped, then nodded.

Will girded his strength and stalked down the hallway, hoping he looked like the consummate professional he wasn't. If he had wanted to hang around dead bodies, he would have become a cop.

But he didn't.

He liked what he did—Investigations that were for the most part, bloodless. It wasn't that he was squeamish. An investigator usually dug into the everyday garbage of mankind, rooting around for clues and information, and he usually surfaced none the worse for wear. You could shower off the stench and live a normal life. But Will believed that constant exposure to blood crimes left a stain on the soul that no amount of showering could remove.

He drew a deep breath, then stepped into the doorway of the room, expecting to see a horrible sight. Or maybe some overturned furniture. Anything that might indicate a level of violence that culminated in the death of a person.

But the room was strangely neat—that is, if you considered a gurney complete with a filled black body bag, as intrinsically neat. A man wearing a blue jumpsuit marked "M.E." stood next to the gurney. He looked up from the notes he was scribbling.

"Can I help you?"

"I'm looking for Detective Trainor. Is he—"

"Will. Good, you're here." Steve Trainor stepped out of the bathroom and dodged a forensics person, dusting the door frame.

Will glanced at the body bag. "What happened?"

Steve shrugged. "That's what we're trying to figure out. Too many unanswered questions. I'm hoping you can answer the 'who' it happened to. Her purse, all her IDs were gone and the room was registered to an 'E. S. Gardner' and paid for with cash. You ready to take a look?"

"Yeah." Will swallowed hard. "Yeah," he repeated.

Steve nodded to the technician who unzipped the bag open enough for Will to see the puffy face hidden within.

It took him a while to reconcile his memory of Celia's cold beauty with the face of the dead woman. But little by little, he started recognizing her features. It wasn't that death hadn't been kind to her; violence was what had robbed her of her beauty.

Will took a deep breath, trying to steady all the parts of him that were on shaky ground. "I'm positive it's her. It's Celia Strauss."

Steve nodded. "I thought so, but I had to be sure." He turned to the technician. "Why don't you take five?" The man nodded and exited.

Will waited until the man was out of earshot. "How did she die?"

The detective pointed to the bed. "At first, we thought maybe it was a case of a sex game gone out of control."

Will glanced at the bed, spotting the remainders of several silk scarves tied to the head-and footboards. The sheets had been removed from the bed, but a white bedspread had been tossed over the striped mattress ticking. The edges of a red stain peeped out from one side of the quilted material.

A sudden image of Celia flashed into Will's mind. She was laughing and crooking her finger with a classic come-hither smile. He cleared his throat, wishing it was just as easy to clear his mind. "She was into that kind of sex...from what I've heard."

Steve jammed his hands into his pockets. "Do you know that by rumor? Or from personal experience?"

Will bristled at the insinuation. "She offered. Once. I declined. You didn't answer my question—how'd she die?"

"Gunshot wound to the chest. The M.E. says the bullet probably nicked the aorta and she bled to death. According to the angle of entry, the killer was probably standing about where you are."

Will moved self-consciously from the spot.

Steve shook his head. "Don't worry. Forensics is through in here."

"Have you found the weapon, yet?"

"Didn't expect to. It was a clean kill. She was an easy target, all trussed up like a goose...in heat." Steve reddened a little. "You see everything in this job." He nodded toward the brass headboard. "She was still...attached to the frame when her body was discovered."

Will struggled to banish that particularly unsavory image from his mind. He shifted his attention as well as his posture away from the bed. "Who found her?"

"Typical story. The maid used her passkey so she could clean up the room." The cop peeled off the thin plastic gloves he was wearing. "Listen, if we're going to play Twenty Questions, then it's my turn. When was the last time you saw the lately lamented Ms. Strauss?"

"Last night. At a bar."

"Business or pleasure?"

"With Celia, it was hard to tell the difference."

Steve nodded. "That's what I've been told. Had she been working on any cases for you?"

"Same old stuff. The bait-and-mate cases."

"She was your usual lure?"

Will nodded. "It was cost-efficient. Celia appealed to a wide variety of men so I didn't have to keep hiring and training female operatives. All the guys liked her."

Steve glanced at the silk scarves that fluttered in the slight breeze that stirred in the room. "All of 'em but one." Trainor pulled a notebook from his jacket pocket and consulted it. "There's one more thing. Before she was shot, someone tried to strangle her. There were bruises around her neck." He gave Will a sidelong glance. "Seeing how she seemed to have a predilection for, shall we say, the unusual, do you know if she was a gasper?"

Will shrugged. "Not that I'd heard but with Celia, there's no telling. Are you certain you have the order of injury right? Attempted strangulation, then shot? Not the other way around?"

"The M.E. says probably not, though he won't go on

the record until he's done a full autopsy. There were
no—'' Trainor pulled a pencil out of his jacket and used
the eraser to turn to a different page of his notebook
'''—signs of occlusion of the veins or telltale redness of
the skin.' Also, she wouldn't have bled this much if she
was already dead.'' He flipped the notebook closed.
''Could this be business related? Had she been working
on any unusual cases?''

''Unusual? No, nothing out of the ordinary.'' Will
didn't like the direction of Steve's questions. He wasn't
ready yet to throw Raymond Bergeron's name into the
fray. There had to be a way to sidestep the issue and
temporarily distract Steve from the inevitable question.

But the detective kept pushing. ''You said you saw her
last night at a bar. Was she working on a case then?''

''Yes.''

''You gonna give me names?''

''Sorry.'' Will felt the blood rush through his ears; he
knew the next two words would be the ones to seriously
pique Steve Trainor's professional interest. ''Client confidentiality.''

A light of challenge flared in the cop's eyes. ''So you're
going to force me to make an official req—''

''Excuse me. Will?'' Sara appeared in the hallway at
the door. She looked distinctly pale.

He wondered how much she'd heard. No matter, she
was a welcome interruption. He crossed the room quickly.
''I thought I told you to stay by the elevator.''

She looked as if she would have liked to. ''I remember,
but…I had to know….''

He leaned closer to her. ''Pretend to get sick,'' he whispered, grabbing her by the elbow.

She took one look at the body bag and paled. Somehow, Will didn't think she needed to pretend. She swayed
against him. ''Is that the body? Is it…was it *her?*'' she
asked in a hushed voice.

"Yes and yes." He turned to the detective, who was frowning at the intrusion. "I think I'd better get her out of here, Steve. She's a little squeamish about these things."

Steve crossed his arms, obviously unhappy to have his Twenty Questions cut off. "You going to introduce us?"

Will turned back to Sara. "It'll be okay, honey," he said just a bit louder than necessary. Sara gave him a look of shock. He continued, praying she had the presence of mind to play along. "We'll get you outside and into the fresh air and you'll feel better in no time." He shot Steve a strained smile. "She's a ride-along. Wants to see what the business is all about."

"And you bring her here?" Steve shook his head. "Sheesh. You got some *cojones,* Riggs." He turned to Sara. "Ma'am? Don't let him fool you into thinking it's always like this. He spends his life sitting on a photo stakeout in alleys drinking lukewarm coffee and in the library looking up information. Being a P.I. is *not* like you see on television."

Sara stared numbly at the body bag, then turned her blank stare to Steve and back to Will again. "I...I..." Grabbing his arm, she groaned. "I—I think I'm going to be sick." She bent over and for one tense moment, Will was afraid she just might fulfill her prophecy all over his shoes. But he suddenly felt a slight pinch. A signal?

A second pinch, this time, a bit harder.

He pinched her back lightly on the arm. Shielded from Steve's view, Sara made an "okay" sign with her thumb and forefinger.

Contact had been made and verified.

Will thought fast. "Uh...Steve...listen, I'll call you and we can continue with the questions. Meanwhile, once I get her settled, I'll go back to my office and pull up the information on what cases Celia had been working on."

"But—"

Sara groaned again and tugged him into the hallway. "Please…now!" She made a gurping noise and pressed her hand to her mouth. They kept up the charade past the cop at the elevator who solicitously held the door for them.

"First body?" the officer asked in genuine sympathy.

Sara released an almost-theatrical moan and Will shrugged. "Some people just aren't cut out for this business." They stumbled into the elevator car.

When the doors slid closed, Sara straightened, pulled away from him and flipped the hair out her face. Will wasn't sure how much of her sickness was an act; she still looked rather pasty-faced.

If he had any doubts, they were quickly dispelled.

She balanced a fist on each hip and narrowed her gaze to an accusing squint. "What in the world was that macho P.I. shtick all about?"

"Then you're not sick." He leaned back against the wall of the elevator and released his breath in a rush. "What a relief. That means it's my turn." He closed his eyes and tipped his head back, mentally commanding his stomach to downgrade from spin cycle to something less agitating. All theatrics aside, he'd just seen the body of someone he knew very well. Someone who had been alive just twenty-four hours earlier. Someone who had died a violent death. Someone who—

A gentle hand touched his arm. "Are you okay?"

Will swallowed back his revulsion, knowing he had a persona to fill, thanks to the wonders of television, which created desensitized heroes, impervious to the horrors of death.

He opened his eyes, took one look at Sara's pale concern and abandoned all stoic baggage that accompanied the mythical trench coat of the American P.I. "No. I'm not okay. Celia's dead and I'm probably the one to blame.'' Will couldn't help but notice Sara didn't remove her hand from his sleeve.

"Why do you blame yourself, Will? You didn't pull the trigger.''

"How do you know she was shot?'' The moment after he spoke, he regretted the slight accusatorial tone to his voice.

If Sara noticed it, she didn't let on. She merely shrugged. "I eavesdropped. I also heard what you said...or failed to say about Raymond.'' She reached over and hit the button for the lobby. "Let me ask two questions.''

In deference to the situation, Will refrained from saying "Shoot.'' Instead he nodded in agreement. "And they are?''

"First. Do you think Raymond could have gotten so angry that he actually killed her?''

Will didn't need time to think. "I think it's possible. He's the type of person who always finds a way to place the blame on someone else. That's what makes him a success as a lawyer—his clients are never guilty. And he isn't, either. The guilty party wasn't the man who was seduced into infidelity, but the woman who tempted him. So the question becomes: What type of revenge would he demand if he had to pay a stiff price for someone else's sins?

"A stiff p-price?''

Will nodded. "Like losing his fiancée. It's evident he was testing you because he wanted to take your relationship to the next plateau. Like marriage.''

Marriage. He could see her repeat the word. In an ideal world, marriage meant lifelong commitment, but right now, they were talking about a life cut short. Will felt the muscles in his arms harden. If Bergeron had betrayed a hidden proclivity to violence, maybe Celia got caught in a booby trap that had been waiting for Sara.

Will glanced at her. By the looks of it, she'd come to the same conclusion.

She swallowed hard, then regained her air of forced detachment with the lifting of her chin. "I hadn't considered that possibility." She paused before continuing, "And second. Although you think Raymond could be the guilty one, you were protecting him. Why?"

Why, indeed?

There was only one simple answer.

For you.

But it was an admission Will wasn't quite ready to make yet, mainly because it was presumptuous. It presumed a potential relationship between Will and Sara and it also presumed that Raymond was guilty. He had no proof to substantiate either theory. Just a reaction from his heart and one from his gut and he knew full well that the internal organ he should be using in both cases was his brain.

He was saved from answering when the doors opened onto the lobby. Sara fell back into a modified version of her sick routine and kept it up as they walked through the elegant foyer. They garnered a few stares but no overt attention. Thankful for the diversion, Will used the time to concoct a suitable-sounding reason why he'd engineered their escape. A squad car sat in front of the entrance, which meant they continued their charade until they reached his car. Unfortunately, divine inspiration failed to provide a convenient excuse for his actions.

When they reached the car, Sara braced her hand against the window, preventing him from opening the passenger door for her. Her gaze met his, questioning, pained.

"Why, Will? Why are you protecting a man who you think is obviously guilty?"

His heart began to hammer and a sudden cold sweat formed across the back of his neck. He reached deep inside himself, looking for the answer supplied by logic, control and experience, but finding only one—fueled by emotion and desire. It took everything he had to maintain his eye contact with her while he made his admission. He took a moment to study her face, watching how she changed from fierce to delicate in the blink of an eye.

"Why?"

Chapter Seven

Will took a step away from the car, evidently disturbed by the boldness of her question. He rocked back on his heels, then crossed his arms. "Hell...you know the reason, Sara. Despite what he's put you through, Bergeron deserves the benefit of the doubt until we have more information."

A shiver danced across her shoulders. It was the answer she expected, but not necessarily the one she wanted to hear.

"After all," he continued, "he's your fiancé as well as my client."

"My ex-fiancé," she supplied automatically.

"My ex-client." Will managed a wan smile. "But I wasn't lying when I mentioned confidentiality to Trainor. It continues even if the business relationship comes to a screeching halt."

Sara stared openly at him. He was impressive. His logic was irrefutable and his sense of loyalty, admirable. How could he be so calm after having just identified his associate's body? Sara didn't even know the woman and she was still shaking at the concept that the black bag contained someone who only a little while earlier had been alive, talking, laughing....

Laughing...

A sudden tremor coursed through Sara's body. Although she would rather have blamed it on the autumn breeze, which stirred the leaves at their feet, she knew it was the lingering echo of the dead woman's laughter that created such a reaction.

"Are you cold? I'll make sure to turn the heat on as soon as we get in the car."

"I'm all right."

He unlocked the door and held it open for her.

"Where to now?" she asked as she slid into the front seat.

"We find Bergeron before the cops figure out how involved he is."

Her stomach performed another flip-flopping dive. "Then you think he did it."

"I have no proof, but I know he's just as involved in this case as we are."

Her stomach lunged with such ferocity that she began to think her "sick" ruse was only a precursor to fact. "We? As in you and me?"

Will started the car and turned on the heater. "We're guilty of a sin of omission rather than commission. I'm afraid Trainor won't be too forgiving of either."

"But we didn't lie."

"We don't have to. It's called withholding evidence. The best way we can make amends is to find Bergeron, get the truth out of him and get him to turn himself in." He rubbed his hands briskly in front of the heater vents.

"What if he didn't do it? What if he has an alibi?"

"Then they check it out and release him. No harm, no foul." Will put the car in reverse and began to back out of the parking space. "Where do you suggest we start? His home or his office?"

Sara looked at her watch. "He has Saturday hours. Let's try his office first."

"Then office it is."

They rode in silence, each lost in their own web of thoughts. Sara looked over every now and then and could tell by the way Will's eyebrows knitted, then released, that he was mired in a mental struggle.

Once they arrived, she directed them into the parking deck. Will scanned the area and pulled into the first available space. "Do you see his car?"

She shook her head. "He parks on a security level. We can't get up there without a decal."

Will grunted in response.

It was the only sound he made during the trip from the car to the elevator and all the way up to the eleventh floor. She led the way to the double glass doors and paused before entering.

"What's wrong?"

She tried to smile but failed. "I don't know what to say or how to handle this. Do we barge in there and ask him point-blank if he killed that woman?"

"We'll play it by ear." He reached around her to push the door open. The gesture brought him close to her, so near that his after-shave tickled her nose. She stopped in mid-breath, refusing to inhale and let her senses be enticed by the inviting aroma.

This wasn't the right time....

"Sara?"

Nor the right place...

"You coming?"

She shook herself back to attention. Will was still holding the door open for her. "Uh...yeah, I'm sorry."

Joanie looked up, her florid face folding into a smile. "Sara...hi! And Mr. Riggs. What a surprise! Is Mr. Bergeron expecting you?"

"No, I thought I'd just stop by and...I met Wi—Mr. Riggs in the parking lot." Lord, when had she gotten to be such a bad liar? "Is Raymond busy?"

Joanie's genuine smile suddenly turned plastic. "Uh…I'm afraid he's not in at the moment."

Sara knew the woman well enough to realize something was amiss. "'Not in' as in out at a meeting or 'not in' as in you have no idea where he is?"

Joanie glanced over Sara's shoulder, her plastered smile starting to weaken in places.

"What, Joanie?" Sara looked back at Will, then gave the secretary an encouraging nod. "It's okay. You can talk in front of Mr. Riggs."

Joanie's expression melted into a frown. "I have no idea where he is," she said with a sigh. "He's missed three appointments and I've called him everywhere. His place, the health club, his beeper, his car phone… everywhere! It's totally unlike him to simply disappear like this. Did you see him last night? Was he feeling sick or something?"

"I didn't.… I—"

"He looked fine when I saw him around nine," Will supplied. Sara suppressed an overwhelming urge to elbow him in the ribs. "I'll tell you what I'll do," he continued. "If I can use his phone, I'll call around and see if I can find him." He took a few steps toward the door leading to Raymond's office. "I have a couple of contacts in town who might be able to help locate him fairly easily."

"Well…" Joanie hesitated like a conscientious secretary should. "I'm afraid I can't let you use his office—"

"It's okay, Joanie." Sara dredged up a reassuring smile. "I'll go in there with him."

The offer seemed to appease Joanie. She nodded anxiously. "Thanks."

Sara grabbed Will by the arm and tugged him toward Raymond's office. She turned back to Joanie and gestured toward the phone on her desk. "Why don't you call and cancel the rest of his appointments for today, okay?"

Joanie sniffed and nodded again. "Good idea." She

managed a strained smile in return. "I feel better with you here. I even tried to call you earlier but Mr. Hilliard said you were out on an errand."

Evidently he didn't mention we were going to view a dead body....

Once the door clicked shut behind them, Sara walked past her accomplice to Raymond's desk. "Okay. It was obvious you wanted a chance to look through his desk for clues or whatever. Here's your opportunity. While you do that, I'm going to see if he's left me any messages."

Sara dialed out on Raymond's personal line, calling the restaurant first. After learning she had no messages, urgent or otherwise, from Raymond, she gave Martin only the sketchiest of details to placate him.

"And if he calls, don't let him know anything's wrong. Get a number, find out where he is and if you can, call me immediately."

"He's in that much trouble?"

She sighed. "Looks that way."

Martin made a noise that sounded suspiciously like a word he only used when the county health inspector came around. "What if I can't get you?"

"Then—" she tapped Will on the arm and gestured at his pager "—call this number...."

Will stared blankly at her.

"Your pager number," she mouthed. "What is it?"

"Oh...555-4212."

She repeated the number to Martin.

"Got it. But if no one answers at that number, I'm calling the cops. Understand?"

"You do what you feel is right, Martin. I'll talk to you later." She hung up.

Will huddled over the keyboard of Raymond's computer. "No news?"

"No." She allowed herself the luxury of a small sigh before dialing her own number. A couple of words into the outgoing speech message, she punched in the code for message retrieval. The machine gave the time in a mechanical voice, then Sara heard: "Hi honey, it's Mom. I just wanted to touch base with you and see how you're doing. Dad's busy—"

Sara advanced to the next message. "9:24 a.m."

"This is Carl and I want to give you a chance to personally view the latest in home security systems. If you'll call—"

Next message. "10:31 a.m."

"Oh, God…Sara, I'm in so much trouble."

Her grip tightened on the phone. The slurred voice belonged to Raymond.

"You sicced that bitch on me and now everything's going to hell. *I'm* going to hell." He drew in a long, gasping breath. "It's not my fault, Sara. It's not. It's yours. You hired the slut."

He was drunk—not merely overestimate-your-abilities-and-drive-fast drunk; he'd sunk far below that to become a maudlin, rambling sot whose ravings told her much more about the real man than she ever wanted to know.

"I've got to go away, f-f-formulate my defense 'fore the cops grab m-me," he stammered. "Need a good d-defense. Heat of passion? Self-defense? Defamation of character? Nev'r mind that. It's your fault. All your damn—" The answering machine clicked and cut off his call.

She stood motionless, still clutching the phone, fearing that the next message would be a continuation of Raymond's rambling harangue. But there were no more. After a moment, she managed to punch in the code that saved the messages.

Saved Raymond's confession for posterity's sake.

For the prosecution's sake?

"Everything okay?" Will asked.

"Uh…yeah." Sara jumped, her mind and heart racing

at the same speed. She replaced the receiver, praying that
her hands didn't shake and betray her. Had she actually
just listened to a taped confession of murder? And more
important, was she going to tell anyone about it?

Including Will?

His sense of—dare she say it?—loyalty to Raymond
was admirable though most likely unwarranted. What sort
of compromising position would Will be in if he withheld
the knowledge of such a taped confession from the police?
She couldn't put him in that sort of position. She tried to
smile, to regain some semblance of control. "I just
checked my messages."

"And?"

"You want a good deal on some aluminum siding?"

"No, thanks." He graced her with a stare that lasted
just a bit too long for comfort. "You sure everything's
all right?"

She nodded, not sure whom she was protecting from a
sense of guilt: Raymond, Will or herself. She feigned attention to the computer screen. "How's it going here?"

He wore a look of grim satisfaction as he leaned back
in the chair. "I love organized people."

"Love?" Sara kept her attention on the monitor, fearing direct eye contact. Something told her that given the
proper opportunity, Will Riggs could take one look at her
and easily see the conspiracy in her eyes.

But he merely nodded. "I especially love the ones who
depend on their computers and datebooks to keep them
on their daily track."

"You found his organizer?" Panic lumped in her throat
and she looked around. Raymond never went anywhere
without his organizer. He'd even told her how once he
rushed out of a smoky hotel shower, clutching nothing
other than his organizer and a towel.

*Maybe Raymond's call was a blind. A forced confes-
sion. He never stutters like that unless he's totally*

stressed. Maybe he left behind his organizer as a clue that someone's holding him against his—

"Sara? Something wrong?"

She drummed her fingers on the top of the desk. "Don't you see? He'd never leave it behind willingly. That must mean someone could be holding him—"

"Slow down, Sara." He covered her trembling hand with his warm one. "It's not what you think. I didn't find his organizer—just his organizer files." Will looked at their hands, then self-consciously moved his in order to tap the monitor with his forefinger. "On his computer. Evidently, he lives in fear of losing his datebook so he keeps copies of all his appointments and notes here." Will hit a few keys and a blue box appeared on monitor.

Print Queue
Number of copies:
Page range: 1-99

He nodded toward the screen. "I want your permission to print out his current case listing and a couple of other files I could use to help locate him."

She studied the document partially hidden behind the blue Print box. "Private files?"

"Some of them were protected by a password."

"Password?" Sara turned her gaze from the computer screen to his face. "You were able to guess his password?"

A small smile quirked his lips. "It was pretty obvious. *Ironside.*"

"Ironside? How in the world did you figure something like that out?" A thousand thoughts flashed through her mind but no matter how she ordered them, she couldn't come up with a logical thread that started at Raymond's password and ended at Ironside.

"Simple. According to Trainor, your fiancé—" Will

signaled his surrender before Sara could object "—ex-fiancé registered at the hotel under the name E. S. Gardner."

"So?"

"E. S. Gardner—as in Earl Stanley Gardner, the author of the Perry Mason books." He waved in the direction of the three large bookcases filling the wall behind the desk. Directly behind the chair, she spotted Raymond's prized collection: a series of small red hardback books sandwiched between two sets of larger law books.

"Perry Mason?"

"Think. Perry Mason...who was played by—"

"What's his name? Uh...Raymond Burr," she supplied.

Will gestured for her to continue. "Who later had another show on television called...?"

"'Ironside,'" she stated flatly. An image of a bearded face flashed in her mind, completing the very circuitous route that started with Raymond and ended successfully with his password. "Raymond Bergeron...Raymond Burr. I never even made the connection."

"Who knows?" Will shrugged. "Maybe the similarity of the names is what spurred him into being a lawyer. I've heard of weirder things. But—" he turned his attention back to the computer "—it's just further proof that you might not have known Bergeron as well as you thought you did."

Sara cringed, waiting for the recriminations to continue. But rather than give her a second chorus about the foibles of dating divorce lawyers, Will pressed on. "Once I found his password, I had access to all his files. But before I print out any of them—" he held out his hand "—give me a dollar."

Sara stared at his outstretched palm. "A what?"

"A dollar."

"Why?"

He appeared mildly irritated. "Just do it."

Sara reached into her purse, found a crumpled dollar and dropped it in his hand. "Here. Now what?"

After pocketing the bill, Will reached into the desk drawer and fished out a sticky pad and a pen. A few moments later, he handed her a neatly printed note: "Received from Sara Hardaway, $1.00 as retainer for professional services."

And in the same messy scrawl he'd used on their barroom cocktail napkin, he'd signed "Wm. B. Riggs."

"There. We've made it legal enough."

Her stomach sank as she remembered the conversation she'd overheard between Will and the police detective. "To assure client confidentiality?"

He nodded. "Our first contract was drawn to handle only the loyalty test. But we need something a little less specific for this new situation. A little exchange of money for services rendered and voilà. Instant confidentiality." He hit a button and the printer began to whine.

A second later, the intercom beeped. "Uh, Ms. Hardaway? There's a gentleman out here who would like to see you."

"A gentleman to see me?" Sara glared first at the speaker, then at Will. "No one knows I'm here. I didn't even tell Martin."

"Then who could it be?"

"Someone looking for Raymond." An aggravating thought hung just beyond her reach. "Something's wrong, here."

Will eyed her closely. "What?"

"It's Joanie. She's never called me 'Ms. Hardaway.' Ever."

He held her gaze for a moment. "You think...?"

She punched the intercom. "Uh, Joanie, does this gentleman have a name?"

This time, there was definitely a strained quality to the

secretary's voice. "He says his name is Trainor. Steven Trainor."

Sara released the button a split second before Will's expletive would have carried over the speaker and into the next room.

"Damn it!" He swiveled in the chair and gathered the papers that had started to collect in the printer's output tray. "Stall him."

She grabbed his shoulder and pointed to the opposite side of the room. "You can get out through the door over there. It leads to the back hallway."

"Trainor's no dummy. He'll recognize you and know I'm involved. What I don't want him to see are these printouts. C'mon...c'mon," he coaxed the printer. "Hurry up."

Sara pushed the intercom button. "Uh, Joanie? I'll be right there."

Will stood by the printer, eagerly snatching each piece of paper as it slowly rolled out. "Stall him as long as you can."

Straightening her dress, Sara shuffled toward the door and opened it just wide enough to pass through, then closed it softly behind herself. The detective stood at the front desk, facing away from her.

It's now or never. "Uh...Mr. Trainor?"

Steve Trainor pivoted quickly, his hand disappearing into his jacket as he turned. For a moment, Sara thought he was reaching for a gun, but she belatedly realized he was withdrawing a thin black wallet from his pocket.

"Ma'am, I need to talk—" He stopped in midsentence. To his credit, his only betrayal of surprised recognition was a raised eyebrow. "I guess I don't have to explain why I'm here, Ms. Hardaway." He tucked his wallet back into his pocket without ever exposing the shield within. He flashed her a cold smile. "I didn't think you looked like one of Riggs's trainees. I need to ask you a few questions about Raymond Bergeron.'' He continued without a pause, as if he didn't expect her to have any objections. ''When was the last time you saw your fiancé?''

Joanie wore a look of complete confusion. ''What's he talking about, Sara? Has something happened to Raymond?''

It was the first time Sara had ever heard the woman call Raymond by his first name. For a moment, for one uncomfortably long second, Sara wondered if it signaled a more personal relationship between boss and subordinate.

She glanced at the photographs of three bright-faced toddlers that graced Joanie's desk. Her grandchildren. *Sara... you're talking about Joanie! Am I going to suspect every woman whose path he's ever crossed?*

Trainor continued, evidently oblivious to her lingering uncertainties. ''We just got through talking to the night manager who was able to identify your fiancé as the man who checked into the hotel with Ms. Strauss. It seems Raymond Bergeron was a frequent visitor to their establishment.''

Sara felt a knot form in the center of her stomach. ''A frequent visitor?'' She swallowed hard. ''Would you care to explain that, Detective?''

Trainor shrugged. ''Mr. Bergeron has a standing reservation for Friday nights at the Fair Oaks Inn.'' He nailed her again with his stare accompanied by a single raised eyebrow. ''You usually work on Friday nights, don't you, Ms. Hardaway?''

The blood rushed to Sara's face, filling it with heat.

''Oh, my God...'' Joanie covered her mouth with her hand.

Trainor spared the secretary only a cursory glance, keeping his attention primarily on Sara. ''I'm sorry to have been so blunt, but I wanted you to know that you won't be doing him or yourself any favors by trying to protect him. If you know where he is, you need to tell me. Now.''

Sara realized that the truth, or at least *most* of it, would be the best defense at the moment. ''In all honesty, if I knew where he was, I'd tell you immediately.'' She heaved a deflated sigh and sagged to the desk, perching on its corner. Tears crowded the corners of her eyes and she quickly decided to use what was an honest emotion to her best advantage. Turning partially, she groped behind her for the tissue box, running her hand over the intercom in the process. She prayed she'd managed to turn it on. ''Unfortunately, I don't know where he is.''

''Are you sure?''

''Positive.''

''Did you know the deceased, Ms. Strauss?''

Sara shrugged. ''I never met her, but I knew *of* her, but not by name. Merely as the person hired to play a role.''

''Then you're saying you knew about your fiancé's...liaisons with her?''

''Liaison, singular. They only met last night.''

Trainor shook his head. ''No, I'm afraid that's where you're mistaken. The night manager identified her, as well. It seems Mr. Bergeron and Ms. Strauss have been...meeting at the hotel on an average of twice a month for almost a year.''

Chapter Eight

Will winced.

"Tw-twice a...*month?*"

The electronic circuitry of the intercom filtered out only a little of the emotion in Sara's voice. "F—for a year?"

"Yes, ma'am."

"You've got to be mistaken." This time it was the secretary who protested.

"There's no mistake. They'd used aliases and always paid in cash, but the manager ID'd them easily."

Will switched off the intercom and moved to the door, praying Trainor would be so overwhelmed by Sara's burst of emotion that he wouldn't notice slight movement in the doorknob. Using slow, controlled motions, he twisted the knob and cracked open the door until he'd created a space big enough to see through.

Sara stood in the middle of the room, her hands clenched into fists. Through the glass front door, he could see the secretary weaving down the hall toward a water fountain, evidently too distraught to talk.

Trainor wore an expression of almost-clinical detachment as he gazed unblinkingly at Sara. "Ms. Hardaway, you're asking me to believe you didn't know about his liaisons?"

"Know? Of c-course not!" she sputtered. Her shock

had apparently transformed into anger. "You think I would tolerate something like that? Me? The woman who hasn't even looked at another man in the last three years?"

Will winced again. *Not one look? Now there's a solid blow to my ego.*

"Can you believe the audacity of that man?" Sara stalked across room, pacing as if the constant motion would bleed away some of the pain. "He hires a private investigator to test my loyalty to him, when all the time he's been messing around with another woman? Even worse...with the very female we hired to test him?" She stalked to the desk, then suddenly collapsed in the chair. All the energy and anger left her voice, leaving it flat and emotionless. "Is that irony or what?"

Trainor remained unmoved. "You tell me."

Although she looked drained, she was able to gather enough energy to shoot the detective a steely glare. "It's Raymond's story to tell, not mine."

Will found himself gripping the doorknob harder, hoping that shock and exhaustion wouldn't entice her into saying something foolish.

"Think about it, Detective," she continued. "If I had known anything about his relationship with any woman at all, would I have spent the time and money to hire a detective to test a man I already knew was unfaithful?"

Trainor crossed his arms. "I've found that people do strange things when they get upset, Ms. Hardaway."

An unhealthy flush colored her face. "I assure you—if I'd known anything about this—" She stopped in mid-phrase, then stood suddenly as if imbued with a new wave of strength fueled by rage. "Listen, Detective Trainor, the police damn well better find him before I do because if I see him first, I'm going to rip him into pieces."

Will winced for the third time. Threats? He knew he was hearing words spoken in the blinding heat of emotion, not Sara's true inner voice. But would Steve and the Blackwater homicide division be quite as intuitive?

Will took one look around Bergeron's office to make sure everything was back in place. Seeing that it was, he drew a deep breath and quietly opened the door to the reception area.

Sara was leaning against the desk, her face buried in trembling hands. Trainor looked as if he was stuck halfway between his good-cop and bad-cop routines, not knowing which direction to take. Bergeron's secretary stood outside in the hallway, being consoled by a couple of cronies who were shooting curious glances toward the office.

It took all of Will's control not to walk over and pull Sara into his arms to comfort her. The gesture would smack of familiarity, a sense of implied propriety he had no right to suggest…no matter how he felt. He closed the door firmly behind him, the noise startling both Sara and Trainor. Will regretted catching her off guard, but he was pleased with Steve's reaction of surprise.

He leaned against the door frame and crossed his arms. "What my client is trying to say is she's highly upset by these revelations concerning her ex-fiancé. You must understand that all this has caught her completely off guard."

Trainor's reaction transformed too rapidly from a moment of surprise to a look of scathing disregard. "There you are. I was wondering when you'd get tired of eavesdropping on the intercom. So she's *your* client, now?"

Will nodded with as much nonchalance as he could manage. "She placed me on retainer shortly after we left the hotel."

Trainor made a rude noise. "So when did *you* go back to practicing law? I thought you swore you'd never do it again."

"Law?" Sara turned around slowly and graced him

with a look of total incredulity. Some of the color drained from her flushed face. "You're an...an *attorney?*" She pronounced the word with enough horror in her voice that she could have used it as a substitute for the word *rapist* without losing any impact.

For a moment, Will lost his concentration. He took a step toward her, obeying an instinct that had nothing to do with business. In a flash, he realized his tactical mistake. He pivoted on his heel to face Trainor. "I go back to law only during times of duress," he said over his shoulder to Sara, taking advantage of his position not to make eye contact with her.

"Yeah, with Riggs, you get a bargain. Two for the price of one." Trainor took a step toward the door, held it open and beckoned for the secretary to return. She wiped her eyes and stumbled in their direction. After she crossed the threshold, he closed the door and scattered the gathered spectators with a single glare. They disappeared back into their offices. Trainor then turned to Will and came dangerously close to smirking. "Care to tell me exactly what's going on?"

Will stuffed his hands into his pockets. Out of the corner of his eye, he could see Sara's gaze drilling in his direction. What timing. Just when she must have decided she hated all lawyers, he had to reveal his earlier career mistake. "The condensed no-frills version?"

"That'll do for the moment." Trainor pulled out his notebook and pencil. "Shoot."

Will flinched, then glanced at Sara who didn't seem to appreciate the policeman's brand of gallows humor. All said and done, neither did Will.

He cleared his throat. "Raymond Bergeron hired me to perform a 'loyalty' test on Ms. Hardaway, who, at that time, was his fiancée. I did the job myself rather than use one of my operatives because he requested that I do it. Since he is...was a steady and valued customer, I saw no harm in doing as he asked. I performed a 'mate and bait' routine myself, but she didn't fall for me. She wouldn't even give me her telephone number. I reported my failure to Mr. Bergeron and he seemed quite pleased with the results. Unfortunately for him, Ms. Hardaway found out about the gambit and was understandably upset. She decided turnabout was fair play and she hired me to return the favor by testing his loyalty, as well. As was my usual custom, I used Celia Strauss as the bait."

"You didn't realize they...knew each other?"

Will felt his stomach threaten to turn. He closed his eyes and mentally ran over his conversation with Celia. Had she done anything, said anything that implied she knew Bergeron? "Celia said absolutely nothing to me about it. I even showed her his picture, but she didn't say anything about recognizing him."

"And in all the cases you've done for him, you'd never mentioned her name?"

Will shrugged. "I tend to shield my operatives."

"Why?"

"To preserve their privacy, both personal and business. I don't want to broadcast their identities to my clients because it pretty much defeats the purpose of keeping things confidential. It works both ways. I give my operatives enough information to perform well, but I don't give them the details that might violate my clients' right to privacy."

Trainor turned to the secretary who had her face buried in a soggy tissue. "As Mr. Bergeron's secretary, did you witness any of these meetings?"

She looked up at him and nodded. "Almost all of them. I always take notes."

"Is Mr. Riggs correct? Did you ever hear him mention any of his operatives' names?"

"Never. He just called them his 'ops,' never referring

to them by specific name. I asked him why one time and he gave me the same explanation.''

Satisfied, Trainor turned his inquisitive stare back toward Will. ''So you set up their meeting for last night?''

Will nodded. ''Ms. Hardaway made a date at a restaurant with her ex-fiancé. I discussed strategies with Celia, then we staked out the location. I was able to watch the whole proceeding without being seen. From my vantage point, everything went according to plan. It looked to me as if Celia dangled her bait and hooked him easily.'' Will felt the muscles in his arms tighten. ''Of course, now that I think about it, everything went off just a bit too smoothly.''

''You weren't suspicious at the time?''

''Not really. They acted and reacted like they'd never met before, but it was evident they were highly attracted to each other.'' Will forced himself to look anywhere but at Sara. Her shock and disappointment were too much for him to handle. Trainor expected him to play a certain role and it was going to take his complete attention to be successful. To help bolster his performance, Will added a nonchalant shrug. ''They played 'My, Aren't You Witty!' for a half hour or so, segued into a basic game of footsie and tongue hockey, then they took off. That's when things went wrong.''

Steve crossed his arms, his gaze narrowing. '''When things went wrong...' Isn't that a bit of an understatement?''

Will recognized the change in posture; the man was making one of his infamous transitions from good to bad cop. Steve Trainor was the only police officer Will knew who reveled in playing both parts.

''Jeez, Riggs, I thought you never let the mate-and-baits reach the 'Let's go to a motel and screw' stage.'' He almost sneered as he spoke.

Will performed what he considered an almost-graceful

shrug. "They're not supposed to go that far. Celia had orders not to leave the restaurant with him. I was more than stunned when she jumped in the car with him. And I might add that she did go willingly. I tried to tail them, but Raymond drives like a Grand Prix champion. He headed straight for Key Bridge and from there, probably I-66. There was no way I could keep up with them."

"What did you do next?"

"The only thing I could do—I staked out his house in McLean on the off chance he'd head home either with or without her. But he never showed. Finally I called Sara to report." A split second after he spoke, Will realized he'd made a slip by calling her by her first name.

Trainor turned to Sara. "What was your reaction to the news, *Ms. Hardaway?*" He placed just enough emphasis on her name to signal he'd caught Will's gaffe.

She sniffed into her tissue and straightened, evidently unaware of the undercurrents. "What do you think? I was hurt by what Mr. Riggs told me. Very upset." She stopped for a moment as if weighing a decision. "Then Raymond called me about two o'clock in the morning. We argued. He was furious at me. He was drunk, too." She shivered. "It was horrible. Accusations, names."

Her face hardened perceptibly. "If I'd known anything about his continuing relationship with her..." She paused, breaking away to duck her head, hiding her expression. A second later, she lifted her chin, facing them with renewed strength. "Needless to say, I ended the call by breaking our engagement and hanging up on him."

She looked at Will as if asking his advice. He nodded, knowing she had one more piece of information she had to tell the police.

"There's one more thing," she stated in a flat voice that reminded Will of a dispassionate witness on "Dragnet."

Trainor leaned forward, his face as expressive as Sgt. Joe Friday's. "Yes?"

"I could hear a woman's laughter in the background. Wherever he was when he called me, he wasn't alone."

"He called you exactly at two o'clock?"

"A couple of minutes either side of two."

Trainor scribbled a few more lines in his notebook.

"Well?" Will prompted.

Trainor affected an accent deeper than his usual soft Virginia one. "I'd say the boy's in a heap o' trouble." He snapped his notebook closed and had the audacity to smile. "You know, I really like it when the cases are practically in the courthouse's backyard. I'll have a search warrant here in a half hour."

"A search warrant? Oh, dear." Joanie clutched the appointment book to her chest. "I can still try to cancel the rest of his appointments for today, can't I? I don't want clients walking in and finding the police tearing up the office."

Trainor gave the telephone a contemplative glare, then turned it on the secretary. "What are you telling people?"

She straightened. "I can assure you I haven't been informing them that he's involved in something criminal. All I knew was he was missing. I didn't know about—" a look of dismay draped her tear-streaked features "—any of this. I've been saying he had to cancel due to a sudden illness."

"That sounds reasonable enough. Go ahead and finish, then."

Joanie nodded, then her face crumpled with a new cascade of tears. Trainor released an exaggerated sigh. Although Will felt compelled to do something, he had no idea how to handle the situation. It was Sara who rushed to the woman's side and started comforting her with quiet, soothing words of reassurance.

Will echoed Trainor's sigh.

The detective motioned for Will to follow him into Bergeron's private office. When he reached out to close the door behind him, Trainor shook his head.

"No, keep it open. I need to keep an eye on what's going on out there." He shot Will a half smile. The good cop had returned. "So, exactly what were you two doing in here when I came?"

Will did some quick mental choreography; it was time to tap-dance a bit. "Ms. Hardaway was understandably upset, but she didn't want to tell the secretary anything more than she had to." Will leaned forward and added a conspiratorial note to his voice. "The woman worships the man, you know."

"But Ms. Hardaway doesn't?"

"Ms. Hardaway has had almost a week to come to grips with sudden disillusionment."

"'Sudden disillusionment'?" Trainor repeated. His features hardened. "I thought she swore she didn't know anything about her fiancé's...dalliances."

Will decided to continue to play to Trainor's good-cop side in hopes it would return. He sneaked a quick look at the women, then kept his voice low. "She didn't. Neither of us did. Her world sustained a pretty big crack in it when Bergeron decided he needed to test her loyalty. The idiot even admitted to me he had no reason to distrust her. I checked her paper trail and she came up clean. I tried to talk him out of continuing but—"

"But he tested her anyway," Trainor supplied. "Strange man. Of course, most attorneys are. Especially the ones who handle divorce." He paused. "So, did she pass the test?"

Will sighed. It was an admission he didn't exactly want broadcast around to everybody. He tried to shrug off what he almost considered a personal failure. "Between you and me? She passed with flying colors. I gave her everything I've got, but there was nothing I could do to get past her outer defenses. It was like trying to break into Fort Knox with a spoon.''

"A looker like her?" Trainor nodded toward the open door. "Funny…she doesn't strike me as the cold-fish type.''

Will knew his part of the game and picked up his cue. ''That's the problem. She's not a cold fish." He added a theatrical sigh. "Take a good hard look at her, my friend. In this day and age, she's practically a dying breed. She's a good-looking, smart, loyal woman. I guess you could say she's loyal to a fault.''

"Loyal to a fault…'' Trainor repeated. "Maybe. I still wonder why she's out there, still being loyal to him. Out of habit? Or maybe she knows more that she's letting on. We're talking about the death of a mistress, here. She's the most likely suspect.''

"Her? No way. Sara's not that type of woman. She—'' Will stopped, realizing he'd been taken in by a master of questioning. "You bastard.''

"That's why they pay me the big money, Riggs. To see through even the most sophisticated con jobs." Trainor shot him a speculative glare that exposed every embellishment Will had made in the last half hour. "Let's can the crap. Do you think she knows something she's not telling us? That she's still protecting him?''

Will contemplated the notion for a full three seconds before shaking his head. "No. I think there's a gap between them that won't ever be bridged again. If he walked in right now and you, yourself, totally exonerated him, I don't think Sara would take him back. She may be loyal, but she's not stupid. She knows when to give up.'' *And hopefully when to look somewhere else…at someone else.*

"And you're willing to swear in court that you were on the phone talking to her at two o'clock this morning?''

Will nodded. "Absolutely. I was in my car and I initiated the call. You can subpoena the phone records to support my statement."

"We'll do that." Trainor glanced out the door and Will followed his gaze. Together, they observed Sara as she was talking on the phone. They could hear enough of her conversation to realize she was in mid-cancellation.

"Terribly sorry for the inconvenience, Mrs. Howard. Er, *Ms.* Howard. I understand.... Yes... But could we call you back Monday and reschedule it then...? Yes... Ma'am, there's nothing I can do between now and then.... No... Thank you."

She wiped a stray strand of hair from her face, consulted the appointment book and started punching in the next number.

"May I speak to Mr. Barnes?"

Trainor gave her a once-over that made the hairs on the back of Will's neck bristle. "So you say you gave her everything you got? The total charm package? And she still didn't tumble?"

Will nodded.

Trainor conducted one more slow survey of her attributes, then released a short bark of laughter. "Definitely your loss. If I'd been you, I think I would have tried harder." He turned back to Will and thumbed toward the desk. "You know the drill."

"What?"

"Oh, come on...I know what you were doing. You sent the lady out to stall me while you searched the office. Or maybe his computer." He reached over and placed a hand on the printer. "It's still warm. Show me what you found."

"Nothing."

"Come, now...you don't expect me to believe that, do you? Spread 'em."

"You're kidding. You want to pat me down?"

"I'd just as soon not have to go through official channels. Chalk it up to professional courtesy."

Will sighed, then bent over to assume the frisk position. Halfway through the search procedure, he looked over and saw Sara staring aghast at the spectacle. He shot her a reassuring wink.

"The printer is warm because it automatically comes on when you turn on the computer."

"And why did you turn on the computer?"

"We didn't. It was on when we came in. Ask the secretary. She probably switches everything on first thing in the morning."

"But you thoughtfully turned it off while you were eavesdropping?"

Will shrugged. "It was loud and I wanted to hear everything you said."

Trainor searched thoroughly but came up with no papers, no computer disks to show for his efforts. He motioned for Will to straighten. "Thanks. That saved both of us a lot of time." He wagged a finger in Will's face. "Listen, if Bergeron surfaces, I want to be the first to know about it, okay? No rent-a-cop heroics, no P.I. grandstanding. Got it?"

Will nodded. "Understood."

"Now let's go see if the ladies are through."

As they walked into the reception area, Sara had just hung up the phone. "I canceled the last appointment for today."

Joanie sniffed, then straightened in her seat. "I'm okay now." She turned toward Trainor. "What should I do about the appointments for Monday?"

The policeman shrugged. "I'd hold off. This could all be resolved over the weekend."

Joanie brightened. "Really?"

Will glanced up and his gaze locked with Sara's hooded one. It was evident that neither of them thought that Raymond would arrive in the office on Monday morning, ready to conduct business as usual. But once that tacit agreement passed between them, she still held his gaze. In it, he read a full spectrum of emotions: fear, disappointment, confusion...

Will turned away first, knowing the intensity of their shared looks could become a red flag in Trainor's book. If the man suspected collusion, their alibis would be useless. Will turned to the secretary. "I assume Raymond has a lawyer, so you'd better call him and get him here as soon as possible. There are a slew of confidentiality elements that need to be addressed before they can search the office."

Joanie nodded. "Yes, sir."

He faced Trainor. "You know how to get a hold of me."

The policeman nodded. "And you, Ms. Hardaway?"

She tightened her lips in momentary indecision, then her gaze hardened. She nodded toward Will. "I'll be with him. Looking for Raymond."

Chapter Nine

"'I'll be with him'?" Will repeated after hitting the Lobby button with the heel of his hand. The elevator doors glided closed, isolating them from the curious who had begun to congregate in the hallway again.

Sara crossed her arms and stared straight ahead. "What was I supposed to say? 'I'll be sitting at home and wringing my hands?' You're going to look for Raymond, aren't you?"

Will nodded. "Damn straight, I am. He killed Celia. I'm going to get the bastard."

"Then I'm going with you." Will started to protest but Sara gestured for him to stop. "You think he's guilty. I think he's innocent. The only way we're going to learn the truth is to find him. And it makes a lot of sense to work together. I know Raymond. I know his habits, his tastes, where he goes when he's mad, where he goes when he's sad—"

"Where he goes when he has something to hide?"

The elevator lurched slightly and the doors slid open to the well-appointed foyer. Sara stepped out, shot Will an almost-venomous look, then marched toward the door without waiting for him.

He followed her across the marble floor, his footfalls reverberating like gunshots. Conscious of the echo, he lowered his voice even though there was nobody visible in the lobby. "You act as if he's completely incapable of killing someone. The Blackwater Barracuda—lacking the killer instinct? I don't think so."

"That's in the courtroom. Outside the courtroom—"

"Outside the courtroom, he's no different. He doesn't stop being a ruthless, lying son of a bitch just because he closes his briefcase and hangs up his jacket. You can't just turn it off like that."

"He can't?" Her eyes narrowed. "Or you couldn't?"

Will jammed his hands into his pockets and turned away. She was too damn perceptive for her own good. Memories laced with old accusations floated to the front of his mind. He released a deep sigh in hopes of clearing away the cobwebs of past guilts. "It's an occupational hazard I decided I didn't want to put up with. I've watched a lot of attorneys suffer through the same problem—people pay you good money to be a bastard in court and it becomes hard to stop once the day is over. It eats into your life, destroys your relationships...."

His voice trailed off as he remembered one-too-many Friday nights that blended into Monday mornings. When you made your career your entire existence, losing a case felt like losing a piece of your life and that turned out to be a mighty stiff price to pay for people who were essentially strangers.

To his shock, Sara lost her look of hostility and even nodded her begrudged agreement. "You get so wrapped up in a case that you don't have time for anybody or anything else. Believe me, I've seen it happen too many times not to recognize the signs or anticipate the consequences. It can destroy a relationship if you're not careful." She gazed across the lobby with an unfocused stare.

"You and Raymond had troubles before?"

"Us?" She shook out of her uneasy reverie. "Uh...no...I watched it happen to some of Raymond's friends,'' she added quickly. Too quickly, in Will's opinion. "So—" she managed a tight-lipped smile "—since we differ in opinion on whether he's guilty or not, can we simply agree to disagree? After all, we do have one thing in common—we both want to find him."

He shrugged. "I guess it's the safest thing to do in this case."

"Good..." Her smile lost some of its strained quality. "So exactly how far does my investment take me?"

He stared at her. "Huh?"

She led the way to the parking deck. "You're on retainer, remember? At least you were. I suspect the dollar ran out while we were in the elevator, somewhere between the second and third floor. When we get in the car, I'll write you a check to cover—"

"Nope." He shook his head as he held open the door for her. "No check. I'm doing this for Celia. I sent her out on that job, so finding her killer is my responsibility. Morally and financially. I figure having you along might simply speed up the process of finding Bergeron."

"Nonsense." Sara waved her hand as if to dismiss his plan as she passed through the door. "We split expenses, fifty-fifty. I have a vested interest as well to prove Raymond innocent." She continued without taking a breath, "So, like I said, where to, first?"

Will opened his mouth to protest, then closed it again. Her loyalty to Bergeron was admirably misplaced. How could she retain any feelings for a fool like him? Even if she believed Bergeron hadn't killed Celia, Sara knew he'd been sleeping with the woman....

"What's wrong?" She stood by his car.

He took one long look at her. Somewhere down the line, "pretty" had become "beautiful." Was it because he'd had a chance to see beyond the outer layer of her personality and get a glimpse of the real person inside?

He shook himself mentally. *Jeez, that's what got me in trouble to begin with. Attraction. Basic animal attraction.*

"Will? What's wrong?" she repeated.

"You." His heart misfired as he realized what he'd said aloud. He swallowed hard as protective instincts swelled up to cover the hole his libido had made in his self-control. "Uh...this sudden surge of loyalty."

"Loyalty?" Her brows knitted together in perplexity, then relaxed. "Oh...to Raymond? If I believe he didn't kill her, then does that mean I still love and trust him?"

He nodded as he unlocked the car. "Something like that."

"Love him? Probably. I can't just turn it off. Trust him? Never again. He broke the bonds that held us together. And he broke them—" she made a face as she slid into her seat "—in a very unforgivable way. Although I don't believe he killed Celia Strauss, I've accepted the fact that he went to bed with her. I've decided it's my mission to find him, make sure he's free and clear of any murder charges and then basically kick him out of my life forever."

He accepted her explanation with a shrug. "Sounds reasonable enough."

She waited until he walked around the car and got into the driver's seat before she continued their conversation. "So our first step in trying to find him is to...?" Her voice trailed off expectantly.

"Go back to my office," he supplied. "I want to check Bergeron's datebook."

"The one from his computer?" A confused look crossed her face. "But how? I watched Mr. Trainor search you. How could you have smuggled out all that paper?"

He smiled. "I didn't. When I realized I only had a couple of minutes before Trainor figured out I was there, I stopped the printing." Will started the engine with a roar and headed for the exit. "I knew there was no way he would let me walk out of the office without being searched. Then I realized good ol' Raymond had a fax-modem in his computer so I simply had the computer fax the file to my office.''

Her look of mild astonishment grew into a genuine smile. ''So that's why you were stalling—so that the computer could finish faxing everything to you?''

Will nodded. ''A high-tech version of 'Desperate measures for desperate times.' ''

She settled back in her seat. ''I'm impressed.''

Will scanned the traffic, hiding his smug smirk. *You're supposed to be.*

Saturday midday

''THAT MUCH?'' Will stared at the large stack of curled paper in his secretary's hand.

Mimi nodded. ''We were lucky there was a new roll in the machine. Once it ran out, I tried to put in a new one as quickly as possible, but once the buffer filled up, the call was disconnected. I thought maybe whoever would call back but they didn't.'' She turned around and picked up a neat pile of papers from her desk. ''I made copies so you didn't have to fool with the originals.'' She balanced the two stacks of paper, one in each hand. ''You know—'' she raised an eyebrow in mock disdain ''—if we had a plain-paper fax, we wouldn't have to worry about the paper running out so quickly or making copies since you hate handling thermal paper.''

Will shot his secretary a smile and took the papers from her hand. ''I get the message, Mimi. Put it on the wish list.'' He turned to Sara. ''Let's go to my office to talk.''

Sara hadn't known what to expect in terms of his office space. The building housed a variety of businesses: importers, construction companies, real-estate offices, dentists'— That was what Will's outer office reminded her of—a dentist's office. The reception area was small but comfortable, painted in soothing colors as if to lull a patient into forgetting about losing a tooth.

Or a fiancé.

But once they stepped into his personal space, the first thing she noticed was a large aquarium that dominated one wall. An exotic collection of fish glided through the water, passing over the obligatory sunken treasure-chest. Only this treasure included a miniature Maltese falcon nestled among the faux pearls and shiny golden coins.

"'The stuff dreams are made of,'" Will said in a fair imitation of Humphrey Bogart's growl.

Sara turned around, surprised to find him standing close by, peering over her shoulder. "What are you talking about?"

He pointed past her to the statue of the small black bird in the water. "That's what Bogey told Ward Bond's character when he asked what the Maltese falcon was. 'The stuff dreams are made of.'"

"So you saw the movie as a kid and that's what made you want to grow up to be a private eye?"

He shrugged and moved away, creating a sudden gulf between them, physically and emotionally. He stopped near a large bookcase that filled the wall to the right of his desk. "I got a new dream each time I saw a different movie or read a different book." He reached out to the nearest shelf of books and ran a finger across the spines of a dozen volumes or so. "I wanted to be a race-car driver, a ship's captain, a fireman, an astronaut—"

"A lawyer?"

His hand stopped, one spine shy of a collection of law books. Evidently self-conscious, he turned his motion into a gesture for her to sit. Once she was seated, he dropped into his own chair behind the desk. "Honestly? I never dreamed about becoming a lawyer. I guess that's what made me think it would be a real profession—because it wasn't the sort of thing kids dreamed about.''

''Unless you're Raymond Bergeron.'' Sara allowed herself a sigh, knowing that any other emotional release might cause a cascade effect. ''According to his family, he came out of the womb knowing he was going to be a lawyer. That's why I can't believe he would violate something that he's revered for so long.''

Will picked up a pencil and began drumming it on his blotter. ''Don't be so sure. He two-timed you.''

Sara tried to ignore the sudden rumble in her stomach, which mimicked the pencil's drumbeat. ''There's no law that says an unmarried man has to be faithful to his girl-friend. It only becomes a point of legal contention when they get married.''

''There's always 'breach of promise.''' Will stopped drumming and tossed the pencil back toward its holder. ''He's a fool, you know.''

Sara smiled in spite of herself. ''I agree one hundred percent. However, I don't believe he's a murdering fool.'' She glanced at the papers on Will's desk. ''And I hope something in his date-book file might help us establish his innocence.''

''We got more than I expected.'' A perplexed look crossed his face. ''In fact, we got a *lot* more than I expected and I'm not sure why.''

''Where do we start?''

He glanced again at the stack of papers and shrugged. ''Where else? At the beginning. I think—'' The intercom interrupted him. He stretched past Sara, his arm brushing her shoulder as he reached for the instrument and punched a button. ''Yes, Mimi?''

''I was wondering if it's a convenient time for me to go to lunch?''

Will consulted his watch. ''Sure. We'll be okay.''

Sara's stomach turned a complete somersault as she

grabbed his outstretched arm. "What time is it?" she asked, straining to see his watch.

Raymond always wore a Rolex; Martin relied on the split-second accuracy of an expensive chronometer Lucy had bought him during their vacation in Switzerland. Sara assumed that Will utilized something with similar precision due to the nature of his business. A leather band peeped from beneath the white cuff of his shirt.

As soon as her fingers curled around his wrist, she felt uncomfortable. Not necessarily a lightning-bolt sensation, but more a static charge that fluttered across the back of her hand and down her arm.

Will interrupted the flow by shifting his obscuring sleeve out of the way, revealing a watch face with a cartoon Martian that pointed to the twelve with his gloved hand as well as his disintegrator ray.

"Noon?" she managed in a strangled voice. "Martin must be going crazy! I didn't even think about calling him."

Will nudged the telephone toward her. "Here. Call him now."

Sara dialed the private kitchen number. It rang several times before someone picked up.

"Blackwater Café."

"Lucy? It's me."

"Good God, Sara, where have you been? Martin's been going crazy!"

"Tell him I'm sorry. I'll get back to work as soon as I can—" She heard the sound of the phone being fumbled from one person to the next.

"Sara? Did that bastard cousin of mine do it? Did he kill that woman?" Martin's voice boomed over the kitchen noises in the background.

Was she hearing him correctly? "Surely you don't think Raymond's capable of something like this."

"Ray is capable of doing practically anything if he thinks it's going to save his ass. Where is he?"

"That's the problem." Sara tightened her grip on the receiver. "We don't know where he is. He's not at home or at work." A shiver shimmied up her spine. "The police are looking for him. They have a warrant."

"So he's on the run, eh? You know what that means—he's guilty as sin."

"Martin—"

"I know...I know. Innocent until proven guilty. I'll try to remember that. But you need to face facts, Sara. He might not be the man you thought he was...that *we* thought he was." There was an uncomfortable pause, then he spoke again. "I suppose you're going to need me to cover for you until this is all over."

"Well..."

"I can do it, no problem...but you need to drop by first and countersign some checks, okay?"

"Thanks, Martin."

"Don't thank me. It's going to cost you. I'll make sure you remember this when it comes to scheduling our Christmas hours." The gruffness left his voice. "You be careful, hon. Don't do anything stupid, because I don't want to have to break in a new partner, okay?"

"I'll be careful, Martin."

"And if you do find Ray, tell him I'll do my family duty and bring him a goody basket in jail, but for him not to expect to find a hacksaw blade baked in the croissants."

Sara felt a good deal of tension flee from her body; having Martin's support meant a great deal to her. It was comforting to know that whether she married his cousin or not, he would always be "family" to her. "Thanks, partner. We really appreciate this."

"We?" He muttered an expletive. "Don't tell me there's still a chance for you and Raymond to be a 'we'?"

"No. I was talking about—" *Admit it. You were talking about you and Will* "—Mr. Riggs, the private investigator you met this morning. He's agreed to help me find Raymond."

"Good. I don't want you out looking for him by yourself. It might not be safe. But before you go too far, swing by here and sign these checks, okay?"

"As soon as I can. I promise. Bye."

Sara hung up the phone quickly, the echo of the word *we* still bouncing through her mind. She'd heard of acting, reacting on the rebound, but this was ridiculous.

"Everything okay?"

Sara glanced at Will, hoping her face didn't betray her momentary aberration. "Uh...Martin was just offering to cater to the jail. Raymond has some eclectic tastes and prefers gourmet food."

"Which may explain why he was going to marry someone who owns a restaurant."

She nodded, distracted by a new flood of thoughts. *Food. Jail. Gourmet to go.* A light was growing, the shadows dimming in the back of her brain.

"What?" Will's eyebrows furrowed and he leaned forward in his chair. "I can tell something's going on. What is it?"

As the thoughts began to link into some semblance of coherence, Sara felt her heart quicken, the sharp intake of breath becoming painful in her lungs. "Raymond is very particular about what he eats. And when he gets stressed, he eats a lot."

Will's scowl deepened. "So? You expect him to gain a lot of weight?"

"No...he's on the run, right? So he can't walk into his favorite restaurant and sit down to order a gourmet meal. Everybody knows him on sight and the news is going to leak out soon. If he wants to eat well, he has only one option."

"What? Cook it himself?"

Sara rolled her eyes. "Good Lord, no! He'll order out. He'll phone a restaurant and have someone deliver it to wherever he's hiding. Chefs, maître d's...those are the people who know him on sight. But the delivery people won't recognize him at all."

Will grimaced as he leaned back in his chair. It was an obvious signal that he found her logic strained at best. "So you want us to stake out every steak house in the metro area? To hire two or three hundred operatives to follow the delivery people and—"

"No, you don't understand! We don't need a bunch of people staking out restaurants. I know Raymond. I know what he's going to order and which of a half-dozen or so restaurants in the area he'd be likely to call for a delivery. I can contact all the probable places and explain what's going on."

"And they'll help?"

"If I ask them to. Think of it as a type of...professional courtesy."

His interest piqued, Will leaned over in his chair, rooted around in his credenza and pulled out the L—Z phone book. "So...what are you waiting for?" She took it and began to flip through the pages. She dialed the first number and Will listened in.

He marveled at Sara's perseverance as she waited with strained patience to be connected with the kitchen of the swankiest restaurant in the District. It was a place with a three-month waiting list and a maître d' who was the reincarnation of Mussolini himself. Will wondered how she would coerce them into cooperating. What lies would she tell them rather than expose her own foibles as well as those of her ex-fiancé?

That is, if she even got through.

He couldn't imagine any self-respecting chef even taking a call in the midst of a busy lunch hour. He'd run into one too many cooks who ruled his kitchen domain with an iron-fisted spatula.

But to his surprise, she got through and when she did, she pulled no punches. She told each chef her fiancé was in trouble and she needed to find him before he got into a worse predicament with the law. If they received a food order for delivery that reflected Raymond's patrician tastes in foods, to please call. She gave them Will's office number as well as his pager number.

It was simple, concise and evidently effective. After the sixth such recitation—one conducted in French—she hung up the phone and pushed back in her chair with a sigh. "They'll contact you night or day, if they get a suspicious delivery order. Then we can meet the delivery-man at the address and see if it's Raymond."

Will glanced down at the restaurants she'd circled in the phone book. They included two in the Virginia sub-urbs, two in D.C., one in the Maryland suburbs near Be-thesda and one practically in Baltimore. He created a men-tal map, wincing at the distances between potential starting locations. "Won't he get suspicious if his food takes an extra-long time to reach him? These places aren't necessarily close by. And if we have to deal with rush-hour traffic…" His voice trailed off.

She smiled. "We're not talking about pizza, which has to arrive in thirty minutes or less. He knows to call at least two hours in advance." She glanced at Will's watch again. "I'd say he's probably getting hungry, now. Since it's too late for anything but a makeshift lunch at this point, I bet he'll be even more anxious about arranging for what he considers a decent dinner."

"Are you sure?"

She shrugged. "I'd better be. And I'd better head back to the restaurant and check in. There're a few things I have to do before I can leave all the responsibility to my partners."

Will stood and fished in his pocket for his keys. "I'll drive you back,"

"That's not necessary. I'll call a cab. You have work to do. I'll be back…around two. If you get a call about Raymond…"

He nodded. "I'll call you. Promise. Until then, I'll go through these." He pointed to the stack of papers with the information from Raymond's computer. "Who knows what I might find."

"I'M SURE GLAD YOU CAME back to sign the checks before you disappeared on us." Lucy pushed a limp strand of hair out of her eyes, then slapped the mop into the wringer.

Sara wondered whose neck Lucy was vicariously wringing as she squeezed the dirty water out of the mop head. The moment Sara walked through the back door, she realized she'd stumbled onto a crisis in the making. Their dishwasher had an uncanny sense of timing, spouting off like a geyser at the most inopportune moments.

"Sorry, Luce. Timing is everything, isn't it?" She twisted the hose clamp-screw another quarter revolution. "There. That ought to hold it." Unfolding herself from her cramped position from under the dishwasher, she rotated her shoulders, trying to loosen her tensed muscles. During her exercise, she sneaked a glance at Lucy who stood, arms crossed, grimace in place.

Lucy was upset—not just about the broken dishwasher hose, but about being left with more responsibility than she liked to handle. Their partnership agreement stipulated that Lucy's responsibilities would be strictly up-front—hosting and such. She didn't deal well with the stresses in the kitchen and now she had both her responsibilities as well as Sara's. And Martin was no help; he became totally oblivious to people and their problems when he put on an apron.

Sara knew it was time for a little relations repair-work, too. She tried to smile. "I guess it looks like I'm abandoning a sinking ship at the moment, doesn't it?" Belatedly, she realized her implication—that the restaurant was the sinking ship. "I don't mean the restaurant, of course. Just with all this water..."

Lucy's scowl faded away. She shrugged and a ghost of a grin lit her face. "Yeah, for a while, this did remind me of the *Titanic.* The water was gushing from the broken hose and I couldn't get anybody's attention back here because the music and the laughter were too loud." Her brief flare of amusement faded. "You can't form a bucket brigade when you only have one person and one bucket."

Sara grabbed a second mop and began to help corral the water toward the floor drain. After they finished, they both sagged toward the counter. She tried again. "Lucy, I'm sorry this is happening right now."

Lucy lifted her shoulders expressively. "Like you're to blame? The way I figure it, it's that woman's fault."

"Celia's? Why? I figure Raymond had a hand in it, too." The words conjured up an image of an intimate tableau, which made her stomach tighten. Not one hand, but a pair of hands.

"But she seduced him, Sara!"

"But he allowed himself to be seduced, Lucy," she mimicked.

Stalemate.

Lucy remained resolute. "It may take two to tango but sometimes, one partner is doing all the dancing."

"So you're saying I shoved him onto the proverbial dance floor by setting him up just like he set me up?"

"Well...no...but—"

"But what?"

"You and he...you're so perfect together."

"*Were,* Lucy. We were good together. Not perfect. Good. Now we're not and he's the one who started the chain of events." It was quite the temptation to spew out the fact that Raymond had had a standing appointment to meet Celia Strauss in a hotel room where their dancing definitely became a pas de deux. But Sara wasn't ready to prove to the world how ignorant she'd been of her fiancé's secrets. Ignorance or stupidity? She wasn't sure which.

Lucy remained quiet for a moment, staring at the wet floor. "What are you going to do?"

Sara glanced down at the dirty wet knees of her pants. "Sign the checks, go home, change clothes and then go back to Will's office and see if I can help."

"Oh."

Although she could hear the cacophony of patrons' voices along with muted music from the front of the restaurant, it faded away as the blood rushed in her ears. Silence clung to the walls of the room like damp towels thrown across a clothesline.

Finally Lucy spoke again. "You be careful, okay?"

Sara reached over and hugged her friend. "Listen. I know Raymond didn't kill her."

Lucy wiped away a stray tear before it dared escape and leave a visible trail of her true emotion. "Yeah—" she sniffed "—maybe Raymond didn't, but remember, Sara...*someone* did."

Chapter Ten

Will thumbed through the stack of papers. There were two sets of calendar pages. He compared the two, discovering they weren't duplicates; they detailed the same period of time but the second set contained only cryptic notes and abbreviations. He knew all about the less-than-legal reasons for keeping two sets of financial books, but two datebooks? Why? The whole purpose of keeping a calendar was to coordinate all your appointments and schedules.

Unless...

These are appointments Raymond doesn't want anybody to know about.

Will started comparing each page and an alarming trend emerged. In the "public" calendar, he found an appointment notation on September 26th for "Crandell, Darlene P.—Mrs. Arthur P." On the corresponding private calendar page, there was the cryptic notation "APC.txt V#247 10k."

Not every appointment in the public calendar had a corresponding memo but when they did, each notation consisted of a trio of initials set up like a text-file name, then a code number starting with either a *V, P* or *R*, and a number ending in a *K.*

It didn't take a genius to come up with a possible explanation. But before Will allowed himself the luxury of formulating a theory, he turned to his own computer. A careful scan of his records substantiated his worst fears.

Blackmail.

In the Crandell case, Will had turned over to Bergeron a videotape of Mr. Crandell propositioning a female operative named Margaret. The former Mrs. Crandell had evidently insisted on concrete proof of her husband's infidelity and Will had complied, generating a six-minute video of the elderly Mr. Crandell in action.

In the Gordon-Garcia case—RGG.txt P#47 15k—Bergeron had said the wife insisted on pictures. Will took them himself. In the Landrum case—CSL.txt R#26 5k—Celia had given Will signed receipts, which proved the husband had checked into a hotel in downtown D.C. rather than gone on a business trip to Sacramento. And Will had promptly handed them over to Bergeron.

V, P, R. Video. Photograph. Receipt.

And the numbers? Considering Bergeron's upscale clientele, it was plausible that he might extort ten thousand dollars from a husband with something to hide. Evidently the figure varied, depending on financial circumstances. But whose? The victim's potential cash flow or Bergeron's need?

Will pushed away from the desk, contemplating his discovery. In some ways, he was almost relieved that Celia had been involved in only one of these three cases. It eliminated her as a common denominator and placed the guilt squarely on Bergeron's shoulders.

And mine.

Will stood and stalked over to his fish tank. Placing a palm against the cool glass, he felt the gentle rumble of the compressor, pumping air into the water. The bubbles shot out of the tube, rose upward and performed a frenetic dance on the surface until they popped. There was usually something lulling, even hypnotic, about the chaotic motion of the bubbles but it wasn't working this time. The cool glass heated under his hand, creating a foggy outline around his fingers.

He was hot, all right.

Hot under the collar.

Raymond Bergeron had played him for a fool, violating professional ethics by taking confidential material supplied in good faith and turning it into extortion. Weren't divorces messy enough without introducing third-party greed into the picture?

Will lifted his hand from the tank's side, curling his fingers into a tight fist. For a moment, he stood there, muscles coiled and teeth clenched. Then he slowly willed himself to relax. Getting angry wasn't the answer. It wasn't the William B. Riggs way.

How about getting even?

Will drew in a deep breath.

First he had to find Raymond Bergeron. Then he would figure out what to do with him. And there was still the matter of Celia's death.

Maybe she'd figured out about his blackmail scheme. Maybe the lawyer had killed her rather than have her reveal his secrets. The mind's eye tried to picture Celia, virtuously trying to stop her lover from extortion. The picture faded before it was even half formed. Instead, Will got a mental image of Celia, trying to cut herself in on the deal and Bergeron unwilling to profit-share.

Will nodded. That sounded much more like the Celia he knew. And it might just explain her murder.

He returned to his desk and the pages. He had to check every notation, single out those cases that included Celia as an operative. If she had stumbled onto Bergeron's extortion scheme, then it was probably in connection with a case she'd worked on.

He started with the Landrum case, trying to recall every detail of Mr. Landrum's wee-hours attempts to entice Celia to his hotel room. The man had slipped her a room

key-card with a whisper about getting together. She'd
countered by suggesting he order a bottle of champagne
for their impending rendezvous while she dashed off to
the rest room for a last-minute check. She'd passed the
key to Will who had hightailed it upstairs to verify the
man had really checked in. The conscientious hotel staff
had already slid a bill under his door, so Will had taken
it as his proof.

Between the lines of Celia's report, there were no additional details. For some curious reason, her writing style
had always been diametrically opposed to her personal
style. Her reports were always neat and succinct—not
what you'd expect from the theatrically vampish persona
she so carefully cultivated. She even turned in her report
on a floppy so that Mimi didn't have to retype—

Will stopped.

On a disk?

*Where there's a disk, there's a computer. And where
there's a computer, there might be additional files....*

He grabbed his Rolodex and allowed himself a tight-
lipped smile. *And where there's a Will...*

Saturday, early afternoon

SARA GLANCED AT HERSELF in the rearview mirror and
tried to use a tissue to scrub away the oily smudge on her
cheek. At first, she didn't want to lose precious time in
something as self-indulgent taking as a shower. But by
the time she drove home and stumbled into her bedroom,
a shower had become less a time-wasting luxury and more
a soul-repairing necessity.

Stripping off her dirtied clothes, she took refuge in the
stinging hot spray, wishing she could wash away her nig-
gling sense of guilt as easily as the mess created by the
malfunctioning dishwasher.

Two voices argued inside her. One kept harping, *"What*

sort of idiot doesn't know her fiancé was cheating on her?" And the second countered with the importance of trust and faithfulness. Sara cut off the water when Voice One went a step too far: *"What kind of idiot falls for someone else when the first relationship is barely cold?"*

She toweled herself off. *Yeah…what kind of idiot?* She looked into the mirror, getting a good view of just what type of…

She made a face. "What kind of idiot talks to herself?" To prove she wasn't the least bit smitten, she grabbed jeans and a turtleneck from her closet rather than linger over a clothing selection. Smitten people mulled entirely too long on their clothing choice, she told herself.

A twinge of hunger informed her that she hadn't eaten much all day. She walked into the kitchen, reminding herself that smitten people didn't eat much, either. Sne glanced at the contents of her refrigerator; a ravenous appetite would dispel any notions that she wasn't the least bit infatuated with anybody, anywhere, she decided.

Nothing caught her interest.

She searched the pantry. Nothing there, either.

But if I'm not hungry, that means…

Sara snatched a package of microwavable popcorn from the pantry. She would eat! She would eat if only to prove she wasn't—the word stuck in her mind.

Smitten.

As she adjusted the microwave's timer, she realized it was one-forty. She would never eat, dry her hair, and get over to his office by two. *I'd better call him.…*

Rather than turn off the microwave, she stepped into her office to escape the sound of popping corn. As she reached for the phone, she realized her answering machine was blinking. Had the phone rung while she was in the shower?

Maybe Will has already found Raymond!

She punched the Play button. "10:32 a.m."

"Oh, God…Sara, I'm in so much trouble. You sicced that bitch on me—"

Her hands trembled as she fumbled to hit the Stop button. Taking a step backward, she crossed her arms and stared at the machine. Its red power light glared back, unblinking. She knew she didn't need to play back the tape again to recall his next words. How could she forget them? There would be that long shuddering gasp of breath and the most damning words he could ever inflict on her: *"It's not my fault, Sara. It's not. It's yours. You hired the slut."*

Not my fault…

It's yours.…

It's yours.…

She sank to the chair, lowering her head to the cool smooth surface of the desk.

Raymond's confession.

But of what? Infidelity or murder?

She fought her first instinct to destroy the tape. Instead, with remarkably steady hands, she hit the Fast-Forward button. Now if she could only put him out of her life so efficiently.

The machine beeped, indicating a second message. Instinctively, she hit Play before realizing she might be subjected to yet another outburst. "1:49 p.m." Then flinched at the sound of another male voice.

"Sara? You there? Pick up the phone."

When she realized she was holding her breath, she released it with a relieved sigh.

"It's Will. Don't panic. I haven't heard anything from any of the restaurants. That's not why I'm calling. I got a hunch about the case and I'm in the car, headed over to a friend's place for some help. I won't be back to my office for at least an hour, maybe two. If anything breaks open, I'll contact you immediately. I spoke to someone named Lucy at your restaurant and she told me about the broken dishwasher.'' He paused. ''Sorry, Sara. Just what you needed, eh? I'm going to be busy for a while so why don't you try to get some rest? It may be a long night. Uh…if you need me, call Mimi and she'll patch you right through. Bye.''

The machine clicked, then stopped. No more messages.

Sara wandered back into the kitchen where the aroma of popcorn was almost overwhelming. She pulled the steaming bag out of the microwave and stared forlornly at its contents.

She sat at the kitchen table, opened the bag and forced herself to eat a handful.

If you don't eat something, you know what that means….

''WELL?'' WILL SHIFTED in the broken chair. ''Can you do it?''

Archie used his bandaged finger to push his glasses back up the bridge of his nose. ''Like I told you, it all depends on whether I can access the system or not.''

Will glanced around the workroom where several dozen computers sat, all in different stages of repair. ''I thought you said you could get inside any computer, anywhere.'' For a moment, he wondered if Archie Koeffler had been bragging about his prowess as a repairman rather than a hacker.

Archie ran his hand over his keyboard. ''Usually I can, but there's a sorta binary aspect we have to consider before I can go too far into this case.''

''A 'binary' aspect?''

Archie rolled his eyes and sighed in the world-weary manner of a nearsighted, fourteen-year-old computer genius. Unfortunately, Archie was forty, wore bifocals and lacked the forgivable illusion of youthful inexperience. ''Binary—as in switching. As in ones and zeroes?''

Will smiled as he reached over and picked up a small

wafer board. He flipped it in the air like one would a coin. "You wouldn't be trying to shake me down for more money, now would you, Archie?"

The small man blanched, intercepting the board in mid-air and cradling it in his palm like a cherished gem.

"Of course not. I mean zeroes and ones. As in *off* or *on*. I can't break into her system from a remote location unless her computer is turned on. There's no remote command I can give to power up her computer if she turns it on and off by using a switching station or a surge protector."

"I understand. But we won't know until you try."

Archie shrugged. "Just as long as you understand." Under his breath he added, "Just as long as Celia doesn't find out."

"Archie…I told you over the phone—Celia's dead."

The man cracked his knuckles, then hunched over his keyboard. "She's the person most likely to decide to come back from the dead and haunt me. She hated for people to pry into her private life." He turned to his monitor and squinted. "Here goes."

To Will, the letters crossing the screen were nothing more than gobbledygook, but Archie harrumphed, snorted, guffawed and sneered at each string of characters. For ten minutes he looked and sounded more like an outcast from the National Zoo rather than one of the pre-eminent computer specialists in the D.C. Metro area. But he stopped snuffling and chortling when a neatly ordered directory list scrolled across the monitor.

"Riggs, I always said your success had more to do with dumb luck than skill. Her machine was already on—we're in." He tapped the monitor with his grubby fingertip. "There's her hard-drive directory. And as an added bonus—" he typed in a command "—she's left a disk in the floppy drive and we can access that, too. Tell me what we're looking for and we'll let our fingers do the walking."

Will handed him a disk on which he'd copied two files: the list of cases Celia had worked on during the last six months and the names of clients from Bergeron's secret date book. "Find me any reference to these people. It could be names, initials, code names. You might be able to corroborate the file by date if not by name."

"You got it. Here…while you're waiting…" He nudged a second keyboard toward Will. "Try out this software and tell me if you like it."

Will made a face. "Games?"

"I'm beta testing for a friend. And if I don't distract you, you'll hang over my shoulder and make a nuisance of yourself."

Will tried to concentrate on shooting cybersquids while dodging death rays from the mother ship but he found his attention wandering. The one time he tried to get a glimpse of Archie's screen, the man inched away and pointed to Will's monitor. "Type in WMTX14Q at the setup screen and then INV, and you'll be invisible when you get to the handmaiden's chambers. If she doesn't see you, then she'll start to undress." A lascivious grin flitted across his face. "I could stay there forever.…"

Will pushed away from the workbench. "Well, I can't. I don't have time to sit here and play games, Archie."

"You never do. By the way, you want me to keep a copy of everything for insurance?"

Will nodded. "Good idea. But consider it sensitive data. My eyes only, okay?"

"No problem." Archie hunched over the keyboard and Will returned his attention to the cybermaiden with the come-hither eyes.

A few minutes later, Archie pounded the arm of his chair in obvious triumph. "Got it."

"What?"

The printer on the opposite side of the room whined, then hiccuped. "I ran three different cypher-search programs checking for coded variations of the names on your list."

"And?"

"Celia wasn't much for playing spy. Everything was listed alphabetically on the disk in her B drive, protected with a simple single-stage password." He ejected Will's disk and handed it back to him. Pushing away from the workbench, Archie expertly skidded his office chair around the piles of electronics stacked on the floor. As he reached for his printer, it belched out a single sheet of paper, then let out a metallic whine, which ended in a disheartening clunk.

He grimaced as he plucked the paper from the output tray. "I was going to make you a hard copy, but looks like the damn printer jammed again and it'll take forever to fix." He held out the lone page. "Sorry, Riggs."

"Don't—" Will swallowed hard as he read the familiar name at the top of the page "—worry about it." The paper crumpled slightly as the muscles in his hand tightened. "Don't worry at all...."

A LOUD NOISE PIERCED Sara's sleep. For a moment, she didn't know where she was or what the insistent sound was. Then she roused enough to understand. She was on the couch in the living room and the sound was the telephone. She fumbled with the instrument.

"Hello?"

"Sara? It's Will."

Adrenaline rushed through her, erasing the last vestiges of sleep. "Did he... I mean, did somebody call?"

"No calls, sorry. It's just that I got some information that I think you need to see."

She rubbed her eyes. "What kind of information?"

He hesitated for a moment. "I...I'd rather not say over

the phone—I'm on my cell. Public airwaves, you know. Can you meet me at my office in a half hour...er...forty-five minutes?''

Sara glanced at her watch. ''I can be there by five o'clock. But can't you tell me something now? Anything?''

''Not over the phone. I'll tell you when I see you at five. Bye.''

She returned the phone to its cradle and swung her feet to the floor, rerunning the conversation in her mind. Will sounded odd. Concerned. How bad was the news? What constituted too-bad-to-be-heard-over-the-phone news?

She shivered, then shook her head as if the action could dispel unwanted thoughts. *Please let fiction be stranger than fact.* Then she padded up the stairs to retrieve her shoes and socks. Catching her reflection in the hall mirror, she stopped in the bathroom long enough to brush her still-damp hair, pull it back into a utilitarian ponytail and find her Redskins cap. *Another ball-cap day...*

Starting her car, she pulled out of the driveway with a little more speed than was warranted. Her aggressive tendencies flared as she battled the irregular pockets of traffic that ebbed and flowed along the route, doubling the length of her fifteen-minute drive. By the time she reached Will's office, her imagination had taken the small shred of information and magnified it completely out of proportion and beyond all reason. Her extrapolation of events had grown so preposterous that even she had to laugh at her own unbridled creativity gone overboard.

I'm overreacting, as usual, she told herself as the elevator doors finally slid open. *Blowing everything out of proportion.* She reached his office door and found a yellow note stuck to the door. ''Be back in five minutes. Mimi.''

Sara reached for the doorknob, half expecting to find it

was locked, but she was wrong. The door swung slowly open, revealing the empty reception area. Sara stepped in.

"Hello? Will?"

There was no answer. She crossed over to his office door and knocked. "Anybody home?"

Her only answer was silence. For a moment, the stillness seemed oppressive, dangerous, then she realized she was simply falling prey again to an imagination that was evidently bent on getting the best of—

She sensed a sudden movement behind her. Before she could turn around, someone slammed into her, knocking her into the wall. One strong arm circled her chest, pinning her arms to her sides. Then her attacker slapped his free hand over her mouth. With a grunt, he hoisted her up high enough so that her feet didn't touch the ground.

Without traction, she was a goner.

Sara struggled valiantly and almost broke free when she hooked a foot around the frame of the door leading into Will's office. Although she managed to throw her attacker off-balance for a moment, he recovered and tightened his hold on her as he carried her forward into Will's office. He removed his hand from her mouth only long enough to open a closet door and bodily throw her in.

She twisted in midair, hoping to catch a glimpse of her attacker's face, but there was no light in the office other than that from the fish tank. Striking her shoulder on the side of a metal file cabinet created more noise than it did pain. The jarring action loosened a couple of boxes that tumbled from the shelves above her and rained their contents over her. In a split second, Sara had decided to remain motionless, praying she could convince her attacker that she'd been knocked out by the fall. Before she could formulate a reason for playing possum or even devise a follow-up plan, the man slammed shut the closet door. The telltale click of a lock made her heart jump in her throat.

She hated small, dark places. Especially closets. That was why all of hers were large and well-lit. Swallowing back her fear, she blindly took stock of her dark prison. The fiercest weapon she could find without making a lot of noise was a metal shelf-bracket and a large can of coffee.

The rich aroma of coffee filled the closet as she reached in and got a handful of fresh grounds. If nothing else, if the man opened the closet door, she would throw it in his eyes and use the long metal bracket to trip him or push him off-balance as she made a break for freedom.

She heard a noise beyond the door and girded herself for combat, should the man open the closet. Instead, she heard a slamming noise.

The door?

Was he leaving? Or had Will arrived?

A strong tremor rocketed through her. Would the attacker attempt to waylay Will as he had her? Or maybe the person she heard was his secretary, returning from her errand.

Coffee grounds leaked from her fist as Sara pounded the door. "In here! I'm in here, in the closet. Let me out!" She tightened her grip on the metal bracket as she listened carefully, not knowing whether to expect a rescue or another attack.

The aroma of coffee filled the room as an odd companion to the silence. She inhaled deeply, hoping that an ordinary scent would help her calm down and deal with an extraordinary situation. It did little to dispel her fears. But a moment later, another smell joined that of the coffee. Sara dropped to her hands and knees and leaned down to sniff the air coming in from beneath the door.

Gasoline?

She knew of only one reason why she would smell gas at a time like this. She dropped the metal bracket and began to pound on the door with both fists. "Don't do it!"

No one responded.

Smoke began to roll in from beneath the door.

ONE FOR THE MONEY...

The flames followed the trail of gasoline that snaked across the room.

Two for the show...

The second match flared to life and its flames leaped effortlessly to the gas-soaked carpet in front of the closet. Would two fires be sufficient?

With the quick flick of a wrist, the burning match landed in the open desk drawer. Smoke began its lazy ascent to the ceiling in graceful curls.

Three to get ready...

The woman in the closet started beating on the door, but for some reason, the sounds of her terror were easy to ignore. It really didn't matter if anybody figured out it was arson. The most damning evidence would be charred beyond recognition and once eliminated, would never haunt them again.

That is...once the fire reached the open gas can.

And four to blow...

Chapter Eleven

Saturday, late afternoon

Will reached up and patted his jacket pocket, making sure the disk was still there. Rather than wait for the elevator, he decided to bleed off some of his nervous energy by taking the stairs.

He'd reached the second floor when he heard the building's fire alarm go off. By the time he arrived at the third floor, a few people began to pass him on the way down.

"I hate these false alarms," one woman grumbled to her companion. Will stepped aside, allowing them to pass by.

"I heard one of the maintenance guys say he thought it was an electrical short in the system," her companion replied.

Another voice echoed in strident waves throughout the stairwell. "It's not a false alarm. Someone smelled smoke on five. Hurry!"

Will took the stairs two at a time, spurred on by instinct alone. He didn't start smelling smoke until he reached the fifth-floor landing. As he trotted down the hallway, his imagination painted a picture of a fiery inferno around each corner. But the odor of smoke didn't grow cloying until he reached his office where he saw a telltale brown-gray cloud clinging to the corridor ceiling.

His heart quickened as he pushed open the door and a bigger cloud of smoke boiled out, hitting him in the face. He stepped back for a moment, caught his breath, then stepped in.

Thick smoke muted the light from the fixtures, forming deeper shadows than usual. Will squinted through the dirty haze. "Anybody here? Sara? Mimi?"

A series of popping noises drowned out any possible responses. Will turned in time to see smoke billow from beneath the door leading to his office. As he neared the door, he could feel the increased heat in the thickening smoke that clung to him.

"Is anybody here?" he shouted, hoping to be heard over the unmistakable crackle of fire consuming matter. He placed his palm gingerly against the door, below the small bronze sign that proudly announced William B. Riggs, Private Investigator. Relief flooded through him; no heat meant the fire hadn't reached the door—yet.

When he tried to enter his office, the door moved only a few inches, evidently blocked by something on the floor. Fear galvanized in the pit of his stomach. A body?

Putting his shoulder against the door, he bulldozed both it and its obstruction aside. But before he could identify the obstacle, a wall of hot smoke knocked him to his knees. Taking advantage of his position, he drew in a deep breath of the fresher air, then reached in front of him, expecting to find a body. Instead, he found a fallen file cabinet.

His guarded relief faded as some of the smoke cleared, allowing him to scan the room. He was almost spellbound by the fiery sight of destruction. Fire scaled the drapes, extending deadly fingers of flame across the ceiling. A too-perfect wall of fire had formed between the desk and the closet. Will sniffed and caught the scent of gasoline amid the other burning odors.

Arson...

He heard someone cough, then a pounding sound from the closet. "In here! Help! It's locked."

It took Will only a moment to recognize the voice and then realize the deadly implications. Sara—trapped in the closet. He lunged toward the expanding barrier of fire, but the searing heat drove him back.

"Sara...I'll get you out!"

He took off his jacket and tried to beat back the flames—to no avail. Stymied, he tried a second route, going around the back of his desk to the closet. Unfortunately, the flames were spreading from his chair to his desk, which created a second, more pressing problem.

Will knew there was a box of ammunition in his bottom desk drawer. If the fire hit the ammo, all hell would break loose. *But*— his feverish mind raced ahead —*maybe a little breaking loose is exactly what we need.*

Sara pounded on the door, again. "Will! Is that you? The door's locked. I can't get out."

"Hold on!" He had neither the time nor enough oxygen to explain. He fumbled with his keys, mentally thanking a power far beyond himself for allowing him to insert the right one in the lock on the first try. He tried to ignore the metal drawer handle as it burned through the fabric of his jacket and seared his palm.

Luckily, the ammo and his gun were in the back of the drawer and hadn't picked up much of the fire's ambient heat. Loading the weapon with an oiled efficiency that rivaled that of any soldier in the field, Will dropped to his knees as close to the closet as the flames permitted.

He drew a deep breath of the fresher air. "Sara...get away from the door. I'm going to shoot the lock."

A muffled, "Okay" was the only response.

The smoke thickened, creating a momentary haze between Will and his target. The fire was shifting, flaring up even closer to the door. Even if he managed to shoot out the lock, she wouldn't be able to escape through the flames. Unless...

Will fired three times. He pumped two bullets into the door, splintering the wood and freeing the bolt. Then he took careful aim and fired again.

The bullet entered the side of the fish tank nearest the door, creating a small hole, dead center in the glass. Cracks in the glass radiated outward, like a deadly spider web. Water arced out of the hole in a gentle stream, doing little to extinguish the flaming carpet. But a split second later, the shattered glass gave way and one hundred and ten gallons of water gushed out of the broken tank, effectively dousing a path to the closet.

Steam rose in great billowing clouds and combined with the smoke to form a dense cloud. Will lunged blindly through it, trying to make himself forget his prized fish struggling for survival amid the shards of broken glass.

"Sara!" He reached into the closet, connected with a hand and pulled. She stumbled into his arms, coughing and clutching him for support.

"Someone locked me in—"

"No time." Will wrapped an arm around her waist and tugged her toward the door. "This way!"

Together, they lurched out of the office and into the hallway. "You okay?" he gasped as he continued pulling her down the hallway to the stairwell.

Sara coughed and nodded. "Yeah," she answered in a strangled voice. "Your secretary..."

He froze. *Mimi!* "You go on. I have to go back—" A small explosion interrupted them, rocking the staircase slightly. They both scrambled for a handhold. The air thickened perceptibly.

A trio of firemen rounded the landing below them just as a second explosion rattled the building. A boiling cloud of smoke poured into the stairwell.

"You two okay?" one of them called up as they approached.

Will nodded, trying to catch his breath but getting a lungful of smoke instead. "My secretary—" He pointed up. "Gotta go back," he managed to strangle out between coughs.

"Her name's Mimi?"

Will felt a weight lift from his chest. "Yeah?"

"Don't worry. She's safe. She spotted your car and sent us up to look for you. C'mon."

It wasn't until they hit the fresh air and his mind and his lungs cleared that Will realized he'd left his jacket and the disk behind in the fire. He sat on the ambulance bumper, watching the paramedic bandage the burn on his hand from the red-hot drawer handle.

Sara was thirty feet away, being administered to by a couple of attentive young men who had insisted that although she seemed otherwise unharmed, she needed to stay on oxygen a little while longer.

While they fretted over her, Will dealt with the other professionals, answering the questions posed by the police and the fire investigators. Yes, it was probably arson; he'd smelled gasoline. Yes, it started in his office, in the vicinity of his file cabinets. Yes, it looked as if someone was trying to destroy his records. No, he wasn't sure what case might be involved. No, he didn't believe Miss Hardaway had been the target; she'd simply been in the wrong place at the wrong time.

No, Mimi wasn't married, but sorry, she did have a boyfriend.

Forty-five minutes later, Will had answered every question, signed every form, dodged a persistent reporter from the *Post* and sent the emotionally-charged Mimi home with her aforementioned boyfriend, much to the firefighters' collective disappointment. Before she left, Mimi promised to have their nightly answering service forward any calls from restaurants to Will's cell phone and to call Archie and ask him to make another copy of Celia's files.

He found Sara standing by herself with her arms crossed and staring at the building. He walked up behind her and called her name softly.

She sighed and didn't turn around. "I don't know what I hated more. The fire or being locked in the closet."

When he realized she was shivering, it seemed a perfectly natural act for him to step up behind her and place his arms around her. His mind rationalized that it was logical to share bodily warmth. His heart explained it away as a sympathetic action that a friend performed for a friend. But somehow he figured his body had another explanation for his actions. Sara complicated things by sighing and settling back against his chest as if she had belonged there for years.

"I'm sorry you got caught up in something like this, Sara."

She turned in his arms. "Then you think it was in connection with another case? Not Raymond's?"

"I didn't say that."

"It wasn't Raymond who attacked me." She spoke with a sense of conviction that he couldn't share.

"How can you be so sure?" he prodded.

"If Raymond had been the man who grabbed me, I'm pretty sure I would have recognized him." Reddening slightly, she turned away but still remained within the circle of his arms where she shivered noticeably. "After all, we were...together for almost three years."

Will fought the instinct to ask how two people who seemed obviously mismatched could stay together for three long years. He knew the probable answer. Even worse, he knew that if he asked, Sara would then feel compelled to defend Bergeron. The last thing he wanted to do was stir up any more protective feelings she might have for the man.

"Okay…maybe it wasn't Bergeron. Then the pertinent question becomes, Who was it?"

"Maybe the same person who killed Celia. Maybe he was trying to destroy any evidence you've found that would prove Raymond's innocence."

"Or maybe they think I'm a potential threat. Who's going to believe I'm an innocent middleman between two blackmailers?"

"Two blackmailers?"

When Sara stiffened, Will suddenly realized how intimate and proprietary his stance had been. He shifted, jamming his hands into his pockets as he took a sudden, self-conscious step away from Sara. "I had a disk in the pocket of my jacket, which was a copy of what I believe were incriminating files from Celia's computer."

"The police let you into her house?"

"Not exactly. But the point is, I don't have the jacket anymore. I left it up there. I assume it was burned along with everything else." Sara followed his glance; even in the darkness, he could see the jagged black streak of soot scarring the side of the office building. "But," he continued, lowering his voice, "I did find out something incriminating and the data's not gone forever. Can we go somewhere to talk?"

"Sure." She paused for a moment, which gave his unchecked imagination time to come up with a thousand different scenarios.

"My place?" she offered.

A thousand and one.

Saturday, early evening

THE LOGISTICS OF GETTING home took longer than Sara expected. She realized belatedly that her keys were lost somewhere in the ruins of Will's office. Their most persuasive arguments failed to get them past the barriers erected by the fire and police investigation teams. By the time they were in Will's car, neither of them was ready to hold an in-depth discussion while negotiating the early-Saturday-night Beltway traffic. Their conversation was strained at best as they limited themselves to innocuous topics.

She noticed him eyeing a pet store as they passed a strip mall at the entrance to her neighborhood. She guessed his thoughts.

"I...I'm sorry about your fish."

He sighed. "That's okay. They probably wouldn't have survived the fire anyway. At least, this way..." His voice trailed off with a wordless shrug.

Sara mentally completed his thought. *At least, they didn't die in vain.* She swallowed hard, then nodded. He'd deliberately sacrificed something important to him in order to save her life, yet he was reluctant to talk about it. Why? She wasn't used to such self-effacing behavior. She was used to Raymond, who wanted to be applauded and rewarded for each time that he negotiated or compromised some small point of contention in their relationship. Frequently, meeting Raymond halfway meant traveling nine-tenths of a mile to his one-tenth.

But that's over....

As they pulled up in her driveway, Sara suddenly realized she'd never given Will any directions to her house. "You know where I live," she stated as he opened the car door for her.

"I know a lot of things about you."

"Like what?"

He followed her to the front door. "Like you missed being valedictorian in high school by two-tenths of a point. You changed majors twice before going into restaurant management. You had to work hard to talk your partner out of the sports theme he wanted for your restaurant."

Martin had been so insistent.... "Thorough, aren't you?"

He smiled. "I try to be."

Sara retrieved her spare house key from its hiding place: a hidden slot in the side of a decorative "Welcome to My Home" plaque. Her purse, like Will's jacket, had been lost in the fire. She ignored Will's look of disapproval. "I know... I know you're not supposed to keep a spare key in an obvious place near the door. But you have to admit, that's not particularly obvious."

He followed her inside. "It is if someone was watching you. They know where you keep the key, now."

She sighed. As much as she appreciated his protective instincts, this wasn't the time to bring it up. They had more important topics to discuss.

Like blackmail.

"Nice kitchen." Will eyed the room, his bleary gaze settling on her coffee maker.

"Coffee?" she offered. "We could probably use the caffeine."

"Good idea."

"Let me go check my messages, first." She ducked into her office, leaving Will behind in the kitchen. As the whine of the rewinding tape filled her ears, she pawed through the desk drawer and found her spare keys. There were two, maybe three messages, from the sound of it. She hesitated before hitting the Play button. Did she expect another rambling diatribe from Raymond?

There was a click and a beep.

A mechanical voice intoned, "2:47 p.m."

"Ms. Hardaway," the recorded voice started. "This is Clifford Heating and Air Conditioning. It's time to have your furnace checked and—"

She released the breath she held as she fast-forwarded to the next one.

"3:02 p.m."

"Sara, it's Lily. Give me a call when you get in, okay?"

Sorry, Lily, you'll have to wait.

Another beep. "5:17 p.m."

"Sara? It's—" The background noise swelled, blotting out the name, but she recognized the voice. "I tried the number you gave me, but no one's there. I didn't know you were working with Mr. Riggs. He's good, I hear. Anyway, the boss asked me to call because we just got a weird delivery order about fifteen minutes ago. See if this rings a bell....Chimney-smoked lobster with saffron pasta, corn cakes with caviar—"

Sara looked up from her rigid stance at her desk to see Will standing in the doorway, listening.

"—fresh turbot with a sweet-potato crust, and seaweed salad. You and I both know that's Mr. B.'s favorite meal. Unfortunately, the hostess took the order so I didn't have a chance to try to recognize his voice. Let's see.... It's quarter after five now, and the delivery's set for seven-thirty to some fleabag motel in the District." The man recited the address and gave a room number. "I hope this helps. Good luck."

Both she and Will glanced at the clock on her desk. Seven thirty-five.

Then his gaze connected with hers. "We can get there in twenty minutes if we hurry."

IT WASN'T UNTIL THEY hit I-395 that Sara remembered why they'd driven to her place to begin with.

"So Celia is...was a blackmailer, too," she stated, keeping all emotion from her voice.

Will spared her a quick glance, then returned his attention to the road. "Looks that way. I had a friend tap into her computer system and we found files and financial records that seem to substantiate it. Luckily, I left a copy of everything with him." His face tightened. "The problem is that in order to prove my theory, I'll have to talk to the people who've been blackmailed and I don't think they're going to be too cooperative.''

"Because it's a touchy subject?''

He shifted in his seat, evidently trying to find a comfortable position. "No, because they'll probably think I'm shaking them down, too." A large truck veered into their lane, cutting them off. Will responded by savagely punching the horn with the heel of his hand.

When the horn's echoing blast had died away, a palpable silence filled the car. After a protracted moment, he broke the stillness with a sigh. "Who's going to believe I didn't have anything to do with the blackmail scheme?''

It was an implication that had never crossed Sara's mind. "Surely no one would—''

He smacked the steering wheel again, this time missing the horn. "Damn it, Sara. Of course, they would. People always believe the worst about others. And even if they don't believe I'm an extortionist, they've got to figure I must be a piss-poor investigator if I didn't realize it was going on under my own nose.''

"No, they'll think you are an honest man who's trying to undo the damage made by a couple of unscrupulous people.''

"Don't bet on it.''

Another uneasy wave of silence clogged the air. Sara remained quiet for a while, out of habit more than anything else. She'd learned to keep a low profile when Raymond got angry. *But,* she reminded herself, *this isn't Raymond.*

"So…" She glanced out the side window, brave enough to speak, but not strong enough to watch his expression as she spoke. "Do you think they simply woke up in bed together one morning and decided to become blackmailers?''

He shrugged. "Who knows? Maybe they worked to-

gether. Maybe they worked independently. Until I can do
a name-by-name comparison of their clientele, we won't
know for sure.''

A second car cut close to their bumper but Will made
no overt response beyond slowing down. ''You probably
don't want to hear this, but it's possible Bergeron killed
Celia because she was horning in on his territory. I suspect
he'd know exactly how far he could push someone financially—how much money he could squeeze out of them
before they became desperate enough to act. Celia, on the
other hand, always lived on the edge. She believed in
extremes. Her instinct might have been to find a likely
target and try to milk him dry.''

''Which gives even more credence to the theory that
someone other than Raymond killed her. Maybe one of
her extortion victims killed her.''

''Maybe.''

It was the last word he spoke until the freeway ended,
dumping them onto New York Avenue. Sara's stomach
began to churn and she gripped the door handle even
though he had decelerated to negotiate the stop-and-go
traffic.

''What's wrong?''

''What do I say to him? How do we confront him?''

''*We* don't.''

Outrage replaced fear as she straightened in her seat.
''You're crazy if you think I'm letting you go in alone.''

He surprised her by shooting her a half grin. ''You're
nuts if you think I'm going in at all. That's a job for the
police, not me.''

''Then…'' She hesitated. ''Uh…what are we doing
here?''

His face relaxed and his smile loosened into something
more genuine. And much more attractive. ''We can't expect the police to follow up on a lead just because someone has ordered a meal that the suspect is likely to eat.

We verify that it's Bergeron and then we call the cops and wait until they get there.''

"No heroics?"

Will solemnly crossed his heart. "No heroics. That's for the guys on television." He pointed across the street. "There it is."

"It" was a squatty, two-story building, which could boast of no architectural style other than "prefab." Someone had rearranged the letters on the marquee sign in front, which now boasted, "Clean TV. Color Rooms." Will doubted either was true; these types of motels made their profit with X-rated pay-per-view movies, and their monochromatic decorations were usually bolted to the wall. For someone who probably preferred a weekend at the Ritz Carlton, this must have been a hell of an education for Raymond S. Bergeron, Esquire.

Sara squinted into the darkness. "I don't see his car."

"If he's bright, he didn't park it here. A Porsche wouldn't last long in this neighborhood. If nothing else, his tag makes him pretty conspicuous." Will gave the lot a cursory glance, then turned his attention to the numbered doors. The one marked 132 turned out to be a ground-floor corner room, signifying the man had some sort of basic survival instinct. Dousing the headlights, Will pulled into the nearest parking space, about three doors down from the room.

He switched off the engine. "Ready?"

She scowled. "I thought you said no heroics."

"I did. I still do. But I have to determine if someone's in there. And if it's him."

"How?"

Will studied the layout. The room had one large window, muffled by a thick curtain. But there was a gap, as if Bergeron had been watching for his dinner delivery and forgotten to straighten the curtain. Will unfastened his seat belt, turned off the interior lights and opened the car door.

Sara looked shocked. "What are you doing?"

He leaned down, peering back into the car. "I'm just going to take a look, that's all." He closed the door gently and headed for Room 132. Before he took more than a couple of steps, Will heard a noise behind him and discovered Sara climbing out of the car. She caught up with him, nabbing him by his sleeve. "Not without me, you don't," she whispered between clenched teeth as she fell in step with him.

They approached the door. Just as they reached the room, a car pulled into the lot, catching them in its glaring headlights. Will jerked her away from the window, folding her into a quick embrace to hide their identities and disguise their motives. A few seconds later, the car turned away, plunging them back into darkness.

Sara looked up at him with a hooded gaze, but she made no effort to break away. A small voice in the back of Will's head mimicked the throbbing pulse that raced through him. *Too-soon, too-soon, too-soon.* But whose job was it to define the term, *soon?* Hers? His?

She sighed and her gaze faded into a blushing smile as she extricated herself from his arms.

"S-sorry."

He surprised her. Hell, he shocked himself. Will leaned down and kissed her.

It wasn't whimsy or curiosity that fueled him. It wasn't concern or compassion. It was passion—a deep longing that had sparked to life the first time he heard Raymond Bergeron describe her. For all his faults, the attorney knew this woman well; he had painted an accurate portrait of her, listing her hopes and dreams, but evidently not sharing them. Knowing her wasn't the same as appreciating her. And certainly, appreciation wasn't the same as love.

But make no mistake.

She was kissing him back.

Will felt the rumble of her heart as she pressed against

him, one hand tangled in his hair, the other wrapped around his waist. And as quickly as they were kissing, they stopped.

She pulled back, panting slightly and wearing a look of confusion mixed with a flush of satisfaction. "Why did we do that?" she asked in a hoarse whisper.

"Because we had to. We had to know."

She pinned him with a look that made him almost shiver with desire. "And do we? Do we…know?"

He swallowed hard. "You know, now. I knew from the very beginning."

"The beginning?"

"From the first moment—"

A loud thump erupted from Bergeron's room. Will pushed Sara out of the way, shielding her from the door, which he expected to fly open.

Nothing happened.

"Was that him?" Sara whispered.

"I'm not sure. Stay here." Will pushed her back into the shadows and moved cautiously toward the room. As he reached the door, he heard a scratching sound coming from inside. He pressed his ear against the door and heard a muffled voice. Girding his courage, he shifted toward the window and took a quick glance at the room through the curtain gap, then pulled back.

Certainly he didn't see what he thought he saw….

Will took a second look, this time longer than the first.

Sara abandoned her shadows and sprang forward, grabbing him by his sleeve. "He'll see you!" she hissed under her breath.

His brain began to process the details of what he'd seen. His stomach began to churn. *Aw, hell!*

"Move back." Will wrenched his arm out of her grip.

"What?" She stepped back in confusion, forgetting to keep her voice low.

Will counted to himself.

One. If I break my foot...
Two. I'm suing the bastard for everything he's worth.
Three!

He connected right below the doorknob, hoping to concentrate the majority of the force where the bolt entered the door frame. Theory and practice met in a rare display of cooperation and the door swung open, slamming into the wall and barely missing the body of a man sprawled on the floor.

Will rushed in and rolled the body over.

Raymond Bergeron gave him a glassy stare.

Chapter Twelve

Saturday evening

The emergency-room doctor drew a deep breath and flexed his shoulders. "It's a good thing you found him when you did," he said, trying to stifle a yawn.

"Yeah...Bergeron's a lucky son of a bitch, isn't he?" Will watched Sara out of the corner of his eye. She looked too pale for her own good.

She crossed her arms, displaying more nervousness than anger. "But he *is* going to recover, correct?"

The doctor nodded. "He'll have to undergo a full course of treatment, plus some cardiac monitoring, but, yes, I think he'll be back to normal very soon."

A new voice rang out. "Just in time to face a charge of first-degree murder." Steve Trainor appeared behind them, commanding their collective attention. "Trainor. Blackwater PD. Homicide." He held his badge in one hand and stuck the other hand out in greeting, which the doctor accepted after a moment's hesitation. "We've already made arrangements to have Mr. Bergeron escorted back over the Potomac as soon as he gets out of the hospital. There's a current warrant out on him in Blackwater." He turned his attention solely to the doctor. "Have you been able to tell what kind of poison it was?"

"Toxicology identified it as being from the fluoride family." The doctor lifted one shoulder. It might have been another attempt to relieve tired muscles or a shrug; Sara couldn't tell the difference.

Trainor raised an eyebrow. "Fluoride?" A look of disbelief filled his face. "You mean as in killer toothpaste?"

The doctor glared at him. "Only if you're in the habit of lacing your toothpaste with roach poison. Luckily, Mr. Bergeron ingested the chemical along with a substantial-size meal, so it slowed the absorption rate."

Trainor pulled a notebook and a pen from his jacket pocket. "You think it was suicide, Dr.—" he glared at the ID clipped to the doctor's lapel "—Hamilton?"

Sara stepped forward. "Of course not!"

Trainor shot her a look of open disdain. "I was asking the doctor."

Dr. Hamilton consulted his chart. "I can't say. I've never seen Mr. Bergeron before so I have no idea of his mental state at the time of the incident. All I know is—" the doctor looked up and leaned down as if to reveal a secret "—if I was going to kill myself, I'd choose a more effective way than this. No one in their right mind would sprinkle roach poison on a gourmet meal, then sit down and eat it."

Trainor looked up, his interest piqued. "Are you saying that the poison was *in* the food?"

"That's what the guys in toxicology say. They tested the food sample the paramedics brought as well as the patient's stomach contents." The doctor glanced down at his watch. "You'll have to excuse me. I have rounds to make. Mr. Bergeron is upstairs but I've left strict instructions that he is not to be disturbed by anyone. If you want to question him, do it tomorrow." He turned to Trainor. "That goes for you, too. If there are any other questions for me, you'll have to ask them after I finish rounds."

As the doctor walked off, Trainor turned and beamed

a cold smile in Sara's direction. "A gourmet meal? Sounds like something up your alley, Ms. Hardaway. In fact, this all sounds a bit too convenient. Your fiancé—" he raised his hands and gestured his surrender before she could object "—forgive me, your *ex*-fiancé sits down to a hearty but potentially lethal gourmet meal and you arrive just in time to save him." His smile evaporated to a hardened stare. "What happened? Had second thoughts?"

Sara felt her hands tighten into fists, but thankfully, she was able to keep them by her sides. "I didn't try to kill Raymond, if that's what you're insinuating. In fact, I was doing your job for you, Detective—locating a suspect so he could be properly questioned."

"We prefer our suspects to be conscious and in good health. And as far as helping us goes, if you knew which hotel he was likely to hide in, why didn't you just tell us?"

"I didn't know where he was. But I did know that Raymond always insists on eating well, especially when he's stressed. So I put out the word among my fellow restaurant professionals and they did the rest. I got a call this evening from a friend's chef who had taken a delivery order for a suspiciously familiar gourmet meal to be delivered to a hotel. We put two and two together and—"

"Added a little roach poison to the meal in hopes of subtracting one from the final total?"

Sara crossed her arms and leveled a lethal glare in his direction. "Why don't you verify my story with the owner of the restaurant who received and prepared the delivery order? Retired Judge Michael F. Russell who owns The Judge's Chambers in Georgetown." She rocked back on her heels, knowing that she'd displayed a winning ace. "He'll verify my story and I think even you have to admit he's a reliable source for information."

Trainor tried to save the moment by raising his eyebrow again and uttering a threatening, "We'll see," but his attempt to save face fell short of its mark. Having tossed his last retort, Trainor stalked off in the direction of the nurses' station.

After he disappeared around the corner, Sara sagged against the wall, giddy with relief and guarded victory. "It felt so good to watch that smug look drop off his face!"

Will's smile was strained at best. "That good, eh?"

She nodded, aware of the thrum of blood that buzzed in her ears, courtesy of an adrenaline surge that had changed from one of fear to one of triumph in the space of a few heartbeats. She leaned forward and gave Will a resounding kiss on the cheek. "That good," she repeated. She suddenly looked at their position; her with a proprietary grip around his arms and him wearing a faint imprint of lipstick on his face. A sudden flush of heat filled her cheeks and she released him. "Uh…what next? Do you think they'll let us question Raymond?" Suddenly, she was babbling. "There are so many things I want to ask him, so many confusing points I need to have explained." She made a beeline for the elevator. "Do you think—"

"Hold it!" It was his turn to grab her. "There's something you need to know."

Sara fought the adrenaline-inspired desire to jump to action and instead, obeyed a stronger instinct to listen. She peered closer, realizing his expression meant that something was wrong. Terribly wrong.

"What?"

He looked around with a conspiratorial glance, then pulled her toward the exit. "It's about the information that I got from Celia's files."

"The disk you lost in the fire?"

He nodded, holding the door open for her. "My friend was able to print out one of the records before his equipment malfunctioned."

"You have a name?"

Will continued to scan the area as he led her to the car. "Initials." He refused to elaborate until they reached the car. Once they'd climbed in, he started the engine and then reached into the glove compartment. He withdrew a folded piece of paper, flattened out the creases and pointed to a line of text. "Here."

MFR -asked 10k, rec'd 0k. Case: H. Wilkinson— sentencing hearing—wife's first husband. Didn't excuse self. W. —max sentence.

The adrenaline subsided, leaving Sara with an empty, hollow feeling. "What does this mean?"

"You don't remember the Harlan Wilkinson case? The man plowed into a crowd at a high-school football rally and killed a teacher and injured several students. Wilkinson pleaded guilty of driving while intoxicated and vehicular manslaughter. Mike Russell was the judge in charge of sentencing and he threw the book at the man."

Sara stared at the words on the paper. "Meaning he gave the man a tougher sentence than normal because...because he'd been married to Mike's wife?"

Will shrugged. "I guess so. Evidently, Celia thought it was something she could use to blackmail Mike. Apparently she asked for ten grand. It says 'okay,' so she must have gotten the amount she asked for."

"If Celia was blackmailing Mike, then maybe Raymond was, too. If Mike poisoned Raymond's meal, then maybe..." Her stomach turned. "He's the one who killed Celia, too?"

Will remained silent, then he slowly shook his head. "I don't think so."

"Why?"

"Then why would Mike have his chef call you and give you all the information about the order and the motel, giving us plenty of time to get the cops there and have

Bergeron arrested? We may not have gotten the message until after seven-thirty, but your machine time-stamped it at quarter after five. If Mike wanted Bergeron dead, all he had to do was say nothing.''

She looked relieved. ''Then there's a good chance it's not Mike. What do you suggest we do?''

Will glanced at his watch. ''His place is still open. Let's go there and ask him.''

''As simple as that?''

Will nodded. ''It can be if we do it the right way.''

Saturday night

MIKE HELD A GLASS UP to the light for inspection. ''So, can I assume that Ray will be remanded over into the custody of the police for questioning after he recovers?''

''I suppose so.'' Will fiddled with the cocktail napkin under his drink, straightening the creased corner.

Mike replaced the freshly polished glass and picked up another one with water spots. ''This is one time that I'm glad I could take advantage of my reputation as a former-but-still-honored-and-respected member of the court.'' He shook his head. ''Roach poison, you say? What a bad way to mess up a good meal. But—'' he performed a shrug ''—at least you found him in time.''

''He's a lucky stiff.'' Will knew his smile would appear genuine. It was a proverbial trick of the trade.

Mike nodded, giving Sara a quick glance. ''He used to be luckier. Sorry you two broke up but, in light of recent activities…'' His voice trailed off, as if it wasn't seemly to congratulate Sara on getting out while the getting was good.

She nodded self-consciously and pretended to study her drink.

''The place is really hopping tonight.'' Will had to

speak loudly to be heard over the noise in the bar. "How come?"

Mike shook his head. "I don't ask why. I just card 'em, serve 'em and take their—" a shriek of laughter from the other end of the bar cut him off "—money. If they start to get too rowdy," he added in a very carrying voice, "I refuse to serve them." He turned back to Sara and Will. "You two want to go back to my office where you can enjoy your drinks in a little peace and quiet?"

"Only if you join us." It was Sara's turn to put the finishing touch on their masquerade. "We wanted to thank you for helping us."

"Sure. Hey, Adam! Cover me, okay?" An employee stepped in, replacing Mike as a bartender. "Come on." He motioned for them to follow him through the crowd and into a room in the back. When he closed the door behind them, the noise level dropped significantly.

Will had never been in Mike's private office. Paperwork sat on the scarred desk in haphazard piles. A couple of crates with a plank formed a table overflowing with even more paperwork. The room could be described as utilitarian at best. But in the midst of the bare-bones setup, there was an obviously expensive Persian rug and a large, comfortable-looking burgundy couch with matching armchair.

Mike indicated that they should take their seats on the couch and he perched on the armrest of the chair. Will couldn't help admiring the furniture, running his hand over the soft leather cushion.

"Nice, eh?" Mike smiled. "They're the last relics I have of my days on the bench." He patted his chair's cushioned back. "I might have been able to give up the prestige of the office, but I couldn't make myself give up my office furniture." His smile grew a bit maudlin. "I made many a decision stretched out on that couch, staring at the cracks of my chamber ceiling."

"Like the decision to give Harlan Wilkinson a maximum sentence?"

The smile faded, revealing Mike's well-trained poker face. Then his gaze narrowed, growing momentarily harsh. "Celia. Right?"

Will nodded. "She left some pretty detailed files." He shifted to the edge of his seat and rested his elbows on his knees. "As God is my witness, Mike, I didn't know she was blackmailing anybody. Especially you."

A deep furrow formed between Mike's eyebrows. "I never once thought you were part of it. You're not that type of man." He shrugged. "At least she didn't get any money out of me."

"But, her files—"

Mike lifted his hand, gesturing for Will to stop. "Like I said, she never got any money out of me...not that she didn't try awfully hard. Celia thought she had me in the hot seat because I failed to disqualify myself on the Wilkinson case despite the fact that I had a connection to the victim. Apparently she'd once dated the poor bastard who did it."

He paused to pay feigned attention to the chair, then shook out of his strained reverie. "Well, anyway...Celia figured she could wring a small fortune out of me to keep quiet but..." Mike stood and stuffed his hands in his pockets. "But she found out she was wrong. I called her bluff."

Will straightened in his seat. "You what?"

"You heard me. I called her bluff." A look of relief replaced the tension in the judge's face. "She threatened. I countered and I guess you could say we reached stalemate."

"You're telling us she didn't get any money from you?" Will still needed to be convinced and after taking one look at Sara, he knew she did, too.

"Not a penny." Mike rattled the coins in his pocket as

he paced, following a time-worn trail on the rug. "I must've been the first person who ever stood up to her and I guess it took her by surprise. She never said another word about money after that."

Will couldn't ignore the little voice in the back of his mind. *Sure, she never said anything…if you killed her.* He shook away the intrusive thought. "Uh…how long ago did this happen?"

"Three years. I *will* admit she raised a legitimate problem issue. I should have removed myself from the case once I realized who the victim was. But if anything, I should have been lenient on Wilkinson. The man he killed, Marjorie's first husband, was a certifiable louse. Sometimes I think Wilkinson did the world a favor. But…I knew in my heart that because of his record, he deserved the maximum sentence allowed by law and that's exactly what he got."

Sara was the one who put the pieces together. "Is this the reason why you stepped off the bench three years ago and opened the restaurant?"

Mike nodded. "I came too close to stepping over an ethical line and I decided I never wanted to put myself in that position again." He slowly scanned the office, his face softening into a smile. "I've never been happier since. And I suppose I have Celia Strauss to thank for that. But to use your own words, Will—" he pulled his hands out of his pockets and drew a solemn cross over his heart "—as God is my witness, I never threatened or made any effort to hurt that woman, then or now."

Will studied the man's face. Although Judge Michael F. Russell was famous for his ability to mask all emotion, there was an undeniable sense of sincerity to his words. Plus, there was proof by Celia's own hand. Belatedly, Will realized what she'd meant when she typed "Asked 10k, rec'd 0k." *0k* wasn't *okay*. It meant *zero k*. Zero dollars. No money.

"One more question, Mike."

"Shoot."

Will glanced at Sara who returned a small nod of encouragement. "Did Raymond Bergeron ever try the same trick as Celia? To extort money from you?"

The judge's smile broadened. "Only around the poker table. No time otherwise. Why?" Realization dawned in his eyes and his expression dimmed a bit. "Wait...you thought I might have been the one who poisoned him?" He crossed his arms in mock anger. "You honestly think I'd jeopardize the restaurant's reputation by poisoning a very public figure like him?"

"Of course not," Sara answered quickly. "That was the first thing I told the detective in charge." She paused for a moment, as if making a decision. "From what we can tell, Raymond decided to follow her example and has been blackmailing people, too."

"Whoa!" Mike rocked back on his heels. "I never expected something like that out of the counselor. I can see that this is going to be a complicated case. Now that you've eliminated me as a suspect, where do you stand in your investigation?"

Will shrugged. "Good question. There's a chance that if we figure out who tried to poison Bergeron, then we might find Celia's killer."

"Why don't you ask Raymond? I presume he'll be able to talk soon."

"He'll probably be up to questioning tomorrow, but being able to talk isn't the same as being willing to talk. We think it might be one of his extortion victims, and Bergeron may not be willing to implicate himself to finger the killer."

"Knowing Ray, I can see your point. Since there seems to be only one case of poisoning, why don't you find out who he ate with?"

Will felt his heart give an extra beat. "What are you talking about?"

"The meal he ordered," Mike offered as if it were explanation enough. "Didn't you know?" He released a noisy sigh. "He ordered dinner for two."

SARA REMAINED inordinately quiet during the trip back. Will tried to tell himself it was the accumulating effects of the fire, the poisoning episodes and Mike's revelation about dinner that had overloaded her system. Everybody knew that even the strongest metals break if sufficiently fatigued. And *fatigue* was the operative word in his vocabulary at the moment. He was bone-tired and he suspected Sara suffered the same fate.

Of course, maybe she wasn't merely being quiet.

He glanced at her. She had propped herself against the car window, eyes closed, her even breath making a frosty cloud on the glass. A convenient red light gave him a chance to study her features. He couldn't call her delicate—at least, not when she was awake. There was too much fire in her eyes, too much energy in her step. But now, exhaustion had muted the fire to a soft glow. She had no energy reserves, he would bet.

As far as that went, neither did he.

He drove as far as he could without waking her. But he knew she needed to make a decision soon.

"Sara?"

She jerked up. "Y-yes?"

"Sorry I had to wake you. We're almost to your home, but I just realized your car is at my office. I thought you might want to swing by and pick it up."

"I don't want to keep you out any later. Can we get the car tomorrow?"

"Sure."

"And for the record—" she attempted a smile "—I wasn't asleep. No chance of that happening tonight."

For me, either. A surge of something strangely like desire knifed through him. He blamed it on her smile. It cut through his usual reservations, touching something inside him. And to see her being twisted and tugged by her lingering feelings for a louse like Bergeron was more than Will could bear. She might kid herself and say she was over the man, but he knew it would take a while before she could trust someone else.

Like him.

A sudden telltale flash of blue light reflected off a signpost up ahead. As Will turned the corner, he tightened his grip on the steering wheel. Sara straightened in her seat and leaned forward, straining against the shoulder belt.

"They're at my house!"

A couple of squad cars were parked at the curb, their lights silently piercing the night with an irritating rhythm. Instead of pulling into the driveway, Will drove on by.

"But you..." Sara turned in her seat, trying to look past him to the house. "What are they doing? What's going on?"

Will reached for his cellular phone, punched in a number and wedged the instrument between his shoulder and ear. The phone rang and a silken voice answered with a simple, "Elliott."

"Elaine? It's Will. Since when did you start working the graveyard?"

"Since I decided to get a week off to take a Christmas cruise in the Caribbean. My boss is jealous and the only way he'd agree to let me have a vacation in December is if I take the shifts nobody else wants. And speaking of people wanting stuff..." Her voice always reminded him of silk sheets and strategic scraps of lace. In reality, Elaine Elliott was a six-foot-three Amazon beauty with a sunny disposition and a devoted husband. It wasn't her fault if her voice tended to make most men dream impossible dreams.

"I'm at 2849 Linwood Way. What's going down?"

He could hear the clicking of computer keys.

"Suspicious person spotted by neighbor. Possible B and E." There was a moment of silence. "Oops..."

"What?"

"You still live at 2683 Capstone Drive?"

"Yeah. So?"

"They sent a squad car there thirty minutes ago to investigate a possible B and E. A neighbor helped them secure the property but said someone definitely broke in. A coincidence?"

"Probably not. Anything else?"

"Just the usual Saturday-night mayhem."

"Thanks, doll. I owe you one."

"Want to baby-sit my kids while I'm away?"

"No, thanks." Will hung up and turned to Sara who had commandeered the rearview mirror in order to see the proceedings behind her. "One of your neighbors evidently saw someone suspicious hanging outside your house and was afraid they were trying to break in."

"That's Martin's car in the driveway so they must have tried to get me at the restaurant and he came instead. I need to go back and—"

He pulled away from the curb and kept driving straight. "You need to get some sleep. You're exhausted. We've both been put through hell's wringer tonight. We don't need any more cops and their questions. If Martin's there, he can take care of things, right?"

"Yeah..." She hesitated. "But where do I spend the night?"

Where indeed? Both of their homes had been invaded. They needed someplace safe. Anonymous. "We'll stay in a hotel tonight."

She pulled her attention away from the mirror and stared at him. "We?"

"Yeah." He suddenly realized the implication. "I

mean we as in you and me in hotel rooms. Rooms, plural. Not you and me...together. My friend told me that there was a reported break-in at my place, too, tonight. I think we'd both be safer if we went someplace where we don't have to worry about burglars, fire or poison or..."

"Speeding cars..." she supplied. A look of awe washed over her face. "You don't think someone was trying to hurt you that first night we met, do you?"

He'd considered the near accident merely an unfortunate circumstance. But what if it wasn't a coincidence?

What if it had been deliberate?

Chapter Thirteen

Saturday, late night

Sara scanned the hotel room, wondering why it made her feel so...tawdry. The decorations were tasteful; the obligatory modern painting consisted of brushstrokes of muted pastels that coordinated with the draperies and upholstered sofa and chair. A couple of lamps added a warm glow to the room, which should have softened her harsh assessment of the situation.

If there had been a bed in the room, then she might have been able to justify her uneasy feelings. A bed would squat there, like a foghorn, announcing, "Two people, one bed. Let your imagination fill in the blanks!"

But there was no bed. Will had rented a suite in deference to both their needs: hers for privacy and his to maintain "basic security." She would sleep in the bedroom and he would remain on the couch, playing sentry. It was, essentially, a perfect layout.

But why did it make her so uneasy?

Don't be an idiot, Sara. You're enga— She stopped herself. She was no longer engaged.

Will shut the door behind them and she jumped at the sound of the dead bolt being thrown.

"This seems nice enough."

She nodded inanely and tightened her grip on the plastic bag in her hand. They'd stopped at a twenty-four-hour grocery store and picked up the barest essentials. Maybe it was the bag that made her feel so uncomfortable. Of course, people who checked into hotels without luggage usually had one agenda on their minds.

Will walked over to a darkened doorway and reached in, turning on a light switch. Sara followed him, moving close enough to see the corner of a quilted pastel bedspread.

"You can sleep in there. And this thing—" he pointed to the sofa "—unfolds to make a bed for me." He paused and gave her a critical once-over. "You look exhausted. It's no wonder, considering everything you've been through today."

"I feel exhausted. And filthy. And maybe a bit scared."

He pulled her into his arms and gave her a hug. "I don't blame you. That's why we're here. I guarantee you'll be totally safe."

There was something comforting about being in his embrace. Perhaps *too* reassuring. Sara suddenly became cognizant of how close they were. She felt his breath on her cheek, the warmth of his chest pressed against hers, the strength of his arms wrapped around her.

She lifted her head, meeting his gaze. They stood there, unmoving, for several seconds. Then Will dipped his head and kissed her.

Initially, she thought it was nothing more than an obligatory gesture on his part, but she found herself quickly reacting to the sweet sensuality of it. For a few moments, a tide of visceral pleasure swept her troubles away, making her forget all the problems that had plagued her for the last couple of days.

But he broke the spell by giving her one last squeeze and pulling back, severing their kiss. He dragged his hand through his hair. "Not now, Sara" he said in a strangled voice. "It's not the right time."

She crossed her arms, not out of anger but out of a need to hold herself together. "By whose standards? Ours or society's?"

He reached out a tentative hand and ran his thumb slowly down her cheek. "Mine." He cocked his head. "You're exhausted, aren't you?"

Sara nodded reluctantly. "Yes."

"So am I."

"You think our defenses may be down?"

He shrugged. "Maybe. We'd know better in the morning."

She closed her eyes. He was right. It was too soon after the painful end of one relationship to leap headlong into another—especially one that seemed to have so much potential intensity. Maybe things would look different in the morning.

Maybe...

She opened her eyes, uncrossed her arms and tried to look resolute. "You're right." After a beat she added, "Thanks."

"Sure." He stared at his shoes for a moment with inordinate interest, then looked up. "Try to get some sleep. Okay?"

She nodded. "Okay. G'night." Somehow, she made it to the doorway without tripping. Once inside, she nudged the door closed. Leaning against the wall, she surveyed the room.

It's going to be a long night.

WILL WATCHED THE DOOR close, then realized he'd been holding his breath.

Why?

Earlier, when they had been wandering through the gro-

cery, looking for the toothbrush aisle, they'd passed by
the condom display. Sara had blushed.

It hadn't been a case of calculated innocence, a feigned
reaction. It had been a real honest-to-God blush that
brought much-needed color to her washed-out features.

Who could he kid?

It had made her sexy as hell.

There they'd stood, like a couple of teenagers, trying
to ignore an extensive selection of Trojans. For once in
his life, he'd prayed they weren't sharing the same
thought. After all, what type of man could think of seduction at a time like this?

A red-blooded, all-American jerk.

He knew Sara was probably at her lowest, physically
and emotionally. Only a real jerk would take advantage
of her at a vulnerable time like this. That was the problem;
a real idiot had *already* taken advantage of her. Why
didn't Bergeron realize how good he had it? Sara was a
smart woman who was beautiful, loyal, funny, well-
rounded, successful....

The perfect woman.

At least, by my standards. Perfect for me.

As they'd turned their backs on the display, making
banal chatter about what type of toothbrush they preferred, Will had made *the decision.* One of the things he
would be protecting her from tonight would be himself.

Will sighed.

He'd come close to blowing it with the kiss. Somewhere along the line, what he truly had meant to be a
simple good-night kiss had become something else—
something that knocked him off his feet with the poten-
tiality of its impact on his life.

God help him, he felt something for Sara. Something
real. Something intense. Something he had no right to feel
at this point in time.

He sighed. At least one potential disaster had been nar-

rowly averted by the emergence of logic. It was his duty
to keep her safe and sound from all dangers, even if one
of those dangers was himself.

But now that Sara was on the other side of the door,
getting ready for bed, his duty seemed harder.

He winced. *Bad choice of words.*

Drawing a deep breath, he knocked on the door. Logic
had to prove it was in control.

"Everything okay?"

The panel between them muted her answer, stripping
any discernible emotion from it.

"Umm…yeah."

"Need anything?"

There was a moment's hesitation. "No. Thank you."

"Just checking. I'm going to take a shower so if you
need anything, or hear a noise you don't like, don't hesitate to pound on the door. Okay?"

"Okay…and thanks."

He walked over to the door leading to the hallway and
checked the locks, then stalked into the bathroom where
he hoped untold gallons of cold water would squelch the
various fires in his body, especially the one growing in
his heart.

SARA WAITED UNTIL SHE got into the bathroom before
stripping off her clothes. Although Will had made it quite
evident she had the bedroom to herself, something still
didn't feel…right about undressing in there.

She shivered as she stepped into the shower, trying to
forget the lingering sensations of their kiss. After she adjusted the single control, the water heated quickly, forming a cloud of steam around her. Looking down, she
traced the adventures of the day by the trail of grime and
inflictions. The soot from the fire had filtered through her
clothes and collected in odd places like beneath waist-
bands and cuffs. She had a bruise on her shoulder from

where she fell against the file cabinet in the closet and small rug burns on both knees from her scrambling efforts to make sure Raymond would stay alive until professional help arrived.

The soap removed the dirt and the hot water soothed her aches, but nothing, not even a vigorous shampoo, seemed to erase the thoughts that tumbled disjointedly through her head. When her mind started to rehash the kiss one more time, she balked and forcibly turned her thoughts to the subject that had occupied her mind previously: Raymond.

She refused to believe he was a lost cause. However, she did acknowledge that he was no longer *her* cause. She would support him by believing he was innocent of murder. But that was as far as she was willing to go. She found herself accepting the fact that he might be a blackmailer, even if no witness had stepped forward to accuse him directly. Too much evidence pointed to his probable guilt, including his known association with a blackmailer.

Known association? I'm starting to sound like a lawyer. Like Raymond.

Like Will...

Suddenly the water became too hot, her skin too sensitive. She batted at the control, turning the water off. She stared at the swirl of water laced with a few lingering bubbles as it swept down the drain. All the dirt, all the guilt...

Whose guilt? Raymond's or hers?

Stepping out, she plucked a towel from the stack and began to dry herself. She rubbed vigorously, hoping that the physical sensation might block her thoughts—thoughts that were going in dangerous directions.

The first moment she'd met Will at The Judge's Chambers, she was attracted to him. There was nothing wrong with that, she'd told herself, especially after she'd learned he'd deliberately baited her. Yet she'd resisted his intentional seduction.

Why?

Because she was a loyal woman...or a stupid one.

Stupid enough to be wrapped up in the righteousness of her loyalty to fail to see that her man was cheating on her. Could she add "stupid enough to be charmed by a man whose business was to fabricate himself into her perfect match"? She thought back to the first time she met Will. How much of what he'd said was true? When he escorted her to the car, they had chatted, almost aimlessly. He'd said he liked to sail, but not to fish; loved old movies, classic cars, progressive jazz and, of course, the Redskins.

How much of that was true?

Suddenly it became important for her to know where the fabrications stopped and the real man began. She slipped on the terry-cloth robe the hotel had so thoughtfully provided, belted it tightly and stalked to her door.

She raised her hand to knock...then her courage suddenly failed.

Did it really matter? What difference would knowing make? All she wanted was Will's arms, his lips, his...

She took in a deep gulp of air.

That's it! Talk shows do programs on things like this— bouncing from one bad relationship right into another.

She plopped down on the floor, stunned by the revelation.

Women on the Rebound and the Men Who Catch Them.

She leaned her forehead on her knees.

Her and Will?

Will and her?

I'll never get any sleep, now.

WILL NEVER EVEN UNFOLDED the couch. He stretched out on it, television remote control in hand, and changed channels for an hour until he found a Bogart movie. It was just what he needed to chase away forbidden thoughts: a healthy dose of macho P.I. action with guns ablazing and general murder and mayhem. Everything was fine until Lauren Bacall stepped onto screen. His imagination blended fiction with reality and he conjured up a mental image of Sara dressed as the high-society dame, veiled hat, prim suit, quick-witted, quicker-tongued....

He groaned and switched off the television. *No* Big Sleep *for me tonight. No little sleep either.*

Sunday morning, early

THE CRACK IN THE curtains allowed a long shaft of sunlight to shine directly into Will's face, burning through to his consciousness and waking him with a start. Once he realized where he was, he remembered to congratulate himself. Not only had he withstood temptation, but he actually had fallen asleep at some point.

Logic had won once again over pure animal instinct. The evolutionary pundits could rejoice.

His stomach growled, signifying that some hungers couldn't be so easily denied. He staggered into the bathroom where he relieved himself and splashed cold water on his face. He pulled on his jeans and found the room-service menu, which used glowing adjectives to describe every food item. They didn't serve bacon, eggs, juice and toast but "Lightly fluffed eggs served with a full rasher of imported hickory-smoked bacon, your choice of sunshine-fresh, hand-squeezed juice and of course, our world-famous hand-kneaded bread toasted to a golden brown perfection, with a selection of piquant condiments."

And judging by the price of the meal, each adjective cost the consumer an extra dollar.

Will tapped on the bedroom door. "Sara. You up?" He

heard a groaning sound and a muted thud. "Sara?" He twisted the doorknob and shouldered the door out of the way, ready to spring into action.

He discovered her half out of bed, outstretched fingers just grazing the electric clock radio, which evidently had been knocked from the bedside table.

"You okay? I heard a noise."

For a moment, Sara wasn't sure if this was a lingering dream, reality, or some oddball combination of the two. She knew sleep was fuzzing her brain, but somehow her instincts assured her that her bare-chested protector was the man of her dreams.

She forced herself to open her eyes and her mind. *It's Will.* He stood in the doorway, framed by the sunlight, which highlighted his flexed muscles.

She swallowed hard when she realized what sort of awkward position she'd jackknifed herself into. Shifting back in bed, she gestured weakly at the radio. "It started playing country music. I can't stand country music, especially in the morning."

He shot her a crooked grin. "Me neither." He walked across the room, bent down and picked up the radio, changing the station before replacing it on the table. "Better?"

She heard a soft saxophone wailing a familiar tune. It was soothing. Very relaxing. Very sexy... She closed her eyes. *Get a grip, girl.* "That's m-much better," she stammered. "I love that type of music."

"Me, too." He thrust a folder toward her. "You want some breakfast?"

Grateful for the diversion, she took the menu and studied its contents. Her stomach lurched at the overzealous descriptions.

He must have noticed her discomfort. "What's wrong? You don't like the selection?"

She shook her head. "It all sounds so...so chipper.

'Sunshine-fresh, hand-squeezed juice?' I don't want happy food in the morning.''

Will yawned and lowered himself to the edge of the bed. ''I know what you mean. Give me coffee, maybe a bagel, and then I'll get something more filling later when I finally wake up.''

''Coffee and a bagel. That sounds good. Do they offer something simple like that?'' She squinted at the menu.

It was a perfectly natural act for Will to shift closer to examine the menu alongside her. It was an equally natural act for Sara to lean forward so he could see it more easily.

They met shoulder to shoulder, which came dangerously close to cheek to cheek. She tried to pay inordinate attention to the menu but he became much too distracting, especially when he kissed her.

She didn't expect the kiss, but strangely enough, she wasn't surprised by it. Sara didn't have time to cope with surprise when she had a whole volley of other emotions shooting through her. As her brain repeated its dire warnings about the perils of getting involved during vulnerable times, her heart swore that this was the right guy, the right time. Her body joined forces with her heart and it was two against one.

Will pulled back, breaking contact. He steadied himself, putting one hand on the bedspread and inadvertently contacting her leg beneath it. He blushed and moved his hand to an unoccupied spot. ''Tell me to stop,'' he said in a slightly breathless voice.

Sara swallowed hard. ''No.''

He flinched. ''Is that 'No, I don't want you to kiss me,' or 'No, I won't tell you to stop'?''

Rather than try to explain, she leaned forward and kissed him, again. Only this time, they were past the introductory stage, past the pseudo-chaste method of introducing two sets of unacquainted lips.

Suddenly she was desperate to touch him, to have him touch her.

"This is wrong," he muttered as they kicked the bed-clothes out of the way and fought to reach each other.

"I know." She wound her arms around his neck and he lifted her bodily into the center of the bed without ever breaking off their kiss.

He clawed at the knotted belt of her robe, freeing the material and stripping it from her shoulders. "We shouldn't..."

"Of course not..." She arched in ecstasy as he showered his kisses slowly down her neck and past the hollow of her throat and finally to her breasts where he caressed and teased her until she was ready to scream.

But before she could utter a sound, he moved like lightning, his lips covering hers, his tongue plunging into her mouth. Meanwhile, he trailed his hand past her navel and toyed softly with the brush of curls between her legs.

She fumbled with the stud at the waistband of his jeans and succeeded in forcing it open. Using his free hand, he helped her push the fabric past his hips.

Under his expert skill, she became suddenly helpless, overwhelmed by the deliciously conflicting responses he induced within her. She wanted to laugh, to cry, to fight the unbearably pleasant sensations as long as she could. The longer she resisted, the more intense they became.

"You're perfect," he growled as he rose up long enough to strip off his underwear.

The urgent need inside her built to a level she could barely endure. But to her dismay, Will pulled away from her. She reached out, trying to pull him back. "Please...don't go."

He snatched up his jeans and she thought surely this was a sign that he meant to leave. But instead, he tore into them, pulling from his back pocket a wallet and from it, a condom.

Will fumbled with the wrapper, his hands shaking, his breath coming in big gulps. She tried to help and between the two of them, they tore the package open, the condom tumbling into the jumbled bed clothes.

They scrambled through the sheets and blankets, looking for the wayward condom. "Where is it?" he gritted between his teeth.

Their quest seemed futile, hampered by their inability to stop kissing each other between search attempts.

"We have to find it," she said around a gasp for air.

Suddenly he growled in triumph, holding up the missing disk. Sara cheered and threw herself at him in celebration.

"Just a...minute... There!"

They returned to their previous intensity, having suffered little interruption in their momentum. He plunged into her, his hips starting a demanding rhythm that mimicked the frenzied palpitations of her heart. Digging her nails into his back, she followed his undulating lead, the pleasure-pain building to the moment when she thought she could stand no more.

Their physical worlds splintered into a thousand shards.

At first, Sara floated on a sea of bliss, savoring the aftermath of pleasure. A sense of well-being overwhelmed her to the extent that she forgot her troubles, even her own name. Then, suddenly, she became intensely aware of the man who rolled off her, the man panting for air, the man wearing a goofy grin of satisfaction.

"We shouldn't have done that," he said, staring at the ceiling.

"I know," she agreed.

"You're my client," he offered as if that, alone, were explanation. "It's a mistake."

"I know," she repeated. She snaked her hand into his and held it firmly.

He drew a deep shuddering breath and a palpable silence filled the room. Sara's sense of logic tried to create a string of weak arguments and accusations in hopes of berating the overbearing, ill-timed needs of the body. But she easily pushed them aside and leaned up on one elbow, offering him her very best come-hither look.

"One more time?"

He closed his eyes and took another deep breath. For one frightening moment, she thought he was going to get up and walk away—out of her bed, out of her life.

Instead, he groaned and reached for her.

Chapter Fourteen

Sunday morning, later

They may have made mad, passionate love, explored each other's bodies, shared intimate thoughts and secrets, but when it came to getting dressed, they did it in separate rooms, behind closed doors.

Sara stared at the wall separating them, wondering what she would see if she had X-ray vision. Did Will still have on his sappy grin or had it faded as the reality of what they had done set in? She knew she had no regrets, but what about him?

A shiver danced across her shoulders.

Okay...she had a couple of regrets, but they weren't about him. After the condom broke, bringing an abrupt end to their third wave of passion, they'd slipped under the covers and started talking. There, she'd discovered that he was indeed everything he had pretended to be when they first met. They'd even gotten into a rousing discussion about the Redskins, an unusual postcoital topic, but strangely satisfying.

After all, she could never love a man who didn't appreciate the Redskins....

But cold reality had penetrated their bubble of security. They both knew Raymond was in the hospital, in unknown condition, and in possession of some very important information—such as which of his blackmail victims had killed Celia and tried to poison him.

Sara tugged on her pants. If anybody was going to get the information out of Raymond, it would be her. He might be able to clam up in front of the police, even stonewall the best lawyers in the state of Virginia, but he was putty in her hands. Especially if she got them around his neck.

There was a soft knock at the door. "You dressed?"

"Come on in."

Sara expected the inevitable discomfort, the inability to know what to say and when to say it. If you made love for the first time at night, then there were certain rules of "morning after" etiquette to be followed. But what rules applied when you made love for the first time…in the morning?

Will solved the problem by breezing into the room, giving her a quick kiss on the cheek and flopping on her bed with his shoes in hand. "First stop, the hospital?"

She nodded. "Hopefully Raymond will be up for some questioning."

"I called the hospital but they won't release any information about him. Trainor probably has a gag order in effect to stymie the reporters."

Sara felt her nerves begin to knot. "Reporters? Do you think there's something in the papers about this case?"

Will shrugged. "Trainor can stall them for only so long. Celia's death didn't make yesterday's paper, but I bet it's in today's edition."

Ten minutes later, they sat in Will's car, their complimentary Continental breakfast untouched. They both stared at the small article.

Slain Woman Found In Hotel

The body of a private investigator was discovered

Saturday morning in a hotel in Blackwater in Fairfax County. The woman has been identified as Celia Strauss, an associate with a local investigation firm. Earlier, there were conflicting reports on how she died, but today, a spokesman for the Medical Examiner's office said she died of gunshot wounds. The police say they already have an unidentified suspect in custody.

Unofficial sources say that the suspect is a prominent Blackwater attorney, but the police will not release any information pending further investigation.

Will refolded the paper. "Bergeron's lucky the police decided to protect his identity. If they'd released his name, this story wouldn't have been buried on the third page of the Metro section—it would have been splashed all over the front page." He raised his hand and sketched an arc in the air as if picturing the headlines. "Prominent Blackwater Divorce Attorney Suspected of Woman's Gruesome Death."

"Don't joke about it." Sara shut her eyes, hoping the image of the stark words would fade from her imagination.

"Sorry." Will started the car. "I'll admit I'm willing to consider at this point that maybe, just maybe, he didn't kill Celia."

Sara opened her eyes and stared at him. "What made you change your mind?"

"I'm not sure." He shrugged. "I know he's an insufferable son of a bitch who might be provoked into doing something rash, like try to strangle someone, but I don't think he'd walk away, then come back to finish the job with a gun."

"Which means..."

"Which means somebody else came in and shot her

after he left. He must have run because he was frightened that he might be the next victim."

Sara's mind jumped ahead. "But he ordered dinner for two, which means he expected company. Do you honestly think he'd sit down and chat amiably over dinner with someone he suspected might be a killer?"

"No way. That means the killer is someone he thought he trusted. And that person poisoned him. The important question becomes who. Who *is* this mysterious person? Is it the same person who set fire to my office and almost killed you?"

Sara ran her finger around the lid of the coffee cup she'd brought from the hotel. "I thought you were convinced Raymond attacked me."

Will shook his head. "I did until last night when I started to create a time line for all of this. According to the message, Bergeron called the restaurant right at five, which is around the same time you were being attacked. I don't think Raymond could have thrown you in the closet and then calmly used my phone to call in a delivery order."

Sara pried the lid off the container and took a tentative sip of coffee. "Mike uses caller ID. In fact, he's the one who talked me into getting it for our restaurant. It's becoming a standard operating procedure for anybody taking delivery calls. If the number that showed up on the display had a Virginia area code, but the delivery site was in D.C., they would have noted that on the order and I'm sure the chef would have mentioned it to us, especially if it was *your* telephone number."

Will tightened his two-handed grip on the steering wheel, his knuckles whitening. "So Bergeron might not be running away from the police as much as he's running away from this second suspect. But who in the hell is it?"

"Raymond must know—at least, now that an attempt has been made on his life."

"But will he tell us?"

She took another fortifying sip of coffee. "Only if he's more frightened of us than he is of the other person..."

Sunday, mid-morning

"RAYMOND, SWEETHEART, can you hear me?" Sara waited for a response, then turned to the doctor. "He is going to be all right, isn't he?" She stared at the elaborate tangle of wires that connected him to a bedside machine.

The doctor, a different one from last night, nodded. "Yes. We're merely being cautious. We have to monitor for cardiac irritability in cases involving fluoride poisoning. However, Mr. Bergeron has no history of heart problems so we're not expecting any real complications."

Sara tried to look adoringly at Raymond. She hated playing the role of the grieving fiancée, but it got them past the red tape and into his room. She admitted to herself he still appeared pale, but he certainly looked better than he had only the night before.

She put on her best "concerned loved one" face and gave the doctor a trembling smile. "Can we just sit here a while and be with him?" She acknowledged Will with a nod, not bothering to identify him.

The doctor nodded. "That'll be fine. If he wakes up, don't let him get too excited. He's had a rough time and needs to rest as much as possible."

Will patted Sara on the shoulder. "Don't worry, Doc. We won't bring up any unnecessary unpleasantries."

The doctor's attention dropped to the handcuff, which locked one of Raymond's wrists to the metal railing. "See that you don't."

As the door closed behind the doctor, Sara glanced down at the Sunday newspaper, which had been carefully laid at the end of the bed. The top section had been folded to reveal the crossword puzzle, which had been partially solved. Sara recognized Raymond's handwriting. She silently pointed it out to Will, who understood the implications.

He stepped closer to the bed. "The doctor's gone. You can open your eyes, shyster."

To Sara's surprise, Raymond opened his eyes, giving her a pale but insolent wink. "I thought I had everybody fooled."

"Think again." Will moved swiftly, grabbing Raymond by the throat before the man could react. With one hand shackled to the rail, he lacked the strength to pry Will's fingers loose and he began to gasp for air.

Sara pulled at Will's rigid arm, playing her role to the hilt. "Will, don't! You'll kill him."

"Why shouldn't I? It's what he did to Celia." Will leaned down closer to Raymond. "You got her into a convenient position, then squeezed the life out of her. Why shouldn't I do it to you, now?"

"I—didn't—kill—her," Raymond managed in choking gasps.

"No?" Will released Raymond's throat. "Prove it."

Raymond massaged the red marks, which were beginning to color his skin. He pointed to the paper. "In there. The police said she died of gunshot wounds. All I did was choke her, but I stopped before it was too late. She was alive when I left."

"Then why did you run away?"

"Because I was scared. Angry. Drunk. I went back to the hotel, hoping to sort things out with her. But I heard someone talking about the dead woman on the fifth floor. They described the scene and it was obvious it was Celia. I thought I'd killed her. I ran."

"You call this proof of your innocence? It sounds more like the story the prosecution is going to present."

"I thought I must have been so drunk that I only *thought* she was alive when I left. I honestly believed I'd killed her until I read the paper today. It says she died of gunshot wounds. I tried to strangle her, not shoot her.''

"How do you know that you weren't so drunk that you went out, got a gun and came back to finish her off?''

"I don't have to prove I didn't do that. The police have to prove that I did. I'm willing to admit the truth. I attempted to strangle her, but nothing more than that. Her killer is—'' he paused, evidently to choose his words carefully ''—out there. Somewhere.''

Will crossed his arms, pulling back from his threatening stance. "Okay, for the sake of argument, if you didn't do it, then who did?''

"I can't be sure. Right offhand, I can only think of one person who might be angry enough at Celia to kill her.''

"Who?''

The gleam in Raymond's eye meant he was going to change tactics. Sara recognized all the signs. He was going from defense to offense. Whether the truth would come out was anybody's guess. She gripped the blanket, pleating it between her fingers.

His gaze hardened. "Sara.''

"Me?'' she exploded, forgetting that they were supposed to be scaring him, not vice versa.

"You're the only person I know who might get angry enough to kill her. After all, she seduced me....'' His voice trailed off when he spotted the glint of rage in Will's eyes. Instead of stopping, Raymond continued, gaining confidence as he gained momentum. "Or maybe it was you, Magnum. Celia told me you and she once had a rather volatile, torrid relationship.'' Raymond's lip curled back in an ugly smile. "Maybe you didn't like seeing her turn those magnificent radars of hers in someone else's direction. Maybe you killed her out of jealousy. See? I'm not the only suspect.''

Sara watched Will fight for control. As much as she would like to slap the silly grin off Raymond's face, she was more concerned about Will, worrying that he might forget his tough-guy Bogart routine was supposed to be merely an act.

As usual, Raymond couldn't leave well enough alone. "No wonder you never made it as a lawyer, Riggs. You stepped right into that one. You couldn't bluff your way out of a paper—"

Will lifted his hand and Raymond flinched, then flushed when he realized the simple gesture had shattered his composure as well as interrupted his soliloquy.

Instead of striking out, Will merely held up his forefinger.

"One. Crandell. The videotape cost him ten grand."

Raymond remained motionless in the bed.

"Two. Gordon-Garcia. The pictures cost him seven grand."

Raymond's blush faded, leaving him paler than before.

"Three. Landrum. The hotel only charged him $180. You made him pay twelve grand." Will crossed his arms. "You want more names?"

Raymond's face contorted with a venomous sneer. "You'll never convince anybody that you weren't a part of it. You're the one who used the video recorder, took the pictures, stole the receipt. I couldn't have done it...without you."

Will parried the threat with a smile. "I'll admit you have your faults, but endless greed doesn't seem to be one of them. That's where most blackmailers make their mistakes. Once they get the taste of extortion money, they don't know when to stop squeezing. But you were logical, figuring out how much money each victim could honestly afford before they started getting desperate. But Celia wasn't as careful, was she?"

Will flipped the mechanism that held the nearest siderail in place. As the metal railing lowered, it pulled Raymond's manacled wrist down, putting him in an awk-

wardly vulnerable position. Will leaned closer and
Raymond pushed back, trying to increase the gulf between
them.

"What are you talking about? I never met Celia until
night before last."

Will pressed on, ignoring Raymond's denial. "Face it,
Celia had no self-control. She was reckless, asking for too
much money, approaching the wrong people. She even
tried to squeeze money out of a retired judge over a small
technicality in one of his cases."

Raymond forgot about trying to ease his position as he
turned his rapt and fearful attention to Will. "You're
crazy! I didn't know her, I tell you."

"Stop lying, Bergeron. We know all about your Friday-
night arrangements with Celia, your standing reservation
at the hotel. But better than that, the police know all about
it. Is that where she learned all about your blackmailing
schemes? During pillow talk?"

Raymond blanched.

"I bet she even tried to hit up some of your victims,
didn't she? That had to upset your sense of order and
balance. You knew to the penny how much you could
milk out of them, but her unreasonable demands upset the
balance of things. It even made some of your victims
think twice about paying you."

Raymond narrowed his eyes, then had the audacity to
smile. "Okay...so you *would* have made a good trial lawyer. I was wrong. Sue me." He actually laughed.

Will took a deep breath. "Are we through playing these
macho lawyer games?"

Raymond nodded. "Yeah. I realize I'm in an awkward
position." He glanced down at his captured wrist. "In
more ways than one. Cards on the table, okay?"

Will raised the railing back into place. "Okay."

Raymond made a point of not looking at Sara. "I was
blackmailing some of my clients' spouses. Not all, just

some. And only some of those cases ended up with money going directly into my pocket. Most of the time, I used the information that you gave me to help stabilize my clients' positions when it came to alimony, child support or property division. You know—'Either go with this settlement or I'll show the wife the video and this'll turn from a simple divorce into a nightmare.' Every once in a while, I'd keep the money as a sort of nuisance fee.''

''How altruistic of you.''

Raymond shrugged. ''Divorce is a messy business. If I couldn't simplify it with a little judicial blackmailing, I figured I should get something extra for my efforts. Now, Celia...she didn't care what she received from blackmailing someone. She simply did it for the thrill of seeing people dance to her tune.''

''What do you mean?''

''She liked to know things about people, to be able to poke her fingers in their soft spots and watch them squirm. Yeah, she tried to blackmail Mike Russell, but he called her bluff. But a little failure didn't slow her down. She kept on plugging, kept on sticking her nose in where it didn't belong. You know what they say about curiosity killing the cat....''

''Then you know who killed her?''

Raymond shot both of them an odd stare. ''I thought I knew...at first.''

It took her a moment to comprehend the meaning of his actions. ''You mean...you really thought I shot h-her?'' Sara couldn't bring herself to say Celia's name.

He nodded reluctantly. ''You know what they say about a woman scorned. It seemed to make sense at the time. You would have been the person most likely to get upset that Celia and I were...together....''

Celia and I...together. The words were like fingernails on a chalkboard, echoing through Sara's mind. He'd said them so easily, without even a fragment of guilt. But in his warped vocabulary, "together" had a much broader meaning.

She realized she must have made a noise because Raymond looked up at her closely for the first time.

"Uh…Celia and I…" His voice faded out for a moment and he turned an unattractive shade of red. He stuttered, stammered and began to sweat. Sara realized that, perhaps for the first time in his life, he was having to deal with real guilt, shame and maybe even a degree of humiliation.

If nothing else, Sara got some puerile satisfaction out of watching him wrestle with his newly discovered conscience.

"After I tried to strangle her for betraying me, I realized that I was the one who was betraying you. When I left the hotel room, I went walking, trying to collect my thoughts—" he turned his wan stare toward Sara "—trying to figure out what I had to do to salvage *our* relationship. I still love you, Sara."

Sara swallowed hard. She understood exactly what he was doing. He knew which strings to pluck, where the cracks were in her heart. He was a master manipulator, but she was no longer his willing puppet. She crossed her arms and stared at him, meeting his impassioned gaze with her icy one. "Can the crap and tell us what happened."

Both the battle and the war were lost and he knew it. He continued his story, telling it to the wall rather than make eye contact with her or Will.

"When I finally got back to the hotel, to end everything with her, I was too late. She was dead. It wasn't that hard to convince myself I'd done it." He pushed back into his pillow. "I panicked, I ran. Simple as that."

"And ended up lying in your own puke in the middle of a cheap hotel room. Cut to the chase, Bergeron. Which one of your extortion victims slipped you the poison?"

Raymond's gaze narrowed. "I thought you weren't going to play the tough-guy role anymore."

"I'm not playing. Not anymore. Whoever you've pissed off isn't stopping with you. This cancer is spreading. My office has been destroyed and Sara was almost killed in the process. Someone broke into both our houses." Will took a menacing step toward the bed. "You and Celia must have jerked one string too many. Who is it? What are they looking for?"

"I—I don't know."

Will leaned over the railing, his words almost a whisper. "We could have let you die last night, which would have simplified things considerably. But we didn't. Who poisoned you?"

"I can't—"

Sara took the lead. "We know you had a dinner companion last night. You ordered two meals. Only one person could have poisoned your food and you know who it is. The longer you protect them, the better chance they have of killing all of us."

"This is your last chance, Bergeron." Will crossed his arms. "Last chance before I turn over all your blackmailing files to the police. Tell us—"

The bedside machine began to beep and started spilling out a ribbon of paper. Raymond's face had suddenly turned a pasty white and he clutched his chest with his free hand.

"Raymond?" Sara grabbed the bed rail. "Are you all right?"

The machine stopped its noise and he released a shaky sigh, waving off their concern. "Yeah…yeah, I'm okay. It's over. Give me a…minute." He took several deep breaths and some natural color returned to his features. "Okay…I'll tell you everything—but first, I want to speak to my lawyer. We've got to arrange to get me out of here. I'm a sitting duck."

Will flexed his fingers, looking as if he would like to take his frustrations out on Raymond's throat, again. "C'mon, you're stalling for time. There's a guard outside and you know you can act as your own counsel."

Raymond shook his head. "No way. I don't say anything until I talk to my lawyer."

Will grabbed the phone and nearly threw it on the bed. "Then call. Now."

Raymond picked up the receiver, then gave them a scathing look. "I'd like some privacy, if you don't mind."

Will grabbed Sara's hand and pulled her out of the room. Raymond waited until the door closed before he stabbed the buttons with his forefinger. He muttered an expletive at the chirpy ringing tone that echoed through his brain.

"Hello?"

"It's me."

"Where are you?"

"Where do you think? In the hospital, handcuffed to the bed. That was the whole purpose of your 'special seasoning,' wasn't it? To get me out of the way so you could settle the case with another lawyer?"

She laughed. "It sounded like a good idea at the time…with you being a wanted criminal and all. So why are you calling?"

"Because you're going to redeem yourself."

"How?"

"Listen very closely.…"

Sunday, late morning

"ANITA?" WILL STOOD, gladly abandoning the sagging couch.

The thin woman who approached graced Will with a tremulous smile. "I haven't seen you in some time, William." She looked around nervously, lowering her voice. "Is Ray all right? Has he had any more seizures?"

Will stared at her. "*You're* Bergeron's lawyer?"

She stiffened. "I'm not strictly a divorce lawyer, you know. I've handled criminal cases before."

He winced, realizing belatedly how rude he'd sounded. "I'm sorry...I didn't mean any offense. What surprises me isn't his choice of lawyer, but *your* choice of client. Aren't you on opposing sides of a couple of cases?"

"He needs my help. I can't turn him down in his time of need." Anita turned her attention to Sara, giving her a critical once-over. "And you are?"

Will hesitated. There was something odd in Anita's manner. Her concern for Bergeron was admirable, if not a bit overpowering. God help them if she was another member of the Raymond Bergeron Fan Club. Will managed to pull together a polite smile. "Sara Hardaway, meet Anita Rooney. Anita and I went to law school together."

If Sara sensed anything out of the ordinary, she didn't let on. She stood and offered a hand, which Anita reluctantly accepted. "I'm pleased you could get here so quickly. I'm sure we all want this to end as soon as possible."

Anita shrugged—a noncommittal answer at best. She glanced at the cop guarding the door. "Is this absolutely necessary?"

The policeman nodded. "Yes, ma'am."

"Will, if you'll excuse me, my client needs me." She pushed open the door, making sure to shut it firmly behind her.

Sara made a face at the closed door. "Is she any good?"

"She's thorough. Conscientious. Competent." He searched for something else positive to say.

"Those aren't the first adjectives I think of when asked

to describe a good lawyer.'' Sara shook her head and sat back down. "I sure hope Raymond knows what he's doing."

"Me, too."

They sat quietly for a few minutes, idle chitchat evidently on neither of their agendas. But the silence between them was a comfortable one. After a while, Will started looking for distractions to occupy his mind. The magazine selection was limited at best.

Will's stomach began to growl, a reminder that he'd never gotten a chance to eat his complimentary hotel breakfast, which they had left in the car. He turned to Sara who had been able to find something interesting in an old magazine. "They're probably going to be a while. You hungry?"

She nodded. "Starved."

"Why don't I go see if they have any vending machines around here?" Will dug into his pocket for change. "What do you want?"

She stifled a yawn. "You'd think with everything going on that I wouldn't have a problem being sleepy, but I do. How about something with caffeine in it? Coffee, a soft drink, even a chocolate bar if you can't find anything else."

Will left her on the plastic couch, knowing she would be relatively safe under the watchful eye of one of Blackwater's finest. It took him ten minutes to find a bank of vending machines in the hospital's basement. Most of the machines had "This machine owes me..." sticky notes posted on them. A sympathetic orderly steered him through the maze of hallways to the cafeteria where he waited in line to get two cups of coffee and two chocolate doughnuts. By the time he found his way back to Bergeron's floor, twenty minutes had passed.

He trudged down the hall, balancing a doughnut on top

of each cup. When he turned the corner, he saw that the plastic couch was empty.

She probably went to the rest room....

Will waited five minutes. No Sara.

Sure, women take longer than men, but... He left the food on the beat-up chrome coffee table and approached the policeman standing guard at the door. "Did you see which way Ms. Hardaway went?"

"She left a couple of minutes after you did."

"Left? She just walked off?"

"She went with the other lady, the lawyer."

"You mean Anita's through talking with Bergeron? Where did they go?"

The policeman shrugged. "I'm not here to keep track of the ladies." He thumbed over his shoulder to Bergeron's door. "I'm here to watch him."

Will returned to the couch and stared at his cup of coffee. Where had she gone? Had Anita pulled her off to some private corner to report on Bergeron's confession? An uneasy feeling began to sprout in the pit of his stomach. He forced himself to wait two more minutes, then another two before listening to any of the unsavory scenarios that filled his mind.

Finally, he stalked over to the policeman and pointed at the closed door. "Have you checked on him, lately?"

The man shook his head. "His lady lawyer said he wasn't feeling well and she was going to come back later."

Instinct, intuition, insight—no matter what name it went under—it made alarms go off in Will's head. He shouldered open the door, catching the guard by surprise.

"Wait...you can't just bust in...." His voice trailed away.

The handcuffs dangled from the railing of the empty bed.

Chapter Fifteen

Will slammed the elevator button with the heel of his hand. Bergeron on the loose, Sara missing—the implications were more than he was willing to consider.

Why would Bergeron take her? As a hostage? Out of revenge? *What about—*

He heard a familiar voice and turned in time to see Sara and Anita strolling nonchalantly out of the rest room. He grabbed Sara by the shoulders. "Are you all right?"

She looked appropriately stunned. "Uh...yes. Why?" She stiffened and peered past him to the hallway beyond. Her gaze stopped at the doorway the policeman had been guarding. "Something's wrong."

He nodded. "Bergeron's disappeared."

Anita's eyes opened wide. "Escaped?"

Will felt a tremor course through Sara's body. "But how?" she asked in a hushed voice. "How did he get out of the room? How did he get out of the handcuffs?"

He shrugged. "Let the police worry about how. The important thing is he's on the run."

"On the run," Anita repeated in shock. She started wringing her hands. "How am I supposed to come up with a successful strategy to defend a second-degree murder charge for a client who's on the run?" She paled. "It's impossible, now. If you run, it's because you're guilty. Every jury knows that.''

Sara released a sigh and leaned forward, placing her forehead against his shoulder. "I guess he wasn't ready to face up to what he'd done."

Anita pivoted, wearing a look of near indignation. "You told me in the bathroom that you believed he was innocent!"

"Of Celia's murder, yes. But Raymond's involved in something...else."

"What?"

"He's been—"

"Hold it." Will stepped between them. "This isn't the place to start a...sensitive discussion. I think we ought to find somewhere else to talk. I think Bergeron ran because he's scared. He has the right idea, you know. He's seeking higher ground and so should we."

"But—"

"I'm going to take you someplace safe where you can brief Anita on what's going on and while you're doing that I'll get the files. The sooner I put all the evidence in Trainor's hands, the safer we'll be."

"You're not going anywhere without me."

"Yes, I am, Sara. And you know I'm right. This is the best way to cover all our bases."

"Why can't we stay here?"

"I don't want you anywhere near this hospital. He might still be hanging around."

Anita bristled. "I thought we agreed that Raymond's not the murderer."

"He isn't, but I don't want take any chances that the murderer might come here looking for him."

"But—"

"But nothing." Will consulted his watch. Mimi would be up by now. "C'mon." He grabbed Sara by the hand

and tugged her toward the pay phone across from the nurses' station.

Sara wanted to balk. She wanted to dig in her heels and remind him that the "Me Strong Man" routine was a thing of the past. But beneath his mask of fierce protector, she saw his level of anxiety and it both alarmed and touched her. Even though her strongest instincts were saying, *He's wrong,* a small voice of reason argued, *What if he's right?*

She and Anita exchanged looks as he held a frantic discussion with his secretary.

He hung up the phone. "Okay…it's settled. Mimi lives with her boyfriend in one of those security apartments in Crystal City." He paused. "It's safe, it's fairly close by, and no one would know to look for you there. After I get the files and turn them over to Trainor, I'll come get you and we'll figure out what to do from there. Okay?" His face and voice softened. "I just want to make sure you're safe. I…care about you."

She swallowed back any arguments that she could find her own place of security. With Lucy and Martin—

The first place Raymond would look….

Will's logic sounded as if it had an emotional edge to it, which she couldn't help but appreciate. Somewhere in the back of her mind, she knew that "I love you" had its roots in "I care about you."

She gave him the best smile she could muster, given the circumstances. "Okay."

Ten minutes later, they'd escaped the gauntlet of police who were searching the hospital. Anita and Sara rode together and Will followed for a couple of miles behind them to make sure no one was tailing them.

Sara kept an eye on his car in the side mirror, reassured by his sense of precaution.

"Is he still back there?" Anita asked.

"Yeah…wait, he's come up here. Slow down so he can

catch us at the light." Sara rolled down her window and Will pulled up in the lane to the right of them.

"No one's following you," he called out. "It'll take me about forty minutes to get to Falls Church and back to get the disk. See you at Mimi's. Be careful."

"You, too."

Will rolled up his window, then shot her a thumbs-up before he turned the corner and headed off in a different direction. He made a second turn and disappeared from sight.

Sara couldn't stop herself from sighing.

Anita sniffed in obvious disapproval. "I thought you were Raymond's...girlfriend."

Sara sighed again, this time for a completely different reason. "We were engaged. We're not anymore."

"The rats are deserting the sinking ship?"

Sara tried to ignore the haughtiness of the woman's question. "I guess it looks that way, doesn't it? Trust me, it's hard to explain without going into a great amount of detail about what happened to whom. Why don't we wait until we get to Mimi's place, then I can tell you the whole story."

"Answer me one question."

"What?"

"You and Will. Is it serious?"

Sara leaned her head against the headrest. "It shouldn't be. We've only known each other a little over a week, but...to be perfectly honest, yes. I think it's going to be serious."

"Oh."

They drove in silence until they crossed the Fourteenth Street Bridge. Instead of taking the exit leading to Crystal City, Anita continued south on I-395.

Sara pointed to the left. "You missed the exit."

The car swerved from one lane to the next. "Oops...

these roads are always so damn confusing. I hate driving around here."

Sara watched the woman negotiate a couple of jerky lane changes. "Be thankful it's not a weekday." She scanned the road ahead, reading the exit signs. "I guess the best way to go is to take the Glebe Road exit and approach Crystal City from the other direction."

Anita snaked her hand into her purse. "Sorry. But we're not going to Crystal City." She pulled out her hand, revealing a gun clutched in her trembling fingers.

Sara's heart wedged itself in her throat, then plunged to her feet. "What's that for?"

The woman drew in a shaky breath. "P-protection."

Sara decided that her best line of attack would be no attack at all. A nervous woman with a shaky hand, unclear motives and a gun; the possibilities might be lethal. "Protection from me?"

"Maybe."

"Anita," she said in the softest, most nonconfrontational voice she could manage, "I didn't kill Celia. Honest."

"That's what you say." She split her attention evenly between Sara and the road. "I know what Raymond thinks. And he's usually right."

"Usually, but not always. He's wrong about me. I didn't kill Celia and I didn't poison him."

"I know you didn't. Poison him, that is. I did that."

Sara couldn't help but gape. "You did? Why?"

"To force him to surrender to the authorities. He wouldn't go of his own volition. I figured police custody would be the only way to keep him safe. Then he called me from the hospital and told me the police allowed you into the room. Since the police failed us, it was up to us to keep him safe. So we simply reversed the process. He's free and I have you in my custody."

"But—"

Anita's hand shook. "I don't want to discuss it."

"But—"

"I said shut up!" A flash of steeled determination filled her face, giving it character where none had existed before. Then, as quickly as it had come, it disappeared, leaving a colorless bundle of nerves in its wake.

Sara huddled in her seat, weighing her options. Until they reached a convenient red light, she wouldn't be able to make a break for freedom. The only break she would get by jumping from a moving car would be the one that broke her neck. She would rather face a psychotic woman with a gun than hit the pavement at sixty miles an hour.

Anita took an exit at an ambitious speed and Sara tensed, knowing there was a traffic light only a few blocks ahead. Anita slowed down as she saw the red signal, but she glanced at Sara as if reading her plans. The woman's hand tightened on the gun. At the point when Anita would either have to make her decision to slow down or run the light, the signal changed to green.

Just my luck... Sara drew a deep breath. "Where are we going?"

"I told Will I'd take you someplace safe. That's exactly what I'm doing." She took a sudden turn onto a side street, then made a second turn, clipping the edge of the driveway curb. The car rocked and the steering wheel jerked to the right. At that moment, Sara made an instantaneous decision to make an offensive move rather than a defensive one.

As the steering wheel jerked, Anita automatically reached for it with her gun hand. For a moment, the weapon dangled loosely in her grasp and Sara lunged out with both hands, attempting to wrench the gun free.

Anita reacted with a miraculous speed and agility, knocking Sara back with one hand and recovering the fumbled weapon with the other.

"Why, you bitch!"

The last thing Sara saw was the butt of the gun as it flashed toward her head.

WILL CALLED ARCHIE from his car and explained that he needed to pick up the backup files, but he was in a hurry.

Archie laughed. "What's wrong? Is it a case of...life or death?" he asked with an Olivier-type flourish.

There wasn't a shred of amusement in Will's voice as he answered. "Yes, it is."

By the time he got to the house, Archie was sitting on his porch, disks in hand. He trotted dutifully to the curb, passed them through the car window with a minimum of chitchat and Will was off.

He had only gone a couple of blocks down the road when his car phone rang. He wedged the instrument between his shoulder and ear as he downshifted. "Riggs."

"Will, it's Mimi."

His hand tensed automatically. There was no reason for her to call him unless... "Sara got there all right, didn't she?"

Her momentary hesitation seemed like an eternity to Will. "Well...not really. But it's okay," she added quickly. "She called me and explained that something came up. She wouldn't say what, but she asked me to call you and tell you to meet her at..." Mimi recited the address. Will recognized the street. It was one that ran through an industrial park not far from his office.

"Did she sound all right? I mean, did she sound scared or nervous or anything like that?"

"Not really. In fact, she seemed almost happy, enthusiastic about whatever she'd found out. She asked you to get there as soon as possible."

"Okay." He paused for a moment. "Mimi, if I don't call you back in...let's say, an hour, call Steve Trainor at the Blackwater PD and tell him what you told me. He'll know what to do. Okay?"

"Sure," she said in a voice that was anything but assured. "Uh…boss…should I start to get worried? After all this business with the office and the fire, I can't help but be…concerned. And this bit about calling the police if you don't check in… That stuff only happens in the movies."

"I know. I'm just being overly cautious. It's been a very strange day and I don't want to take any chances. Okay?"

"Sure. Be careful. Bye."

Will turned off the phone. An industrial complex? The skin on the back of his neck prickled.

A very strange day, indeed…

SARA REMEMBERED BITS and pieces—being pulled from the car and being dragged into a warehouse of sorts. She remembered the unmistakable clang of a chain-link fence being opened and recalled being dropped in a heap onto a rough floor. As her eyes focused, she stared at the harsh green carpet beneath her.

Grass?

Dizzy, she tried to dig her fingers into the ground to help her regain her balance, but belatedly realized that the impossibly green lawn was artificial. *AstroTurf?* She fought the wave of dizziness that threatened to take over, forcing herself to focus on something besides the floor.

She was in a warehouse, inside a chain-link cubicle with some sort of machine at one end. Her thoughts started to congeal. The machine had something to do with AstroTurf. Something to do with sports. Something to do with balls. With baseballs.

I'm in a batting cage.

A memory overwhelmed her for a moment—a memory of a cousin pumping a quarter into the change box at an outdoor batting cage and taking a bat in hand to show her how easy it was to learn to hit. While he concentrated on

his stance, she'd turned the selector from Little League to
Major League.

Twelve balls. Eleven strikes and one wild pitch that
gave him a bruise that lasted for a week. Then there were
the lingering echoes of his friends' taunts, which, she suspected, lasted a lot longer than the bruise.

Sara's initial reaction was to scramble out of the way
of imaginary balls, but she remembered that same cousin
had taught her the finer art of playing possum. To her
relief, the ball-hurling machinery was still. It would give
her time to get her bearings, regain her sense of balance
and figure out how she got there, what to do next.

I know how I got here. Sara's head throbbed. *Anita
Rooney, the person voted least likely to have backbone. I
guess you don't need guts if you have a semiautomatic.
Where is she, anyway? I'd like to return the favor....*

From her slumped position, she could see that there
were at least four batting cages in a row and beyond them,
a waiting area with a couple of benches and several sets
of shelves holding bats and helmets. She could also see
the end of a glass case, which evidently operated as a
service counter as well as a concession area. Between a
rack of potato chips and a display of batting gloves, Sara
spotted a curtained doorway.

I wonder if it's an exit—

"Hello, Blazer? It's me."

She froze at the sound of the voice coming from beyond
the door. *Raymond...*

"Listen, I've reached a settlement agreement with Diane's lawyer and they're willing to sign the papers.
Yeah... No..."

Sara suddenly realized she was overhearing one side of
a phone conversation.

"As soon as you can get here—no, not my office. How
about yours? Yeah, at the Sports Barne. Good. I'll be

waiting there. You gave me a key, remember? Okay. Bye.''

Raymond appeared in the doorway, then seemed to stumble forward. Anita trailed only a few steps behind him, the gun aimed at his back. Although she wore a prim dress with a lace collar, Sara suspected that Anita's matching lace gloves played a more utilitarian role—no fingerprints.

"Anita, you don't have to do this."

"Y-yes, I do. She's making me. She knows. She knows everything and she'll ruin my career."

"But you don't need the gun, honey. I want Blazer to sign the papers. I want this whole thing over with so I can straighten out this mess with the police about Celia." He took a step forward. "I didn't kill her, you know."

Sara pulled herself to her feet, dug her fingers into the chain-link and rattled her prison wall. "Don't be so sure about that, Anita."

The empty warehouse magnified the noise, diverting Anita's attention for a moment. Raymond took advantage of the distraction by knocking her off-balance and wrenching the gun out of her hands. Anita attacked him in return and as they struggled, Sara leaped toward the gate, only to find it locked. The fight between Anita and Raymond was destined to have a captured audience of one.

Anita did an admirable job of fighting Raymond, but that was no surprise. Sara had realized in the car that Anita wasn't as delicate as she pretended to be. A sudden gunshot rocketed through the warehouse. Sara dropped to the ground instinctively. Raymond stood back from the melee, the gun firmly clenched in his hand, his finger still curled around the trigger. Anita stepped away, covering her mouth with one gloved hand.

"Anita," he asked in a hushed voice. "Are you all right?"

"She's fine." Another woman stepped out from behind the draped doorway. She trained her gun on Raymond. "Drop it."

He didn't move. "What are you doing here, Diane?"

"Playing cleanup batter." She moved closer, her weapon held in a very steady hand. "I said drop it."

Sara stared at the woman who looked almost familiar. *Diane. Diane who?*

Raymond reacted quickly, grabbing Anita by the arm and pulling her toward him. Sara couldn't tell whether he was using the woman as his shield or as his hostage.

"Now what?" Diane taunted.

"She's your lawyer. You won't shoot her and you don't want me to, either." Anita stiffened, her stricken look degenerating to one of sheer unadulterated panic.

"I suppose you're right. But what about the other one?" Diane shifted slightly to the left, aimed at Sara and fired.

The sound became permanently etched in Sara's memory; the gun's percussion, the whine of the bullet, the zing as it created an instant furrow in the concrete only a foot away from her head. She stayed perfectly still, knowing that there was no place in her cage where she could protect herself from a second shot.

"Like shooting fish in a barrel, Ray...." She lowered her gun. "Or should I call you Mr. Barracuda in a Barrel?"

Raymond knocked Anita aside, took aim at Diane and fired three times in succession. The blasts rocked the warehouse, their echoes almost deafening.

Sara closed her eyes and waited for the scream, the sound of the body hitting the floor...any sound at all....

She heard laughter.

Long, harsh laughter.

"Give Anita the gun."

Sara opened her eyes in time to see the prim-and-proper

Anita taking the gun out of the hands of a very shocked Raymond. She slipped it into her lace-trimmed pocket. "Sorry, Ray," she whispered, "Blanks."

"Now put him in the cage with her."

Raymond complied numbly, without a word of objection, but Sara could see the emotion that seethed beneath the surface of an artificial calm. As the gate slammed behind him and the lock clicked, he lifted his gaze from the freshly-cut groove in the floor and made eye contact with Sara. "I'll kill that heartless bitch. I swear it." Then he stopped, evidently realizing it was the second time in so many days that he'd called someone a "heartless bitch."

Sara took a step away from him, no longer sure. No longer willing to give him the benefit of the doubt. No longer caring.

He sighed. "Sara, I swear on my mother's grave that I didn't kill Celia Strauss."

Diane approached the cage. "Yes, you did." She pointed to Anita's bulging pocket. "And now, thanks to you, we have the murder weapon, complete with your fingerprints on it."

"You bitch, you killed Celia, didn't you?" Raymond threw himself at the fence, but Diane didn't take as much as a flinching step backward.

"You're directly responsible for that woman's death," she stated as if it were an unavoidable fact.

No emotion entered his voice. "What are you talking about?"

"We—that is, Anita and I—didn't know until later that the...person who rode up with us in the elevator and overheard us discussing our...legal strategy was your—" she spared Sara a brief glance "—fiancée. You even mentioned the happy little coincidence to us over the lunch she had so lovingly prepared. Remember?"

Elevator? Sara recalled the ride up with the loathsome

lawyer and her milquetoast client, only to learn later that she'd reversed the roles. This was the odious one, the client—Diane...Barnes. The soon-to-be ex-wife of the man with the inexplicable name of Blazer. Sure, Anita and Diane had been talking in the elevator, but Sara couldn't remember any specifics. She really hadn't even been listening....

"We also had no earthly idea until we saw in the morning paper that the woman you took to the hotel was anybody other than that same fiancée." She turned a malicious face toward the shaking Anita. "I thought I already knew who your latest mistress was." She faced Raymond again. "Put it this way—we killed the wrong woman. We won't make that same mistake again."

Raymond shoved his hands into his pockets and adopted a surprisingly natural smile. Sara recognized it as the calm before the storm, a technique he used to distract potential combatants in the domain of debate. "It seems to me that you've gone the long way around to achieve a relatively short-lived victory. Granted, Blazer isn't a genius, but even he's going to think twice before signing papers when he sees his attorney being held in a cage at gunpoint."

Diane started to speak, but Raymond cut her off. "And if you think that holding a gun to Sara's head is going to help keep me in line, think again. She's not a part of my life anymore." His features hardened. "And from the looks of things, she's already found a replacement for me." He turned toward Anita. "You saw them together. You know what I mean, don't you?"

Anita nodded nervously. "She and Will Riggs. They're together now."

Will...

How long would it take for him to realize she'd never gotten to Mimi's apartment? How long would it take for him to figure out that the one person who seemed a totally innocuous figure, actually had a key role in everything that had plagued them in the past week? How long would it take for Diane to realize Will knew too much?

Sara sagged against the fence. *Not 'How long'...but 'How much longer...'*

Raymond's voice dropped to nearly a whisper. "Let me out, Diane. I don't care what you do to her or Riggs. Let me out and I'll get Blazer to sign whatever you want."

If Sara hadn't been holding on to the fence, she would have collapsed; Raymond was selling her out.

Diane shifted her harsh stare from Raymond to Sara and back to Raymond. Her dark brows knitted in thought for several seconds, then slowly relaxed. A smile blossomed on her face. "Don't look so defeated, Sara. It's a bluff. You might hate his guts for screwing around on you, but I think he'd take a bullet for you if necessary. That's what this crap is all about, trying to get out so he can become the hero and save you." She shrugged. "It's almost...touching. Unfortunately, Raymond, that sacrifice won't be necessary. I don't need your cooperation to get Blazer to sign any papers."

Anita came to life for the first time in several minutes. "What do you mean?"

"I've been thinking. At first I thought a selective strike would do. You know, take out a key player, implicate another...but things have a way of snowballing. I thought killing just her would be sufficient. I was wrong."

"How wrong?" Anita asked, betraying her anxiety.

Diane ignored her lawyer's question. "But consider what a nice little triangle we have here that we can exploit. The lawyer, his ex-fiancée and the man who came between them. We already have Ray's fingerprints on the gun that killed Celia. What if he goes on a jealous rampage, kills the other two and then shoots himself? Wouldn't that be a neat way to tie this up?"

"Kill all...*three* of them?"

"Oh, don't be so squeamish. You know that Ray isn't worth crying over. He cheated on his fiancée with you and he cheated on you with Celia." Diane began to rock on her heels, almost absentmindedly. "Of course, technically, we only have two of the three in custody, so to speak. But Riggs should be showing up pretty soon. I took a chance, figuring his secretary wouldn't be that familiar with Sara's voice. It worked. He'll be here any minute and I'd better get ready for him."

Will? Here? A burst of frantic energy filled Sara. There was no way in hell she would let him unexpectedly stroll into a trap. She grabbed a double handful of chain-link fence and began to shake it for all she was worth. The sound vibrated throughout the room, the rattling of one fence setting the next in motion.

"Will!" she screamed. "It's a trap!"

Raymond grabbed her around the waist and pulled her away from the fence. He slapped his other hand over her mouth. "Shut up," he hissed. "If he *is* out there, all you're going to do is break his concentration and make him do something rash."

Diane nodded. "Very wise decision, Ray. Thanks. If you hadn't stopped her, I would have simply shot her."

Raymond loosened his hold a bit and Sara wrenched herself free. "Don't you ever touch me again."

"Tsk, tsk, you two." Diane pivoted and took a couple of steps toward the counter. She stopped. "You know...it would be nice if we could get rid of one more person while we're at it. You know...work Blazer into this triangle, somehow?"

Raymond had already turned his attention to their prison, evidently looking for a means of escape. Only Sara saw Anita's telltale reactions to Diane's proposition. The woman's eyes widened and she drew in a sharp breath.

Sara cocked her head in thought. *Anita and Blazer?*

A familiar voice echoed through the warehouse. "If you add a fourth person, then you can't call it a triangle."

"Will!"

She allowed herself to entertain wild thoughts of rescue and reunion until he stumbled forward as if someone was pushing from behind. "Haven't you heard enough, now?" he asked over his shoulder.

A hulking figure carrying a bat appeared in the doorway behind him. "I found this creep prowling around outside. You know him?"

Diane nodded. "Unfortunately I do. Hello, Will. I see you've met Blazer. It's been a while. Been busy?"

"Business is good. Haven't seen you since husband number...three, I think it was. How's it going, Diane? Another marriage down the toilet?"

Blazer merely growled and pushed Will again until they were out from behind the counter and into the main room. Will crossed his arms as if waiting for the man to comprehend the scene before them as well as its deadly implications. Will glanced at Sara, giving her a quick reassuring nod that said, *Whatever it is, we're in it together.*

Blazer drew in a long breath and let it out slowly. Evidently, the dawn had cracked. "It doesn't need to come to this, Diane."

"Put down the bat." She gestured with her free hand.

He made a great show of bending down and placing the bat on the floor. She crooked her finger, then pointed to the batting cage. "Over here. With the rest of them. Hands on head, both of you."

Will complied, lacing his fingers behind his head. Blazer sighed and stomped toward the batting cage, his beefy fists clenched at his sides. "I'm so tired of this game. I told you, Diane. I'm willing to sign anything. I want out. Now!"

"How badly do you want out of this marriage?" Diane

gestured for Anita to unlock the gate and for them to step inside.

"I'm not greedy. Just give me this business, my car and the apartment. You can keep the rest."

The door swung closed with a loud clang and Diane relocked it with one hand. "You are the soul of generosity, Blazer Barnes. I'll think about it." She took two steps away, then pivoted. Her smile was one of pure malevolence, a painful reminder that there were some people in this world who could embrace their own greed without any apparent guilt.

"There, I thought about it. Here's your answer." She raised the gun, planted her feet and—

"No!"

Anita swung into action, literally. In the length of time it took Diane to sight the gun, Anita picked up Blazer's discarded bat and let it fly. It sailed through the air, striking Diane in the back of the head. The gun flew from her hand, clattering against the fence and then skidding a few feet away.

Raymond let out a whooping cheer and started banging the fence in triumph. Sara fell into Will's arms, burying her face in his shoulder. She felt him tense and she pulled back.

Anita held the gun in one hand and was unlocking the door with the other. Raymond rushed out and enveloped her in a big hug. "I knew you weren't like her! I knew you couldn't let her kill me, darling."

"I'm not like her at all," Anita replied as a smile crept across her face.

"No, you're not." Raymond brushed the hair from her face and kissed her. "You understand what love is all about."

She nodded. "Yes, I do...."

She pulled the trigger.

Chapter Sixteen

Anita stood over Raymond's body, the gun pointed in the general direction of Will and Sara, who had entertained brief thoughts of escape. "Sorry." She turned to Blazer. "Are you all right, sweetheart?"

He stepped out of the cage, snaked an arm around her waist and squeezed lightly. "Sure, other than being scared out of my wits. I didn't think you were going to let her go that far."

"She caught me by surprise. I didn't know she was going to change plans in midstream. She actually had some initiative. Scary, isn't it?"

Will nodded. "Now…you sound more like the Anita Rooney I've heard about. The Oscar-winning Anita." He turned to Sara. "One of her old boyfriends once told me she could do more with a trembling lip and a tear-filled eye than any actress in Hollywood. Of course, I didn't believe him. I was like all the other dolts in the class. We believed the outside package. 'Poor little nervous Anita. Let's cut her a little slack.'"

"That's what I wanted you to believe. You felt oh-so-altruistic and I walked away with everything I ever wanted in life without ever getting my hands dirty. It's a wonderful way to live."

Sara stared at the woman. Anita didn't even stand the same way as she had before. She didn't fidget. Her gestures were firm, not fluttery. She even seemed taller, perhaps even prettier. Then Sara looked down at Raymond who groaned and clutched his bloodied shirt. *And deadlier.*

Sara took a step toward the open door, but Anita shook her head. "Honey, I've done you a favor in the long run. Ray decided that the best way to win the most lucrative settlement for Blazer was to seduce me. When he got bored with me because I refused to tell him any of Diane's secrets, he passed me over to Blazer, hoping that his client would have more luck."

Will shifted in front of Sara, slipping his hand in hers, giving her a reassuring squeeze. "Looks like Blazer got lucky, all right."

Blazer nodded. "I sure did. Not only do I get Anita, but I get all of Diane's assets, too. I'm in the will, you know."

Will tsked-tsked softly. "You mean you're in the old will. And the new will that Anita drew up after the separation has mysteriously disappeared, right? Pretty smart, Anita."

"Pretty and smart," Blazer corrected. "She could have told Ray about the money Diane was supposed to have lost in the spec-spec—"

"Speculative," Anita supplied.

"Uh...that type of land deal in Arizona, but if he'd included that as part of the settlement, then feds would have stepped in and claimed half of it for taxes and penalties and stuff. Of course, knowing Ray, he'd probably try to use it as blackmail material. Either way, I would have gotten a whole bunch less of the money than I'll get now."

Will managed a halfhearted smile. "Lucky you."

"But not so lucky for you, I guess." Blazer turned to Anita. "I'll go drag her into the next cage and set everything up. I always told Diane not to go into the cages without a batting helmet. Those balls can kill an unprotected person." He winked. "Ain't that too bad?"

Anita waved the gun at them. "I'll take care of these two."

Sara knew this was her only chance. She squeezed Will's hand, then pushed him aside. "No...wait!" She flung herself at Blazer, then sagged so he would be compelled to reach out and support her dead weight.

"How could you!" She pummeled his chest with her fists, then dissolved into tears, which were surprisingly real. "You said she didn't mean anything to you. You said you only slept with her so that you could get your hands on as much of Diane's money as possible. And you said you did it for us!"

As Sara had hoped, he responded to her outburst immediately. And strongly. He gaped, then pushed her back, raising his hands as if to prove he'd never ever touched her in his entire life. "I swear I don't know what she's talking about, Anita. I don't!"

The strength of his denial planted a momentary seed of doubt in Anita's mind, causing enough of a distraction for Will to act.

Sara was in the middle of crying, shouting, "You swore you loved me!" when Will lunged for Anita. Blazer realized too late that Anita was the objective of Will's trajectory. The man tried to stiff-arm Sara out of the way in order to intercept the tackle, but she dodged his hand. Instead of trying to knock him over—a useless goal, considering the difference in their sizes—she jumped up, wrapped her arms around his neck and hung on for dear life.

Blazer initially fell to one knee, thrown off-balance by her additional weight. Judging by his groan of pain, Sara had discovered his Achilles' heel, or hamstring, as the case might be. As he struggled to rise, she managed to clip him beneath the chin with the top of her head. She saw a couple of stars herself, but he roared in pain, and like an injured animal, he became twice as dangerous. He tore her arms from around his neck and tossed her aside like an empty beer can.

As she hit the concrete, she heard a hideous sound. It was a combination of a scream, a roar and a gunshot. She realized belatedly that the scream was her own.

The roar belonged to Blazer. "Anita!"

And the gunshot?

Blazer stood stock-still, gaping at the sight of Anita and Will in a tangled heap. Sara's heart lodged itself permanently in her windpipe until she watched Will scramble away on all fours, trying to regain his traction to stand. Anita, left behind in an uncomfortable mound, made no effort to move.

Sara doubted the woman would move ever again.

Blazer bellowed and made a flying leap at Will who barely managed to shift out of the way. But Blazer reached out with his impossibly long arms and snagged Will's ankle, literally dragging him back into battle. They rolled and punched, Will's agility and training barely evening the odds against Blazer's brawn and righteous indignation.

Out of the corner of his eye, Will saw Sara rummaging through one of the cases where the batting supplies were kept. Blazer took advantage of Will's diverted attention and landed a good hard punch in the center of his chest. Will fell backward in a momentary oblivion, his sole attention riveted on learning how to breathe again. He looked up to find Blazer towering over him, panting, blood dripping from his broken nose. The man reached down with one meaty fist, gathered Will's shirt in his hand and hauled him to his feet.

"To the moon!" Blazer croaked as he cocked back his arm and prepared to land a blow that Will honestly doubted he would survive.

Suddenly, Blazer jerked. His chin dropped down to his chest and his fist loosened. Will wrestled out of the man's grip, able to take a stumbling step to the side. Blazer lifted his head and stared blankly at Will. Then his eyes rolled back and he collapsed like a marionette with no strings attached.

Blazer fell and behind him, Will could see Sara completing the swing that had saved his life. Instead of a bat, she held a batting helmet in her hands.

As she turned back to face Will, the helmet slowly separated into two parts. She stared down at Blazer in shock, aghast at what one person could do when properly provoked and suitably armed.

Will managed to smile somehow. "Is this your way of telling him you don't love him anymore?"

One week later

SARA SAT CROSS-LEGGED in the middle of the bed, the Sunday paper spread in front of her. Once upon what seemed a long time ago, the crossword had been Raymond's sole domain, no matter in whose paper it appeared. He'd never learned how much fun it could be to solve it together.

"What's an eleven-letter word for *asexual*? First letter *M*?" she called out.

Will stuck his head out of the bathroom. "Um, try… Wait." He closed his eyes and began to count on his fingers. Um…nine, ten, eleven." He opened his eyes. "Try *monogenetic*."

She wrote the letters in order, not surprised at all to see that they fit in with two other clues. "Thanks."

"You're welcome. Do you have any toothpaste?"

"In the side pocket of my case."

"Uh…how about a spare toothbrush?"

She wadded up the crossword puzzle and threw it at him. He dodged it and shot her a smile that made the familiar itch start again.

"What can I say? I'm a lousy packer." He shuffled across the room and sat on the edge of the bed, letting himself fall backward across the pillows. "Ouch!"

"That bruise on your stomach still hurts?"

He pulled back his robe and probed the discoloration gingerly. "Yeah."

She turned around. "I'll make it better." She placed a gentle kiss above the edge of the bruise, then shifted so that her head rested in the crook of his arm.

"You hungry?"

Sara smiled. "I ordered breakfast already. Bagels and coffee."

He sighed. "Perfect. Can you reach the sports section without getting up?"

She used her leg to slide the paper toward them. She grabbed several sections indiscriminately and handed them to him, assured that at least one of them contained the sports. She realized her strategic error when she saw the picture of Raymond.

She'd been avoiding the front page, knowing that Will's prediction had come true. This time, the story wasn't buried on the third page in the Metro section. This time, it was front-page news. Will held up the paper and they stared at it together.

The reporting team had done their homework, calling the series of connected stories "Anatomy of a Crime." They traced the Howard-Barnes marriage through from its dubious beginning to its tragic end with the death of Diane Howard-Barnes at the hands of her own lawyer, Anita Rooney, who died in a struggle over the murder weapon. Each branch, each participant got a separate story, explaining what brought them into what the reporters called "the final bloodbath."

Sara thought they'd taken a bit of literary license with that description. She remembered seeing some blood, but the reporters made it sound like the entire Sports Barne was drenched in it by the time Will called 911.

Will was the only one of the principals to come out unscathed by the articles. He'd been exonerated by statements made by the survivors and, as well, by some of the unidentified blackmail victims.

Perhaps, Raymond caught the worst of it, his weaknesses and greed splashed across the front page for everyone to see: his family, his friends, the Bar Association.

Sara, for some inexplicable reason, was barely mentioned at all, which proved either the reporters hadn't paid enough attention to the facts or that Mike Russell still wielded an incredible amount of influence on both sides of the Potomac. Considering he was one of the unidentified blackmail victims who volunteered information, she figured she had him to thank for her own anonymity.

Finally Will released a sigh. "Well?"

"I don't exist."

"I noticed that." He tossed the paper over the side of the bed. "Relieved?"

She nodded, shifting onto her side. "Actually, I am. I didn't really want to go back and face everybody."

"What about the restaurant? Lots of your customers know you were engaged to Raymond."

She shrugged. "We live in Washington, D.C., where today's scandal lands in tomorrow's recycling bin. Heck, there's probably more disbarred lawyers than garbage men in this area. Lots of my customers have been involved in their own scandals. They've learned to cultivate convenient short-term memories. What about you? Your business?"

He smiled. "It's what we call good P.I.P.R."

She wrinkled her nose in thought. "Piper?"

"No. P.I., private investigator. PR, public relations. The phone will be ringing off the hook tomorrow. Now all I need is a new office to house that phone."

"Do we have to go back tonight?" Sara wondered if it sounded as much like a whine to him as it did to her.

He stretched his arms out over his head, laced his fingers together and flexed his muscles. "'Fraid so. Life goes on."

She girded her courage to ask the one question that had haunted her all weekend. "What about us?"

"Us? As in you and me? Together? Forever and ever, amen?"

Sara felt herself blushing. She turned onto her side, propping her elbow on the bed and her head on her fist. "I wasn't asking about a lifetime commitment, not quite yet. Just how we were going to fit into each other's lives."

"Well…" He turned over onto his side, and mirrored her position so that they were face-to-face. "You're going to have to let me cook every now and then. I really enjoy it and I'm pretty good, even if it's not quite gourmet fare."

"I agree only if you let me buy a new tank and fish for your new office wherever it ends up. I feel very responsible for the destruction of the last aquarium."

"Okay. So far so good, wouldn't you say?"

"Here comes the acid test." She winced in anticipation of an unacceptable answer. "I have to work lots of weekends. I almost never get Friday off. What are you going to do on Fridays?"

He pondered her question for only a moment. "Well, back in the old days, if I wasn't working on a case, I'd stay home and watch 'The X-Files.' But now—" his smile grew "—maybe Mike can teach me some of the finer points of bartending. I could pinch-hit on Friday nights at the Blackwater Café. Maybe…help out." He began to peel the robe from her shoulder. "Anything I can do to make some extra brownie points with the owner."

She toyed with the sash of his robe. "Sounds good to me."

He leaned toward her, brushing his lips across her bare shoulder. "Just one more question."

"What?"

"Do you have a TV in the bar?"

COMING NEXT MONTH

#409 MIDNIGHT PREY by Caroline Burnes
Lawman
Her Montana horse ranch was half-Lakota Shadoe Deerman's lifeblood. But renegade U.S. Wildlife agent Hank Emrich seemed intent on destroying her land—and winning her heart. Could he also protect Shadoe when someone else seemed to want her: dead or alive?

#410 LULLABY DECEPTION by Susan Kearney
Max Braddack appeared to be a smooth operator—Brooke Evans expected as much from a man who was protecting his wealthy twin, the man whose biological child she had raised. But while Max's charm was intoxicating, Brooke was sure he had something to hide.

#411 SUNSET PROMISES by Carla Cassidy
Cheyenne Nights
Colette Connor prayed she wouldn't deliver her baby on the Connor ranch doorstep. With no recollection of who she was, how she got pregnant, she had nowhere else to turn. Only the knowing eyes, the incendiary kisses of stranger Hank Cooper disturbed her more. Did he have the answers to all of her questions?

#412 THE SILENT GROOM by Kelsey Roberts
The Rose Tattoo
Gabriel Langston was everything Joanna Boudreaux disliked—and desired—in one sexy package. He was also the last thing she needed while defending Rose Porter on a murder charge—but he wouldn't take no for an answer. He showered her with kisses and compliments, and told her everything she needed to know—except why he was so sure Rose was innocent.

AVAILABLE THIS MONTH:

#405 HERO FOR HIRE
Laura Kenner

#406 THE VALENTINE HOSTAGE
Dawn Stewardson

#407 FOR YOUR EYES ONLY
Rebecca York

#408 FEVER RISING
Maggie Ferguson

Look us up on-line at: http://www.romance.net

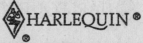

Heartbreak RANCH

Four generations of independent women...
Four heartwarming, romantic stories of the West...
Four incredible authors...

Fern Michaels
Jill Marie Landis
Dorsey Kelley
Chelley Kitzmiller

Saddle up with Heartbreak Ranch, an outstanding
Western collection that will take you on a whirlwind
trip through four generations and the exciting,
romantic adventures of four strong women who
have inherited the ranch from Bella Duprey,
famed Barbary Coast madam.

Available in March,
wherever Harlequin books are sold.

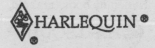

HARLEQUIN ®

Look us up on-line at: http://www.romance.net   HTBK

HARLEQUIN®

I N T R I G U E®

Cheyenne Nights

by Carla Cassidy

As little girls the Connor sisters dreamed of gallant princes on white horses. As women they were swept away by mysterious cowboys on black stallions. But with dusty dungarees and low-hung Stetsons, their cowboys are no less the knights in shining armor.

Join Carla Cassidy for the Connor sisters' wild West Wyoming tales of intrigue:

SUNSET PROMISES
(March)

MIDNIGHT WISHES
(April)

SUNRISE VOWS
(May)

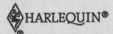